Praise for **JANE ISENBERG**'s **BEL BARRETT MYSTERIES**

"Bel Barrett brings killers to justice with her wry sense of humor and handy estrogen patch."
Bergen Record

"Jane Isenberg delivers a well-plotted, light mystery peopled with likable, realistic characters and skillfully served by sharp wit."
Ft. Lauderdale Sun-Sentinel

"Wonderful mysteries."
Aarp.com

"Bel Barrett is distinguished even among a crop of increasingly diverse fictional detectives by punctuating the discovery of clues with bouts of hot flashes."
New York Times

"Glows with heart, humor, and hot flashes."
Publishers Weekly (*Starred Review*)

"The Bel Barrett series keeps getting better with every book."
Cozies, Capers, and Crimes

"[A] funny, fast-moving . . . series."
The Seattle Times

JANE ISENBERG

HOT WIRED

A
BEL BARRETT
MYSTERY

AVON BOOKS
An Imprint of HarperCollinsPublishers

This is a work of fiction. Names, characters, places, and incidents are products of the author's imagination or are used fictitiously and are not to be construed as real. Any resemblance to actual events, locales, organizations, or persons, living or dead, is entirely coincidental.

AVON BOOKS
An Imprint of HarperCollins*Publishers*
10 East 53rd Street
New York, New York 10022-5299

Copyright © 2005 by Jane Isenberg
Excerpts copyright © 1999, 2000, 2000, 2001, 2002, 2003, 2004 by Jane Isenberg
ISBN-13: 978-0-06-057753-7
ISBN-10: 0-06-057753-3
www.avonmystery.com

First Avon Books paperback printing: December 2005

Avon Trademark Reg. U.S. Pat. Off. and in Other Countries, Marca Registrada, Hecho en U.S.A.
HarperCollins ® is a registered trademark of HarperCollins Publishers Inc.

Printed in the U.S.A.

10 9 8 7 6 5 4 3 2 1

To Phil Tompkins, with love

Acknowledgments

Once again, I am indebted to members of my writing group—Susan Babinski, Pat Juell, and Rebecca Mlynarczyk—for their insightful cross-country critiquing and support. And I'm forever grateful to my agent, Laura Peterson, for her encouragement tempered with realism. I'm also thankful to my editor, Sarah Durand, for approaching my work and hers with humor, intelligence, and sensitivity. Alice Acheson, my publicist, has earned my gratitude for her skilled and tireless efforts to help me get the word out about *Hot Wired*. Thanks also to my kids and grandkids, who offered love and understanding while I was working on this book. Friends, both old and new, did the same, and to them I also offer thanks. But a very special thank you goes to our neighbors for not once complaining about the loud music I blasted while I researched hip-hop!

HOT
WIRED

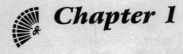

Chapter 1

www.pickurprofs.com

River Edge Community College
Jersey City, NJ

English Professor Bel Barrett

beef wid barrett

profesr barrett she think she ill
been teachin speech since before da pill
she think she stylin wid her rules n crap
but when she get ta rappin it time ta nap
she spit bout her kids n all da rest
but dey aint never nuttin bout her family on da test
she aint got no time ta help u learn
n da book she pik I hope it burn
in her class it only bitches get de A
she hate stuntin niggaz so mabe she gay

pik another prof if u wanna pass
cause barrett suck n so do her class

Evaluation: -1

Whoever wrote this had been a student of mine in a speech class, and he hated me. Worse, he thought I was a terrible teacher. I could feel my stomach churn as I stared, transfixed, at the ugly words on the computer screen. Blinking, I read them again, and then again, all the while struggling to deny them. Even though my limited familiarity with current urban slang kept me from fully understanding the author's every nuance, I certainly got the idea. His lines challenged and then demolished the image I had cultivated of myself as an accomplished and caring prof.

"Here," said Wendy, my longtime officemate and friend, pushing toward me the jar of M&M's that I kept on my desk for emergencies. But for once the little multicolored mood elevators held no allure for me. Swallowing rapidly to avoid gagging, I shook my head. "What kind of site is this?" I asked, squeezing my words out while still trying to keep my lunch in. "How long has this been here? Who has access to it?" As I spoke, I didn't look at Wendy, but continued to stare at the malignant lines on the monitor.

"I told you the post was off the wall. There are a couple of negative evaluations on the site about me too, but nothing quite like that one. I assumed you'd want to check it out." Wendy's rising inflection gave me the impression that she was rethinking this assumption. "According to its home page, *pickurprofs.com* is one of those Web-based bulletin

boards that give students the opportunity to evaluate
their professors and post their critiques anonymously.
Then other students who are registering for courses
can read them when they're deciding what to take. Lots
of colleges have these websites now." As she spoke, I
recalled a few dog-eared, typo-ridden leaflets critiquing courses and professors that had passed from
senior to freshman during my own student days.
Wendy paused and reached over to touch my shoulder.
"Hey! Get a grip! I thought you'd get a giggle out of it.
This posting is clearly the revenge of some F student.
You can't be taking it seriously. Look, you have two
other entries that are raves. Just scroll down. You'll
see."

When I didn't react, Wendy reached over and moved
my mouse herself, revealing the lines: "Take every
course she teaches. She's an inspiration." When I remained motionless, she manipulated the mouse one
more time to bring up another student's opinion of me.
"Her classes are intresting and she grade fair. She
make sure you can speak good in public before the
course ends."

I didn't really take in these students' praise, though,
because I was imagining other students all over the
wired world reading about what a boring and biased
bitch I was. I grasped the mouse and scrolled up again,
praying that the angry diatribe had somehow vanished
into the virtual void from which it had emerged. No
such luck. It was still there. "Bel, you look like the 'before' photo in one of those old Alka-Seltzer ads. Forget
it. Most students love you, and you know it." Like the
academic that she was, Wendy proceeded to document
her assertion. "Last month you racked up your second

RECC Professor of the Year Award in five years, for God's sake. Look." Wendy pointed at the two plaques on our wall before she went on. "The student government polled the students, and they chose you. Twice. Count 'em." A rueful smile lit up her elfin features for just a moment. "I've been teaching here since the seventies just like you, and I don't have even one of those."

I was shaking my head before she finished her sentence. "Only the students who happened to be in class on the day they gave out the surveys got to vote. And I don't think they polled the evening students this year," I said. My stomach had settled slightly, but I felt hot tears brimming and burning. One escaped and scalded a path down my cheek.

"Would you look at you? I swear, Bel, if you shed one more tear over this, I'll cut off your supply of M&M's for good." Concern had moved Wendy's voice up a register, so her shrill rasp was at odds with her flip words. "Bel, you know those faculty evaluation forms that students fill out every semester?" I nodded mutely while another tear, oblivious to Wendy's threat, seared my cheek. "Yours are always so good. Of course, every once in a while somebody says you give too much work or you expect too much, but you almost always get high scores. And your students write really nice comments, too. Remember the one last semester who wrote that your ESL course changed his life? And the other one who said that what he learned in your speech class helped him to get a job? Come on, Bel."

At the sight of a third tear, vexation ridged Wendy's brow. She began to swivel back and forth on her chair, something she did without realizing it whenever she was seriously stressed. "I told you not to go off estrogen. A drama queen like you isn't meant for the rigors of estrogen withdrawal. Now come on. Pull yourself together," she cajoled, holding out a Kleenex as she rotated by me. "You have a class in just a few minutes."

For the first time in many decades of teaching, the thought of entering a classroom filled me with dread, but there was no way around it. My overdeveloped work ethic ensured that no matter what, I would arrive at my class on time and do the best I could. That, in fact, was how I had come close to delivering my second child at RECC during a final exam. I was collecting blue books when the EMTs arrived. On Wendy's next swing-by, I snatched a Kleenex from the box she was still offering and blew my nose. It was as if the action had triggered my usually unreliable memory. Suddenly I knew with absolute certainty who had posted that damning description of me. Wendy was still unaware of my epiphany when she handed me another Kleenex and said, "Oh good! A sign of sanity. Now turn that thing off." She nodded in the direction of my PC.

"In a minute," I answered, moving the cursor to the print icon and jabbing the mouse. I wanted a hard copy of the offending message. "I need to think about this some more. I know who posted it."

"Why do you care?" Wendy asked. Before I could reply, Wendy restated the obvious. "The author has to be some male student who's into rap. He failed Speech with you and blames you rather than himself." Wendy stopped midswivel and added, "You know, Bel, now that I think about it, you ought to be grateful that he's expressing himself this way rather than stalking you like that crazy woman did a few years ago or . . . or worse." She hesitated, perhaps realizing that this was not the time to bring up the occasional headlines about psychotic college students shooting, stabbing, or blowing up professors who displeased them. "After all, sticks and stones . . ."

I yanked the printout from the jaws of the printer and plunged it deep into the depths of my oversized tote. Then I gathered my books and left before Wendy got to the part about how words could never harm me.

Chapter 2

Spring semester 2000 • English 103 • Speech
3 credits • Wed. 6:30–9:20 P.M.

Thompson, Naftali
 Introductory Talk A+
 Journals X, X, 0, 0, 0, 0, 0, X, X, 0, 0, 0, 0
 Informative Speech Outline 0, Informative Speech C-
 Persuasive Speech Outline 0, Persuasive Speech D
 Midterm Exam 65
 Speech 3 Outline ½, Speech 3 D
 Speech 4 Outline 0, Speech 4 0
 Final Exam 60
 Final Grade D
 # Absences 6½

I didn't have a chance to unearth my grade book
until after my next class, Cultures and Values. It went
smoothly in spite of the crisis of confidence I was experiencing when it began. It's impossible to dwell on
your own problems when confronted by the needs of

twenty-odd people relying on you to provide them
with an enriching, nurturing, and, in some cases, life-
changing educational experience. I facilitated several
lively small group discussions about the impact of
colonialism on the West Indian island of Antigua as described in Jamaica Kincaid's *A Small Place*. Later I
conferred with three students who had come up with
excellent topics for research papers.

But my spirits sagged when I returned to the office.
Wendy was gone for the day. I appreciated her concern
and her efforts to put the on-line critique in perspective, but I was relieved that she wasn't there. Although
she herself was an extremely conscientious and effective children's lit professor, I could tell that she didn't
understand why so much of my self-esteem depended
on my being seen as a good and concerned teacher. But
it did. Over the years making a difference in the classroom had become crucial to my very identity. Maybe
that's why I was determined to confirm my suspicion
that the message that had so scrambled my stomach
had been posted by Naftali Thompson, a student whom
I had taught in an evening speech class several years
ago. I thought knowing those mean words were, in
fact, Naftali's would make me feel a little better. So instead of packing up my books and papers and heading
home, I pulled open the bottom file drawer, where I
stored old grade books.

We all hung on to our records in the event that a student protested a grade or the registrar misplaced the
copies we turned in or experienced a computer glitch
when entering our data. While some of my colleagues
had computerized their grading long ago, I had done so
only recently. Luddite that I had been in this one re-

spect, I now faced an entire drawer of old-fashioned grade books, each filled with handwritten class lists and neat squares. These squares were filled with symbols that only I understood.

It took me less than a minute to locate the book I sought, which was near the front of the drawer. It was so accessible because I'd had to refer to it several times in the course of Naftali's formal appeal for a grade change. I grabbed the thin blue ledger, flipped it open to be sure it was the right one, and stashed it in my book bag. Only then did I gather my belongings and leave the office.

I didn't take much work home with me that evening because my husband, Sol, and I had a dinner date with my mother and her housemate. Ma and Sofia had met a few years ago at Hoboken's Senior Center and quickly discovered that they were sisters under the skin. They were both eighty-something widows in delicate health with concerned daughters. Ma had been eager to move out of Sol's and my home, where she had been forced to take refuge after my dad's sudden death. I did not want her to live by herself. Sofia had her own home a few blocks away and balked at her own daughter's repeated suggestion that the house was now too big for Sofia to manage alone. Both Ma and Sofia became tight-lipped and tremulous at even the mention of an assisted living facility.

But it was not only their approach to age-related issues that drew them to one another and solidified their bond. Their shared passion for gambling and their crusty defenses against loss and fear also united them. So when Sofia Dellafemina played her ace and invited Sadie Bickoff to share her home, Ma raised the ante

and accepted. Every time I praised their arrangement
as providing both women with companionship and security, Sol would laugh and say they were just two
hardcore codependents, enabling each other's gambling habit.

But we had noticed with concern that lately their bus
jaunts to Atlantic City were less frequent. Ma had a
dizzy spell one day after changing the bed linen, and
they both had bad arthritis. Determined to keep them in
their home, Sofia's daughter, Marie, and I had insisted
on our mothers hiring a cleaning service to take over
most of their housework. And when Marie and her
family presented Sofia with a DVD player for a recent
birthday, it had seemed like a timely and thoughtful
gift. Sol had offered to install it and teach them how to
use it. In return, Sofia and Ma had extended a dinner
invitation.

I was to meet Sol at their house because he was ar-
riving early to hook up the DVD player before dinner.
I parked the car in the vest pocket parking space we
rented across the street from our row house in downtown Hoboken. It was easier to walk the few blocks to
Ma's house than to spend an hour looking for a parking place any closer. I stopped to pick up some canno-
lis for dessert, hoping the extra walk and the promise
of a little sugar would make me feel better. While I
waited for someone to answer the door, I took off my
shoes and added them to the others in a row on the
floor of the vestibule. Ma and Sofia had instituted a
"no shoes in the house" policy. It was a nuisance, but
Paul, their new house cleaner, claimed it made his life
easier, and they were only too happy to oblige.

I did not want my black mood to spoil the evening

for everybody. In that spirit, I was determined not to mention the message that was burning a hole in my tote and in my bruised and humiliated heart. That resolve was challenged within minutes of my arrival. Concern clouding his round face, Sol followed me into the relative privacy of the pantry between the dining room and the kitchen. "Bad day, love?" he asked, pushing a wayward lock of hair back into the mass of mostly silver frizz fanning out from my face. "You're not coming down with something, are you?" Although Sol and I had been living together for years, we had celebrated our first wedding anniversary only recently. If I had ever entertained any notion that legalizing our relationship would dim his ardor, I had been dead wrong. He had become more solicitous, more devoted since we had exchanged vows. Sometimes his attentiveness drove me crazy, but at that moment I appreciated it.

"Not now," I muttered. I feared that even the briefest reference to the piece of paper in my bag would reduce me to tears, and I was still trying to hold it together. "I'll tell you later." I squeezed his arm and went into the kitchen to help with the final flurry of bringing food to the table.

"So what do you think of the salmon?" Ma asked after we had begun to eat. "And the mango salsa? Marie brought the salsa over. Isn't it delicious? I bet you thought you were going to get either my brisket or Sofia's eggplant again." The Odd Couple, as we had nicknamed Ma and Sofia, who bickered like Oscar and Felix, lived on brisket and eggplant parmigiana, two dishes they both made really well and kept on hand in their freezer.

"It's a treat! The salsa is delicious," I replied, grateful to Marie, who had been so worried about their monotonous diet that she had done something about it. "And the house just sparkles. That Paul must really be the miracle worker you say he is." Ma and Sofia had resisted having the cleaning service, but, to my relief, once it had started, they raved about the young man who showed up every week and made everything spick-and-span.

"He does the whole place in about four hours. He's amazing. And he's so polite and cheerful. It's a pleasure having him around," said Sofia. "Right, Sadie?"

"Right. And he's not bad looking either," said Ma with a wink. "He's studying voice." Marie had interviewed the cleaning service administrator and been reassured that Paul had good references and was reliable and competent, so I wasn't surprised that he was getting high ratings. And there were many aspiring Broadway and cabaret stars waiting tables and cleaning houses in Hoboken and Jersey City, so the young man's ambitions didn't surprise me either.

"Next week he's going to empty the fridge and defrost the freezer." Sofia sighed with pleasure at the prospect of a clean fridge.

"But I bet he didn't make this salmon. It's great," Sol interjected, lest we fail to compliment the part of the meal that one of the Odd Couple had actually made.

"Yes. It's nice and moist," I added.

"So, Sybil, if it's so good, why aren't you eating? You've hardly touched your food. What's the matter?" I was already so upset that I didn't even flinch when Ma called me by my given name, a habit of hers that usually made me crazy. And her injunction to eat was also a refrain that had echoed through my childhood, a period filled with her references to the starving orphans in Korea, who would have loved the lima beans or cauliflower I was rejecting.

"Nothing, Ma, I'm just a little tired. It's been a long week." I forced my mouth into a smile.

"Your mother's right, Bel. Something's wrong. You're usually the first one to ask for seconds. Now your mother's worried. That means she won't be able to sleep, and she'll keep me up. You know we're both too old to be up all night, so you better tell us what the problem is," Sofia chimed in. Another thing Ma and Sofia had in common was the ability to induce guilt in their now middle-aged offspring. Even Sophia's daughter, Marie, who has always been a model of filial devotion, once confided to me that by merely raising one corner of her mouth, Sofia could still inspire waves of soul-crushing guilt in her fifty-five-year-old firstborn.

"It's nothing, really," I stammered. Then, realizing that neither of them believed me, I added, "Okay. A student posted a very negative review of my teaching on-line and I read it. That's all. And I'm tired, so it got to me. But I really don't want to talk about it." Ma and Sofia both nodded, as if acquiescing to my request to table the topic. Relieved, I turned my attention to my plate and willed myself to have a few more bites.

My relief was premature. "Sybil, you're the best professor they've got over there," Ma said, waving a forkful of pink salmon at me. "You spend hours reading those damn papers. You work so hard planning your classes. And look at all the trips you're always taking those kids on. Who else takes them to museums and libraries and plays? So one of them just doesn't appreciate you, that's all." Ma's knee-jerk defense, an echo of Wendy's, didn't exactly surprise me. When my high school crush, Harold Goldstein, whom I'd been tutoring in French for months, invited Ellen Goldman to the junior prom, Ma had said, "It's his loss. He's afraid to ask you because he knows you're too good for him." I'm not sure she was right about Harold's motivation, but she just might be right about Naftali Thompson's.

When Sofia chimed in, she echoed my thoughts, "I hate to say it, but on this topic your mother's one hundred percent right. Remember that article they wrote about you in the paper? The one about how you went back to school at fifty-three to learn how to be a better teacher. And what about those awards you're always getting? Anybody who doesn't appreciate all that you do has a problem." I flashed back on Naftali Thompson, and I felt my hurt feelings crystallize into anger. Did Naftali have a problem? He sure did. He had earned a low grade that prevented him from transferring to State right away. And, now, three years later, thanks to the damn Internet, his problem was my problem.

# *Chapter 3*

To: Bbarrett@circle.com, Shecht@rutgers.edu
From: Rbarrett@uwash.edu
Re: Thanks
Date: 04/20/04 06:10:16

Hi, Mom and Sol,

Thanks to you two for all the interviewing tips and for the feedback on my résumé. You guys rule! I think I aced the interview with the recruiter from Omaha General today! Their starting salary is way cool. Attached are new photos of Abbie J from the time I took her to visit Cindy and Ted in Wenatchee. Oops, gotta go.

Love,
Rebecca

I couldn't focus on my daughter or check out the photos of my granddaughter when Sol and I got home that evening because he was so eager to pull up Naf-

tali's post. On the way home from Ma and Sofia's I'd
told him all about how I'd been bad-mouthed on *pick-
urprofs.com*. As soon as we were inside, I'd dug
around in my purse and found the printout, as well as
my grade book. Sol unfolded the sheet of paper I thrust
at him and read it quickly. Shaking his head, he strode
to the PC and logged on. I stood behind him, my eyes
on the monitor. Once we had skimmed Rebecca's message, we saved it so I could reread it and download the
photos of my adorable grandchild another time. In seconds, Sol brought up the home page of *pickurprofs.com*.
"Damn, you have to register to get onto this site," he
said, typing my name onto the appropriate line even as
he spoke. In a moment, the odious ode glowed on the
screen.

Sol read it again. When he turned to face me, he was
grinning. "C'mon, Bel. Where's your sense of humor?
This is hilarious."

"Not to me." Upset by Sol's lack of empathy, I practically spat out those three words. When I spoke next,
I lowered my voice, hoping to make him understand.
"In fact, I almost threw up when Wendy first showed it
to me. I felt like I'd been blindsided."

"And now?" Sol asked, turning toward me, his grin
gone, his tone tender. Before I could answer, he shut
off the PC and led the way to the kitchen, where he
poured two glasses of Merlot. He handed one to me.
"How do you feel about it now, love?"

"Mad," I said. I took the glass he offered and sat
down at the table. Since we'd had our kitchen reno-
vated a few years ago, we spent as much time in it as
possible. Sol took a seat across from me.

"Good. Anger's a more appropriate response to that

drivel. This wannabe rapper is clearly a nutcase. I'm sure I told you about the graduate student I had who used to send me hate mail." As a retired economics prof at Rutgers, Sol had a store of classroom anecdotes of his own. "He thought I was an ambassador of the devil because I suggested that unchecked capitalism might lead to unforeseen and undesirable consequences." I nodded. Sol and I had spent much of our courtship swapping teaching stories.

"Was he the one who cursed you in the parking lot when you called him on plagiarizing a chapter in his dissertation?" I asked.

Sol's bushy brows converged in a V as he tried to recall the incident. Then he chuckled, and vestiges of that chuckle lightened his tone as he answered me. "Hell no, that guy was a mountain. He must have been about six-five and he weighed over three hundred pounds." Sol, who was a mere five feet nine inches tall and weighed in at a relatively modest two hundred pounds, made a big circle with his arms. "His name was Damian Allen. But tell me about your secret slanderer." Sol's demeanor became grave as he refocused the conversation on me. One of the things I loved about Sol was that he actually enjoyed listening to me. Unlike even my closest friends, he seldom tired of my stories, no matter how long or digressive they were.

"See for yourself," I said. When I slid the grade book across the table, it was open to the page featuring the roster and entries for Naftali's speech class.

Sol, who had computerized his grades as soon as he got his first PC, laughed and passed the book back to me, saying, "You know I can't decipher this code you use. Translate for me, please."

"It's easy." I pointed to the A+. "He gave a good informal introductory talk. It was really a rap." I smiled in spite of myself at the memory of the wiry young man in the requisite baggy jeans, sweatshirt, and chains speaking to beats blasting from a small boom box he had brought in for the occasion. The class had been charmed, and so had I. "I could tell he was used to performing in front of people. He wasn't nervous or hesitant the way most of the other students are. He could have done well in that course if he'd even half-tried." My smile faded as I uttered the last sentence. The failures of able students upset me more than the failures of those who were less gifted.

"What did he say about himself?" Sol wanted to know.

"I don't remember exactly. He gave his rap name, but I can't say now what it was. Something with a T, not Ice-T, but something like that. He talked about his neighborhood, how he always wanted to be a rapper, tell it the way it is." I paused for a few seconds, thinking back, but drew a blank. "Their introductory talks only had to be a couple of minutes long. They serve as icebreakers." Annoyed that I couldn't dredge up more details from Naftali's rap, I added, "I might even have a draft of it somewhere in the office because he never picked up his portfolio at the end of the semester."

"So how did this clever, verbal, and confident young man wind up with a D?" Sol asked. "Want a refill?" He pointed to the bottle of wine on the table.

"No thanks. I'm good." I covered the top of my glass with my hand and then pointed at another line in the open grade book. "You can see here he only did four out of twelve journals."

"I see. But what the hell's a journal?" Sol asked. "I thought this was a public speaking class."

"I'm sure I've told you before," I said, a trace of resignation in my voice. Sol's memory was not much better than mine. "A journal is a written response to the textbook. I don't have time to test them on the reading or even to discuss all of it, but their textbook is filled with useful information. So they have to discuss their reactions to the major points in writing. It's good for them to write," I added.

"Yeah, love. I know." Again Sol sounded resigned. He was all too aware that many of my students needed a lot of help and practice with written expression. No doubt the resentment he felt at the many hours I spent reading and responding to their writing made this fact stick in his head.

"Then will you look at his grades on the speeches?" I pointed at the grade book. "He didn't outline them. Hell, he didn't even show up for the last one. It's not that he did it and failed it. He was a no-show and he never made it up. That's why he got a 0 on it instead of an F." My anger grew as I recalled the young man's casual approach to the class.

"His midterm and final exam grades speak for themselves," Sol said. "And I take it the class met only once a week, so he missed six and a half out of fifteen classes." When I nodded, Sol went on. "I would have failed him. That D you gave him was a gift."

"Well, he didn't think so," I said. "He appealed to the dean for a grade change."

"You're kidding. On what possible grounds?" Sol leaned back in his chair as he waited for me to explain.

"I have a copy of the paperwork on file in the office.

But as I recall, his argument was all about that A+. Naftali felt that he was a better speaker than many in the class, so his natural ability should have been sufficient to assure him at least a C." I shook my head, recalling how Naftali's argument had ignored the requirements of the course, which included acquiring and demonstrating the skills needed to research and outline, as well as speak and listen in a manner appropriate to the college classroom or workplace. "You can't rap your way through life unless you really do make it big. I suppose he was ambivalent about being in school in the first place." I sighed.

"Don't play shrink, Bel," Sol admonished, not for the first time. "But speaking of shrinks, you know, love, that website performs a valuable service." I was expecting a lecture on how useful it would be for students to have a little information about courses and profs before registering. I would have supported that argument wholeheartedly until I read Naftali's hostile diatribe. So I was really surprised when Sol went on to echo Wendy's observation. "After all, if he's a psycho, as long as he's making up nasty rhymes about you, he's not, you know, coming after you with a gun." Sol's tone was suddenly grim, and he spoke slowly as he considered the likelihood of an armed and dangerous gangsta rapper at large in the corridors of RECC.

Sol had suffered from post-traumatic stress after he witnessed the attack on the World Trade Center, and even several years later, he still tended to overreact, especially to the sounds of planes and helicopters overhead. It would not be out of character for my devoted husband to read Naftali's angry words as the ranting of a homicidal psychopath. I spoke quickly, wanting to reassure him. "Not to worry, love. Your bride is safe. Only her feelings are hurt. I haven't seen the kid in years, not since he took his final exam. He filed his appeal in writing. When he didn't get the grade change, I bet he dropped out of school."

"Well, that's a relief," Sol replied, taking my hand across the table and twisting my wedding ring. "But I thought you had recovered from your hurt feelings and were pissed off now."

"Well, I am. If students take this ditty he posted seriously, they'll think I'm a sexist and racist bore, and they won't register for my courses." I pictured row upon row of empty seats in my classroom.

"Well, if they don't take your courses, they'll miss out on one of the finest professors I've ever had the privilege of marrying." We both giggled. Sol's first wife had also taught, and I loved to tease him about his penchant for brainy women. "And mind you, there's no bias here." I giggled again, relieved by Sol's gallant and goofy line of patter. It was the first time I'd really laughed since I'd seen Naftali's poisonous poem.

"You're right," I said, my voice sharp now. "They *would* lose out. And I *am* pissed off. Naftali's no different than lots of other students who want a good grade for doing absolutely nothing." I grabbed my grade book and snapped it shut as I spoke.

"You know I can't resist you when you're mad. Let's go to bed." Giving me an exaggerated wink, Sol put our wineglasses in the sink, turned out the light, and led the way upstairs.

Chapter 4

River Edge Community College
Jersey City, NJ

English Professor Bel Barrett

professor barrett, she the bomb
sometime she act jus like my moms
she run her mouth but what she say, it tight
always makin u read n makin u rite
she don give a shit bout sex or race
jus do ur work n show ur face
she got no heart for a nigga who lazy
take it from me, IM Kra-Z

Evaluation: 5

I might have missed IM Kra-Z's posting on *pickur-profs.com* if it weren't for my friend and colleague Il-

luminada Guttierrez. Illuminada, our friend Betty
Ramsey, and I were in Illuminada's new silver VW
sedan on our way to a long overdue lunch together that
Illuminada had instigated. "So, Illuminada, what's
going on? It's not like you to take a long lunch without
a good reason." Betty posed her question before she
had even fastened her seat belt. She had clambered into
the backseat while I was getting in front. I was curious
myself about what had inspired our workaholic friend
to take time away from the busy private investigating
firm that she headed, but I let Betty do the heavy
lifting.

Illuminada's delicate hands were relaxed on the
steering wheel as she expertly maneuvered the car
through the snarl of midday traffic in Jersey City. Her
sleek black hair fell to her ears and swung across her
face when she moved, obscuring her profile. From
where I sat, I couldn't see the silver streak highlighting
her center part and softly framing her even features,
but I knew it was there.

Betty repeated, "What's up, girlfriend? I can't wait
until we get to Newark." As executive assistant to
RECC's president, Betty wanted to justify abandoning
her own overflowing desk and her needy boss for a
couple of hours.

"One of the young geeks on my payroll is taking a
couple of criminal justice courses at RECC over the
summer. When John was registering, he came across
this." Taking one hand off the wheel, Illuminada
reached between the gear shift and the driver's seat,
pulled out four sheets of paper, and handed them to
me. "*Chiquita,* give Betty copies and then check it
out."

I'd planned to share my newfound notoriety with my friends and had looked forward to their laughing off Naftali's ludicrous lyrics as sour grapes from a sore loser. That Illuminada had already discovered his post made me confront anew how many others had access to it. It was unsettling to be reminded of the huge number of people who, thanks to the ubiquity of the Internet, could read Naftali's putrid poem. I'd practically memorized it by then and had no urge to reread it, but I dutifully handed Betty her copies before I spoke. "I know. I saw it already." There was no comment from Betty yet. I could see only the top of her Afro over the paper as she read. "I was pretty upset at first. But then I figured it's just some kid who wasn't happy with the D he earned in my speech class."

"There are two postings. Have you seen the other one?" Illuminada asked.

"Oh no. I figured you'd just made an extra copy of the original," I said. My gut tightened at the thought that Naftali had posted a second vilifying rap about me. I had to force myself to read the second printout Illuminada had handed me. As relief surged through my body, I felt my stomach unknot and my shoulder muscles loosen. I took a deep breath. "This one is a big improvement over the first. I actually remember IM Kra-Z. His real name is Derek Watson or Whitworth or something like that, but he calls himself IM Kra-Z. He's trying to become a rapper. So many kids think they're going to rap their way out of poverty." I shook my head. "Derek was a fairly competent student, though and, as I recall, he earned a B." I paused for a moment before adding, "But even though I'm pleased he came to my defense, I'm still really angry that this website lets anyone post anything without monitoring."

Illuminada pulled the car into the lot next to the restaurant where we planned to lunch. It was one of many Portuguese restaurants in the Newark neighborhood known as the Ironbound because it's bounded by railroad tracks. The area has long been home to immigrants from all over who work in the nearby factories. But in the seventies there was an influx of thousands of refugees fleeing a military coup in Portugal. Since then the Ironbound has featured shops, bakeries, restaurants, churches, schools, and businesses reflecting Portuguese culture. The neighborhood has long been a destination of choice for New York and New Jersey foodies looking for huge portions of delicious steak and seafood served with old-world grace at bargain prices. It was nearly two when we entered the dimly lit restaurant, so we ordered before continuing our conversation.

"That nasty rap is absurd. If any students take it seriously, they'll miss out on a great prof," said Betty. "And it's awful for you to have to read it after all the work you do. We know you take pride in your teaching. I'm sorry you had to bear the brunt of this kid's hostility." I reached over to squeeze Betty's arm. She wasn't exactly laughing off Naftali's post, but she was offering support, and I appreciated it.

"Betty's right. So what are you going to do about it?" asked Illuminada. As usual, her response was practical rather than sentimental.

"I know who posted it." Both of my friends raised their eyebrows. "Naftali Thompson." In a dismissive tone, I added, "He's another wannabe rap star, but he got a D in one of my speech classes a few years ago. He wanted to transfer to State, so he needed a better grade, but he didn't deserve it. He asked for a grade change, and he didn't get that either. It's a familiar story. He's not the problem."

Leaning forward as I continued, I could feel rekindled anger animating my voice. "The webmaster is the problem. I want to talk to him because these entries should be monitored. People shouldn't be able to slander professors or use that kind of language either, come to think of it. Can you find out who the webmaster is?" I addressed this query to Illuminada, whose agency staff included many people adept at cyber research. "I'd like to have a talk with him."

"Sure," said Illuminada. "In fact, I've got someone working on it now." She hesitated and then added, "After John showed me the website, I checked out my own fan ratings." Illuminada, herself an alumna of a community college and eager to "give something back," taught part-time in RECC's Criminal Justice Department. "*Chiquitas,* would you believe there's a posting about me there that says, and I quote, 'She's a good professor, considering that she's a Puerto Rican?' " Illuminada's family was from Cuba, and she took great pride in her heritage.

"It's pretty pathetic when a bigot can't even get his own biases right," said Betty. "Somebody definitely should screen the posts. They can do that without interfering with freedom of speech, can't they?"

"I would hope so, but I'm not at all sure," said Illuminada. "I had a case brought to me last year by the parents of a teen with a weight problem. She was being harassed and mocked by posts on a site that existed solely to spread gossip among kids in her high school. They made her so miserable that she tried to kill herself." Illuminada stopped speaking to acknowledge our horrified gasps. "Now she's getting counseling and all her instruction at home." Illuminada's voice was grave. "The website was not run under the auspices of the school or the school board nor did the students access it from the school's computers, so it couldn't be regulated or eliminated."

"What kind of teenaged sadist runs it?" I asked. "I just can't imagine who gets off by running these things."

"We traced it to a computer geek and his father," said Illuminada. Betty and I gasped again, aghast at the idea of a grown man collaborating with his son to torment the boy's peers. "Go figure. The girl's parents, the principal, and the PTA are trying to get their local paper and TV station to expose it in an effort to pressure the hosts into closing it down. Who knows if they will?" Illuminada shrugged her shoulders. "But I'll get you the name of the *pickurprofs.com* webmaster. We can go talk to him together. He's probably some RECC techie geek with too much time on his hands."

"That's all well and good," said Betty. "But that's only part of the problem. Bel, you say you know who posted that god-awful thing, and you're not worried, but you should make sure you're right. There are a lot of wackos out there. It wouldn't hurt to at least verify that this Thompson kid is, in fact, the author and that he's not enrolled this semester or registered for summer courses."

Illuminada nodded. "Sad to say, Betty's right. It's a lot better to be safe than sorry." Just then our waiter arrived and poured our wine. "To world peace," we said as we raised our glasses. No sooner had we taken our first sip of wine than our waiter reappeared carrying a tray filled with huge bowls heaped with steaming shellfish redolent of garlic. For a few moments, conversation stopped as we dug into the daunting portions.

"So, what do you hear from Lourdes?" I asked Illuminada. As parents of adult kids, we liked to catch up on the doings of each other's progeny whenever we got together.

"I don't," said Illuminada, her lips shiny with oil. "Ever since my birthday dinner, she's been avoiding us. It's because of that toast. Remember? You were there."

"You mean when you raised a glass and said, 'Here's to my daughter, the woman who will be the mother of my grandchildren if I live long enough?' " asked Betty.

Illuminada nodded. "You got it." She turned to me. "Don't say a word, Bel. I know it was my bad. I had too much wine. But that was weeks ago, and I left an apology on her answering machine. But she's still very aloof. Her father and I want to take her and Randy to a concert or a show for her birthday next month, and we'd like to set a date now so we can order the tickets. Raoul's called her. I've called her, but she doesn't pick up and she hasn't returned our calls. It's so infuriating. I'm tempted to scratch the whole thing."

"Why don't you just stop in at the bar and talk to her there?" Betty couldn't resist trying to help.

"Because the last time I did that, she said her boss gave her a hard time about it. I don't know if that's true, but I got the message." Illuminada shrugged.

"Are Lourdes and Randy still dating?" I asked. Illuminada's daughter, Lourdes, and Betty's son, Randy, had connected over a year ago at Sol's and my wedding and had been having an on-again, off-again relationship ever since.

"Who knows?" said Betty. "Every time I ask Randy, he just jokes his way out of giving me a straight answer. He's not the easiest person to stay in touch with either, you know." Illuminada and I glanced at one another. Betty was notorious for micromanaging the lives of family and friends. "The last time I called him, I left a message inviting him and Lourdes to dinner. He hasn't called back."

"You better be careful or you'll jinx their romance," I said, grateful that my two kids stayed in touch more or less regularly. Rebecca e-mailed her news from across the country pretty frequently. And even her younger brother, Mark, made time to phone or e-mail from whatever remote outpost his wanderlust had most lately led him. Sol's daughter, Alexis, whom we had nicknamed The Professor, called from upstate New York whenever she needed a baby-sitter, which was often. I allowed myself to indulge in just a moment of smugness.

I felt guilty about using my friends' parenting problems to elevate my own mood, especially when Illuminada, returning to the subject at hand, said, "*Chiquita,* do you need help to check out this Naftali kid? I'd be glad to have someone in the office make a few calls."

"No thanks. I still have his address and phone number. I'll just dream up some pretext and call him myself. Hey, maybe he really did make it big, and I should be looking for him on MTV." As I pried a succulent

clam from its shell, I said, "Seriously, I'm kind of relieved that you're pushing me to contact Naftali because there is one tiny thing that does worry me about
him."

"What's that?" asked Betty, sopping up her green
garlic sauce with a chunk of Portuguese roll.

"It's his timing. Why did he wait so long to write
this critique and post it? Derek is still taking classes,
but I had Naftali a few years ago." Inspired by Betty's
example, I broke off a piece of my own roll and dipped
it into my bowl before I continued. "Maybe he *has* re-
registered at RECC this semester, and our paths simply
haven't crossed."

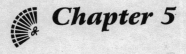

Chapter 5

www.pickurprofs.com

River Edge Community College
Jersey City, NJ

English Professor Bel Barrett

u wanna battle u hoodrat gully wannabe
u cant rhyme ur jus a crybaby
teachers pet n thas no maybe
aint got no beats n u cant sing
u got no balls n got no bling
i gotta ring thas 24 carat
u gotta boner fr fat bitch barrett

Evaluation: -5

i'll battle u this time fr good
u got no rep, no cred in the hood
no demo CD no contract in ur future

u nuttin but a lowlife loser
later fr u gotta rap wid my producer
 IM Kra-Z n i got game
n the *cojones* to sign my name

Evaluation: +5

Increasingly appalled by my new role as muse to hip-hop's battling bards, I was only too happy to join Illuminada at a table in a corner of the bustling cafeteria at State. This was where *pickurprofs.com*'s webmistress, Sarita Singh, had agreed to meet with us during a break between her classes. "I'm embarrassed to admit how shocked I am that the person who dreamed up and runs this slanderous cyber site is female," I said to Illuminada as soon as she arrived.

"Does it matter?" asked Illuminada.

"Only insomuch as it makes me realize that I *am* a bit sexist," I said. "Naftali wasn't all wrong on that one, I'm sorry to say."

Before Illuminada had a chance to reply, a dark-haired young woman approached our table and looked inquiringly at us. "Sarita Singh," she said, extending her hand. Her voice was cool, her diction precise in the manner of Indians educated in British-English. She wore jeans and a white jersey that was clingy enough to set off her slender figure but not so tight as to be provocative by current standards. Her cropped black hair spiked out from her head like rays of the sun in a child's drawing. One ear was the setting for a selection of delicate jeweled studs in a rainbow of colors.

"I'm Professor Bel Barrett," I said, trying to modulate my own voice to match Sarita's. "I'm a member of the English faculty at RECC." The ringed hand Sarita offered was as cool as her voice.

"And I'm Illuminada Guttierrez. I teach criminal justice at RECC." I noted that Illuminada made no mention of the fact that she was a private investigator. An awkward silence followed their handshake. Sarita seated herself and looked expectantly from me to Illuminada and back.

"Thanks for agreeing to meet with us, Sarita," I began.

"No problem. I have a break now anyway," Sarita answered with a slight shrug.

"We wanted to talk with you about your website," I plowed on, annoyed that I hadn't realized how awkward this conversation was going to be. I should have spent more time preparing for it. Sarita raised an eyebrow and waited. She wasn't making this any easier.

"Both Professor Barrett and I have been featured on your site." Illuminada spoke in her let's-get-on-with-it voice. She took copies of the posts out of her briefcase and handed them to Sarita. The young woman scanned them and shrugged again. "I'm not from Puerto Rico," Illuminada said. "I'm Cuban-American. But so what? What does that have to do with my ability to teach?" Illuminada's slightly raised voice betrayed her anger, which I suspected was as much in response to Sarita's shrug as to the contents of the post.

"And I'm neither sexist nor racist," I added. "Nor very fat nor a bitch. But there are people who would find some of the language used in this post"—I poked at the piece of paper on the table between us as I spoke—"both sexist *and* racist."

"*Pickurprofs.com* got over six hundred hits a day

during fall walk-in registration this semester." Sarita's voice was matter-of-fact, but with an undertone of self-righteousness. "The site performs a valuable service for RECC students. When I registered there for the first time, I had no clue which professors to choose. I made some big mistakes. One of my profs kept hitting on me." She held down the index finger of one hand with the same finger on the other hand as she began to enumerate the professors who had inadvertently inspired *pickurprofs.com*. "Another had a problem with foreign students, period." She extended another finger and held it down. "And one was just so boring I thought I'd die." Now Sarita mimed a yawn. "I want to prevent other students from going through what I went through."

As a longtime devoted crusader for all manner of liberal causes, I recognized a world saver when I encountered one, and Sarita qualified. In the sixties she and I would have been protesting the war and marching for civil rights together while waving our flaming bras overhead like torches. As she spoke and I listened, I realized that much of what she was saying was valid. I decided to try a different approach. "Sarita, your site has the potential to perform a valuable service. But the lack of monitoring reduces its credibility. We're not suggesting that you censor the opinions, but rather that you at least monitor the posts to see that they're free from racist and sexist language."

"It also undermines the site's credibility to include comments that are not directly relevant to the professor's ability to teach," added Illuminada. "Whether or not I'm Puerto Rican should not be an issue. Nor should Professor Barrett's weight."

Sarita nodded, taking in what we had to say. When she did reply, what she said was: "The site isn't perfect, but even so, I get very positive e-mail from students who tell me how much it's helped them. In fact," she continued with a smile that was just a hair short of being smug, "I'm working with representatives of the student government at Essex and Bergen community colleges right now. They want to be included, and by next year I hope to extend *pickurprofs.com*'s services to all of New Jersey's community colleges."

"Are you saying that you won't make any effort to implement the suggestions we've made?" I asked, knowing the answer, but wanting to give Sarita a chance to reconsider.

"I'm saying that it's all I can do to run this site the way it is, work on the expansion, and keep up my GPA here at State. Frankly, I don't see any changes in the near future. After all, *pickurprofs.com* is for students, not faculty. And students aren't complaining." Sarita stood, indicating that our meeting was over.

"Well, thanks for meeting with us," said Illuminada. "I hope you'll give some thought to what we've said."

"Yes, Sarita. Thanks," I added, my words a feeble echo of Illuminada's. Sarita nodded. We watched her walk away, her bearing almost regal, her hair a spiky crown. "Well, she certainly is a self-possessed and confident young entrepreneur. In a lot of ways, she's an alumna to be proud of," I said. "Have time for a cup of tea?" I was hoping to get Illuminada's read on Sarita and brainstorm what, if any, action to take in view of the young woman's refusal to even consider modifying her website.

Illuminada shook her head. "No, *chiquita,* I have to

get back. I have a court appearance tomorrow that I
need to prepare for. Did you check out the author of
that mean message yet?" Illuminada's question was
really a reminder.

"Not yet, but I'll do it now. It shouldn't be too
hard." I left the noisy cafeteria with Illuminada and
drove back to my office at RECC. I figured it
shouldn't take more than two phone calls to find out
where Naftali was this semester. First I called the registrar, who assured me that he wasn't currently registered at RECC. Breathing a sigh of relief, I decided to
walk over to the office of the newly appointed Director of Alumni Affairs, Abelard Constantine. The Dean
of Student Affairs and the college's resident statisti-
cian had written a grant to fund Abelard's position in
the hope of tracking alumni to approach for support
and to poll for information. I could use my curiosity
about Naftali as an opportunity to meet and greet a
new staff member.

The sign over the door reading OFFICE OF ALUMNI AF-
FAIRS in nearly illegible Gothic script was misleadingly
pretentious. In fact, until two weeks ago Abelard's office had been a supply closet for maintenance materi-
als. Now it was fitted with a cast-off computer and a
battered desk. Cartons of folders towered where cartons of paper towels and cleansers had once been
stored. A large mop was still propped against the wall
in the corner of the room. I heard whistling as I entered. Abelard Constantine, a short, round individual
with a brown beard and a bald pate, seemed remark-
ably cheerful in view of his dismal surroundings.

"Hi. May I bother you for a moment? I want to introduce myself. I'm Bel Barrett. I'm in the English De-

partment. Welcome to RECC." He took my hand in both of his and squeezed it.

"It's no bother. I'm delighted to be interrupted. I've heard a lot about you, actually. Thanks for stopping by." Although Abelard's voice was warm, I shivered, wondering if he meant he'd heard about Naftali's post. I felt immediately reassured when he went on to say, "I have a work-study student, Jamal Kahn, who's been helping me, and he has you for Composition. He says you're the best teacher he's ever had." Abelard smiled broadly as if he could imagine the pleasure this praise brought me.

"Well, that's always good to hear," I said. Naftali's critique had made me more appreciative than ever of praise for my teaching. "Jamal is an excellent student. I always look forward to reading his work." I leaned against a pile of cartons backed by a wall and surveyed the small room. I couldn't help but shake my head at the number of boxes. "Abelard, this is a huge job! How is it going?"

"You know there are more cartons in a storage unit somewhere?" He chuckled. "But I'll just do the best I can." Hearing this decidedly upbeat response, I wondered how Abelard would fit in with faculty and staff at RECC, where whining was a way of life. Wendy and I whined all the time about our cramped and shabby office, a luxurious setup compared to Abelard's makeshift digs.

"They've only given you one work-study student? You should have at least three or four. Otherwise it will take you years to enter all this data. That's what you have to do, right? And they haven't even given you a new machine. That PC is older than I am," I said, figuring that I could at least model for him how he ought to be sounding.

"Well, it is a challenge, but I like challenges. Besides, I'm grateful to have work. They're not going to ship all these heavy boxes to Bangalore anytime soon." He smiled and shrugged his shoulders.

I felt stupid. The man has probably been out of work for ages, a victim of downsizing or outsourcing or whatever the wordsmiths in human resources were calling it now when they fired you. He was grateful to be working at all. "Well, I'm glad you're here," I said. "We've neglected our alumni long enough." When I spoke again, my tone gradually became more passionate. "I'm always wondering what happened to my students after they graduate or transfer. Of course I run into some of them here and there, but there are others I never hear about or see again. It would be great to have reunions, to invite them back for conferences, to have them mentor current students."

Abelard smiled. "Well, I'm starting to enter data," he said, pointing at the antique PC.

"Oh really?" I asked. "Gee. There are a couple of kids I'm especially curious about. But I don't suppose you've had a chance to track any recent alums. You're probably starting at the beginning, back in the seventies." My theory was that a man who sees himself as a problem solver would jump at the challenge implied in my assumption.

Bingo! I was right. "Try me." Abelard's eyes gleamed. "I'm actually working for Dean Haskins on a priority project that has required me to familiarize myself with recent graduates."

"How about recent dropouts?" I added. "Are you

keeping data on them? Or transfers?" I mentioned the second category of student to camouflage my interest in dropouts.

"Give me the name," said Abelard, his playful tone taking the sting out of his use of the imperative.

"Naftali Thompson. I can go to my office and get you his student ID number if you really need it," I added, silently cursing myself for having forgotten to bring that crucial bit of information with me. I felt the despair of a modern traveler finding herself at the airport without a picture ID.

"No problem," said Abelard. To my surprise, he reached for some papers on his desk and scanned a few of them. Suddenly he looked up at me, his eyes alight now with pleasure and a touch of triumph. "Dean Haskins is tracking RECC dropouts so we can survey them as to why they left. It's part of the college's latest effort to improve retention." I sighed. The college's struggle to retain students was an ongoing one. Work, ill health, and family problems often competed with school for the limited resources of our urban population. "Naftali Thompson enlisted in the armed forces in September of 2002. His unit was deployed to Iraq as part of Operation Iraqi Freedom in March of 2003. They're still serving there."

Chapter 6

www.pickkurprofs.com

River Edge Community College
Jersey City, NJ

Children's Literature Professor
Wendy O'Conner

She good but she don't want the kids watching no TV, she go on about how parents should be reading to them. How we suppose to keep up with are shows if we be reading to the kids all the time? Tell me that.

Evaluation: 4

Knowledgeable about books for children, but avoid if you suffer from motion sickness. She paces back and forth in front of the room when she lectures.

Evaluation: 4

Really immoral. After my wife left me, Professor O'Connor suggested I get books for my five-year-old about kids in single parent families. I don't want my kid to think that sick stuff is normal.

Evaluation: 1

She think I should let my son read books in spanish and english, but I want him lern only english, beside she kinda old. and she make us to read to many books.

Evaluation: 3

"You're right, these comments aren't very enlightened, but they aren't nearly as nasty and hostile as that one I got," I said when Wendy finished scrolling down the contributions some of her students had made to *pickurprofs.com*. "And these don't read like tabloid headlines either. Anybody with half a brain can tell that you're a good teacher who rubbed a few people with personal problems the wrong way. "It's not as if you're the one with the problems."

"According to that last one, I am. I'm old," said Wendy. "The person running the website really should give guidelines to help students phrase their critiques and maybe a checklist or something, so they don't include things like age that have nothing to do with teaching." She was using the crisp tone she used when, as President of the RECC Faculty Senate, she chaired our sessions. "I've put *pickurprofs.com* on the Faculty Senate agenda."

"Good idea," I said. "Our colleagues should know about the site. Maybe a response from the Senate will be more effective at persuading Sarita Singh than Illuminada and I were." I had told Wendy about the conversation Illuminada and I had had with *pickurprofs.com*'s uncooperative webmistress.

"Meanwhile, I'm still really curious about who posted that first rap riff about me. I'm going to talk to the other rapper hopeful, IM Kra-Z. I bet he knows who he battled." When Wendy looked confused, I added, "He's the one who defended me in another rap posted on *pickurprofs.com*. He battled for me." I felt silly even as the words left my lips. Wendy arched an eyebrow, so I explained. "Rappers fight each other in rhyme, and they call it 'battling.' I learned about it in the movie *8 Mile*. I told you to see it. Anyway, his real name's Derek Watson or something that starts with a W. He's still here. He took Comp I with me a few semesters ago, but he hasn't graduated yet. I run into him every now and then."

Wendy shrugged and said, "I don't understand why you're so interested in who posted that vicious evaluation. I'd just as soon not know who authored those pathetic comments about me." She pointed to the screen, where the evaluations of her were still visible.

"Frankly I'm curious because he does sound so hostile," I answered. "I'd just feel better if I knew for sure that he wasn't taking classes here now."

"Okay, I can see that." I was grateful that Wendy didn't try to diminish my concern. In fact, the readiness with which she accepted it reinforced my desire to learn the identity of my detractor. "But, Bel, I thought you had him pegged."

"The student I thought was responsible for it has been serving in Iraq since he dropped out of RECC.

Who knew?" I tapped my head to indicate how surprised I had been to learn of Naftali's distant whereabouts. I shouldn't have been surprised, though. Traditionally young people with poor grades and worse job prospects had been drawn to the military. And in the post-Vietnam era many high school graduates had enlisted in the armed forces or the reserves, not only to serve their country and earn a paycheck. They had also sought and found support, training, and meaning that enriched and directed their young lives. But in the post 9/11 era, enlistment, even in the reserves, almost certainly meant combat duty.

"So what? They have laptops and DVD and MP3 players over there," said Wendy. "I read that they have hip-hop or punk rock music wired right into their helmets. It psyches them up for battle." Wendy clenched her small fist and raised it in the air to illustrate her point.

"I know, but I just can't imagine him having the time or the motivation to trash a former teacher and battle a local rap rival while he's trying to stay alive and fight real battles. It's got to be somebody else, somebody here. I'm going to talk to Derek." As I spoke, I lifted the phone and called the registrar. With her help I established that Derek's last name was Wilson. She read his current class schedule to me, and I jotted it down. After I thanked her and hung up, I glanced at my watch. According to his schedule, at that very moment Derek was studying Psychology I right downstairs. If I moved fast, and if the instructor did not dismiss the group early, I would be able to catch Derek on his way out of class.

I was only slightly breathless and flustered when I

arrived at his classroom. It was a relief to see Derek still inside, collecting his books. As he walked out the door, I greeted him. "Hi, Derek, do you have a moment? I'd like to talk to you."

"Hi, Professor B," said Derek. His smile slowly broadened into a wide grin. "I always got time for you, Professor B. Sup?" Derek's long legs looked longer and skinnier than they probably were because his baggy, almost skirtlike jeans ended midcalf. I figured he was modeling a hip-hop fashion statement modified for warm weather. He wore sandals and a voluminous black T-shirt with IM KRA-Z emblazoned on it in squiggly purple letters.

"Well, I wanted to thank you for that nice evaluation of me you posted on *pickurprofs.com*." I paused and lowered my voice. "I felt so bad after I read that other one, but yours made me feel a lot better, and I appreciate your doing it. And thanks for battling that other guy on my behalf too."

Derek seemed taken aback by my reference to his on-line chivalry. His wide lazy grin had faded as I spoke. "No problem, Professor B. You a good prof. That other dude jes' mad, tha's all. He got no call to take it out on you. But I gotta go. I got another class in the lab." He jerked his shaggy head in the direction of the building on the next block housing RECC's science and technology classes.

A bit bewildered by his ambiguous response and his desire to flee, I put my hand on his arm to delay him. "Derek, I'd feel a lot more comfortable if I knew for sure who he is. I was hoping you could tell me."

"Mus' jes' be some student failed your class. Tha's what I think," said Derek. "Don' let it get to you. He ain't gonna post another one. Trus' me." Derek literally raced off down the corridor, his outsized pants-legs flapping as he ran.

Disappointed by what I interpreted as Derek's evasiveness, I returned to the office and pulled open the bottom drawer of my file cabinet and stared once again at my cache of old grade books. "No luck," I announced to Wendy, who sat as I'd left her, poring over a set of papers. "He just stonewalled me. He had no problem battling on my behalf, but he's not about to rat out a peer, even a rival, to a prof. So . . ." I inhaled as if about to dive into a lap pool. "I have to go through these damn grade books after all and see if the name of another disappointed student pops up." My shoulders slumped at the sight of the rows of books lined up in the drawer, and I heard myself sigh. Reviewing them would take a long time, and I lacked Abelard Constantine's penchant for cheerfulness in the face of drudgery.

"Bel, going through all those record books would be a viable strategy if you had nothing else to do." Wendy paused while I sat wondering where she was going by reminding me of my overbooked schedule. "Besides, maybe the person who posted that rap isn't a student from one of your classes." Before I could question this seemingly illogical conjecture, Wendy continued. "Maybe someone who came before the Disciplinary Committee when you were serving on it is the author. Duh." Wendy's suggestion seemed so good that I instantly forgave her for the insulting and overused monosyllable with which she ended it.

But then I realized that Wendy's timesaving brainstorm was not, in fact, on target, so I said, "This nasty rap is all about my speech course. He must have been in one of my classes."

"So what? Everybody takes Speech, and a lot of us teach it. It's a required course. If some screwed-up kid harbored a grudge because he thinks you voted to suspend or expel him, he could easily get back at you by smearing your teaching on *pickurprofs.com*. So far the Web offers no forum for evaluating the performance of the Disciplinary Committee. Besides if he even mentioned that committee, he'd lose a lot of his anonymity." Wendy smiled, pleased once more with her logic. "Or maybe he was disciplined by the committee when you were on it and later had you for a course. That happened to me, remember?"

I must have looked puzzled because she refreshed my memory. "I voted to expel that kid who was selling copies of the New Jersey Basic Skills Test to other students. Two years later he appealed, reenrolled, and turned up in my children's lit class." Wendy's voice became shrill at the recollection of this nasty episode and its awkward aftermath. "He probably made and sold copies of all my tests." One corner of her mouth twitched at the thought of the rogue entrepreneur in action.

I thought about what she said for a moment. "You know something? You just may be right. There were several students who were expelled or suspended or otherwise penalized by that committee while I was on it." I remembered all too well the many hours I'd spent deliberating with colleagues over how to handle a student who had cursed out a professor and another who had come to class stoned and babbling. There had been many such cases, many hours spent trying to decide them, many unpopular decisions. "I'm going to look through the minutes of some of those sessions right now."

This time I tugged open the drawer reserved for the detritus of my extensive committee work. There weren't as many folders in it as there were grade books in the other drawer, but each folder was fat with paper. RECC committees, with their minutes, agendas, reports, drafts of reports, proposals, counterproposals, and statements of goals, were responsible for the destruction of entire forests. For once I was glad that my inner pack rat had forced me to hang on to all that paper. I extricated the folder labeled DISCIPLINARY COMMITTEE and began to flip through the pages, scanning each one. Before the end of the afternoon, I'd found what I sought.

That night after Sol and I had finished dinner and done the dishes, he settled on the sofa with the *New York Times* on the table beside him. I was lugging my book bag to the nearby dining room table, where I was about to start reading student papers. But Sol, always loath to lose me to my work, continued a conversation we had begun over dinner. "So you think it's this Brent kid who was suspended for bringing a weapon to school?" Sol posed this question as I passed. He patted the sofa, inviting me to join him there. I had spent a good chunk of time going through Disciplinary Committee records, so I was behind on my preparation for the next day's Composition II class. I wanted to return essays and schedule conferences, and I still had about fifteen papers left to read and comment on. Torn between duty and desire, I stood in front of the sofa. Sol reached for my hand and pulled me down beside him. My book bag landed on the floor at our feet. "Those papers will keep a few minutes. Tell me more about this Brent character. You said he came before the Disciplinary Committee when you were on it, and he was suspended for threatening another student, maybe with a knife. If he's still armed, still mad, and still at RECC, of course I'm going to start worrying. Anybody else on that committee get a nasty write-up on-line?"

"Good question," I said. I was already feeling guilty about the unread papers, so I answered brusquely and resisted Sol's effort to pull me closer. If I got too comfortable, I'd never summon the energy and will to finish what I had to do. "Here's what I learned from the minutes. On the way out of political science class, Brent Rente threatened to 'hurt' another male student who had been paying attention to Brent's girlfriend. Professor Dyson overheard the threat and was afraid Brent might carry it out because on another occasion he had seen Brent take something that might have been a knife out of his pocket." Sol stretched out his legs and lowered his stocking feet to the coffee table. He sighed with contentment.

Determined to get my work done that evening, I kept my own feet firmly planted on the floor. Impatient, I spoke a little faster. "Dyson told Brent he had to see a counselor if he wanted to return to class. Brent was resistant, so Dyson walked Brent over to the counseling service himself. Tom Coffin, our best counselor, had had a cancellation. Dyson introduced Brent to Tom, explained the situation, and left. According to Tom, Brent was furious and responded inappropriately, so Tom referred him to the Disciplinary Committee. We suspended him until he sought and got further counseling on anger management."

"Sounds reasonable. Did the kid do that?" Sol asked. He had relinquished my hand and put his arm around me. I gave him a peck on the cheek, pulled away, and stood up.

"I have no idea. I'm going to ask around tomorrow. Now let me get at those papers," I said.

"Yeah, yeah, yeah," said Sol, who had never appreciated competing with my students for my time. "You and your damn papers. I should've married a math teacher." With that, he turned to the newspaper at his elbow and began to read.

Chapter 7

www.pickurprofs.com

River Edge Community College
Jersey City, NJ

Professor Maurice Jarkesi

Makes you sleepy with long lectures but grades fair. Gives retakes on tests.

Evaluation: 4

Professor Emily Connechy

She forget half the time what assignment she give, but she nice when you got to bring a kid to class. She don't return papers fast enough for you to learn what your mistakes are befor you got to write the next one. she grade good though.

Evaluation: 5

Professor Rudolph Tyndall

Came late to almost every class, left early. The bad news is he teaches right out of the book. The good news is if you can read you can get a good grade without too much effort.

Evaluation: 2

Gives only short answer tests. Seems like a high school teacher not a prof. But the class is an easy A.

Evaluation: 3

The next day I looked up my colleagues on the Disciplinary Committee on *pickurprofs.com*. While their reviews were not exactly raves, none of them had been totally trashed. And there was no trace of rap in any of their critiques. My phone call to the registrar revealed only that Brent Rente had graduated last year. Still not convinced that Brent was not my detractor, I made an appointment to talk with Tom Coffin later that day. It was always good to chat with Tom because he was really in tune with students and took the college's mission seriously. As if that weren't enough, he was an extremely attractive man in his late forties. Wendy and I often speculated about whether or not Tom was married or divorced, gay or straight.

I ran my fingers through my hair and sucked in my gut before I knocked on the door of his basement office. "Come on in, Bel. Have a seat. I'll be right with you," he called. When I entered, Tom was seated behind his desk holding a phone in his hand. A crinkly graying beard covered his lower jaw and spilled over his throat. It hid the laugh lines that I was sure radiated out from his mouth and made more prominent the ones that pointed like arrows to the corners of his mischievous green eyes. His head was a mass of matching crinkly gray curls. Wendy thought Tom looked like a modern monk, but he reminded me of a bearded and younger Jack Nicholson, perhaps because Tom shared the actor's expressive eyebrows and impressive girth. Tom pointed at a coffeepot brewing on a small stand in a corner of the tiny office. I shook my head, sat down, and waited for him to finish his conversation. "Glad to hear it, Larissa. Stop by my office tomorrow and pick up those forms, okay?" He put down the phone and treated me to a grin of welcome.

"Sorry, Bel. Good to see you. You don't get down here often enough. What can I do for you?" Tom took a swig of coffee from a thermos on his desk. In spite of the warmth of his greeting, I could tell the man was in a rush. I had walked past three students waiting in the corridor, presumably for him. RECC only had two full-time counselors at the moment, and even Batty Hattie, Tom's less than competent colleague, was always busy. Grateful that he had made time for me at all, I got to the point.

"There's a really nasty rap critique of me on *pickurprofs.com*." To my dismay, Tom nodded, apparently familiar with both the site and the rotten rhyme. My stomach churned, but I went on. "I'm trying to figure out who put it there. Brent Rente was brought up before the Disciplinary Committee while I served on it, so I wondered if, maybe, he posted it to get back at me." Tom's eyes had brightened at the sound of Brent's name, but his dark eyebrows contorted into a scowl as

I continued. "He's not registered this semester. Any idea where he is and what he's doing?"

"As a matter of fact, I do, Bel. Brent's at State, majoring in psychology. You folks on that committee did that kid a big favor." It was my turn to scowl in consternation. Tom continued. "You gave him a choice between suspension and anger management counseling. At first he was really resistant to having his psyche plumbed in order to continue his education. But I told him if Tony Soprano could benefit from therapy, so could he. He agreed to try it." The curve of Tom's smile was barely visible through the tangle of his beard. "I ran those sessions myself, and Brent came, and he really got into it. Bel, believe it or not, Brent's one of my success stories." I gave Tom a thumbs-up to show that I appreciated the import of Brent's transformation as well as of Tom's role in it.

"Like I said, he's at State, majoring in psychology. He calls in every now and then to say hello and brag about how well he's doing. Wants to work with troubled teens." Tom's voice fairly purred with pleasure at the thought of his protégé's total turnaround. "Besides, he probably couldn't come up with a rap like that. He's not much of a wordsmith."

"You've seen that review?" My question was purely rhetorical. It was clear that I was notorious.

"Yeah, I advise students to consult that website before they register. You may be a good and caring prof, Bel, but some of your colleagues . . ." Tom shook his head. "It's good for students to have access to information, even if it's not all accurate."

"I know," I said. It felt odd for me, a civil rights advocate from way back, to be perceived as opposed to students expressing their opinions. "But I'd prefer it if the site was monitored for racism and sexism and comments unrelated to one's teaching ability."

"Me too, but even as is, that site is better than nothing. It encourages students to be proactive rather than passive during the registration process. And you know as well as I do, that's a good thing." Tom glanced at his watch. "But I don't blame you for wanting to know who posted that rap review. It's pretty hostile. I'll keep my ear to the ground, and if I hear anything, about who might have written it, I'll let you know. You be careful, Bel, because, unfortunately not all of our students have gone through anger management counseling."

"Thanks, Tom," I said, smiling. But my smile was superficial as I realized that I was back to square one. Bad boy Brent Rente had become a poster person for mental health. I spent the rest of the afternoon going through my grade books, searching the rosters of speech classes past, trying to find someone who had both the motive and the verbal ability to have posted such a scathing critique.

I got through about half the books and noted many students who'd failed or gotten poor grades, but only a few of those might have been able to construct a rap poem—and they had retaken the course and done well. It didn't help when Wendy breezed in after her last class and punned, "Still trying to figure out who gave you such a bad rap? It's a good thing you're so obsessive. I'd have given up already." Then she gathered her things and left for the day. I stayed a half hour longer until four when, bleary-eyed and depressed, I too left the office.

Wearily I scanned the lavender Post-its lined up on

the dashboard of my car. Each of them served to remind me of a chore or appointment that I might otherwise forget. I had a handheld organizer, but often failed to consult it until after I'd missed out on a meeting or neglected an errand. But these little flags were hard to ignore, and in the past few years they had provided reliable cues to prod my midlife memory. The one closest to the steering wheel read GROCERIES. GOOD DEAL AFTER CLASSES.

Once every couple of weeks either Sol or I made a run to our local big box discount store and stocked up on everything from toilet tissue to salad greens for ourselves and for Ma and Sofia. When we'd persuaded those two to stop driving, we'd offered to help with their errands. Sol had done it last, and that day it was my turn. I was not in the mood to navigate my way through the always crowded parking lot and then to join the throng of other thrifty shoppers, prowling the miles of aisles for bargains and buys. Nor did I relish the prospect of loading the unbagged groceries into the car, hauling them into the house, dividing the enormous quantities of paper towels, Kleenex, cereals, produce, and meat, and then hauling half the stuff back out to the car again to take to Ma and Sofia.

I flashed my Good Deal card at the greeter and made my weary way inside. Once I reached the grocery department, though, I experienced a mood shift that, for once, had nothing to do with hormones and everything to do with timing. They had started serving samples! I'm a self-confessed sample slut, one of those shameless shoppers who makes her way from tidbit to tidbit, accepting every morsel offered. There was no wedge of apple crisp, chicken quesadilla, or three cheese ravioli that I had not tasted. I planted myself in front of a woman nuking small slabs of chocolate chip cookie dough and hovered. When she thought the cookies were finished, she removed the tray from the microwave and began to place the tiny disks carefully into little paper cupcake holders on the table between us. I reached out. "Give them a minute," she cautioned. "They're still very hot."

"That's okay," I said, trying not to sound desperate. "They look so good." I thrust my hand out again. And it stayed there, frozen over the tray of cookies. On the other side of the small table stood Naftali Thompson. I gaped at him. There was something different about the short wiry figure in the baggy green camouflage pants and the oversized black sweatshirt who was staring back at me, his eyes narrowed and his lips locked in a straight line across his face. I retracted my hand and moved around the table to greet him. He was, after all, a former student and a vet. I extended my right hand to take his, but his right hand was not there. My own hand dangled awkwardly between us, a reminder of all that he had lost. "Oh, Naftali. I'm so sorry. Oh my God." Naftali snatched a cookie with his left hand, turned on his heels, and strode away.

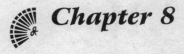

Chapter 8

**Jersey City Native
Wounded in Iraq**

by Josiah Dibbons
The *Jersey City Herald* staff reporter

Jersey City native Spc. Naftali Thompson was among those wounded this week in Iraq when the vehicle he was driving struck a mine outside of Tikrit. Thompson was a passenger in a Heavy Expanded Mobility Tactical Truck or "hemmit," an eight-tired vehicle carrying rations and water, to troops billeted two miles south of Tikrit on Highway One when the explosion occurred.

The nineteen-year-old Thompson, who aspired to a career as a rap artist and performed as NasT, is well known in local hip-hop venues as a clever lyricist and dynamic rapper. Thompson's sister and brother, Olivia Durango and Marcus Thompson, learned of their brother's injury two days after it happened and after he had been flown to a hospital in Germany. Since then they have been in frequent phone contact with army medical personnel. According to Olivia, the wounded GI is being flown to Walter Reed Army Medical Center in Washington, D.C., for further treatment. She and Marcus are planning to visit him there. "I raised Naftali. He's my baby," she explained. "Yeah and he was doing good over there. His commanding officer told me Naftali was going to be promoted to sergeant when this happened," added his brother. The extent of the young soldier's injuries is not yet known.

In spite of being a newspaper junkie, I'd missed the brief article about Naftali that had appeared in our local rag nearly a year ago. If I'd read it, I might have been better prepared when our paths had crossed that afternoon at Good Deal. But believing Naftali to be still in Iraq, and unaware of his injury, I was badly shaken by our encounter. "Wendy, I'm telling you, after I saw that poor kid, I flew out of Good Deal. I didn't shop or anything. I just got out of there. I'm in the car heading home." Clutching my cell phone in one hand, I maneuvered my old Toyota around the corner with the other. I was breaking my resolution never to use a cell phone while driving, so I didn't bring much expertise to the activity, but just then I didn't care. I had to talk to somebody who would understand, and I knew Wendy would. "It was like a nightmare seeing him there with that empty sleeve dangling from his sweatshirt."

I pulled the car into the vest pocket park across the street from our house and wedged it between Sol's car and a pickup truck. "Oh God, Wendy, when I gave him that D, it cost him his arm."

"Bel, get a grip. That boy's injury is *not* your fault. He probably did poorly in other courses beside yours." I could tell by the shrillness in her voice that Wendy was once again worried about my state of mind. "And remember what you always tell me. 'We don't give students grades. They earn them,' and that kid earned a D. The fact that he enlisted is not your fault either, and the fact that he got his arm blown off is certainly not your fault." The more adamant Wendy felt, the faster and louder she spoke.

"But if I'd given him an incomplete or even a C . . ." I stammered. I didn't make any moves to get out of the car. "Wendy, did you ever have a student who enlisted and was injured?" I willed her to say yes, so I wouldn't have to bear this awful guilt alone. There just had to be other nitpicking profs whose grading practices pushed kids into the service where, during wartime, they were likely to be maimed and even killed. There must be legions of us in colleges all over the country, each upholding some outdated version of academic standards in an era when a D or an F could be a death sentence. I didn't wait for her to answer my question before I went on. "Wendy, you should have seen the way he looked at me. His eyes were so cold and hard. He hates me for sure now. And you know what, Wendy?" Again I didn't wait for her to answer. "I don't blame him. I don't blame him one bit. No wonder he wrote that rap about me. He must have written it after he got back."

"Bel, remember I told you I taught high school in the sixties?" Now it was Wendy's turn to continue before I could answer. "Well, I had a bright but lazy student who got a C in my college-level English course. His name was Peter O'Dowd. Because of that C, he didn't get into the only college he'd applied to. He went to Vietnam, and when I saw him years later . . ." I could hear her intake of breath. When she spoke again her voice was barely audible. "That kid was a blind beggar panhandling on the street. He was so stoned he could hardly stand up. And when I approached him and spoke to him, he said he didn't remember me." I was disgusted with myself for feeling somehow relieved by Wendy's sad story. It explained why some educators trace rampant grade inflation at many of the nation's top four-year colleges back to the Vietnam era.

I started when I heard tapping on the car window. It was Sol. His eyes were clouded with worry. "Wendy, thanks. I guess misery really does love company."

"Think nothing of it, Bel. I'm always happy to dredge up the worst moments of my life to make you feel better. But remember, you and I may know it's not your fault that poor kid got hurt. But it sounds like he blames you. And now he's not in Iraq. He's here. Be careful. See you tomorrow." I heard the click of the phone when she hung up.

As Sol and I crossed the street and entered the house, I repeated the story of my encounter with Naftali. Of course, Sol began to worry as soon as he learned that Naftali was back in Jersey City and seriously injured. "I don't like it at all. This kid's got a grudge now that's more complicated, more serious, than before, and I think that makes him dangerous. Besides, in the army they train people to kill. He's probably got a gun." Sol was so concerned about my safety that he couldn't focus on my feelings of guilt and remorse. "Damn, I wish I hadn't agreed to baby-sit for Maya, but Alexis is desperate. I told her I'd drive up tonight so I could be there first thing tomorrow. She has to leave early to make that conference. She's presenting in one of the morning sessions."

"It's okay," I said. And usually it was okay for Sol to take off whenever his professor daughter phoned and drive several hours to her home in upstate New York to baby-sit for his granddaughter. This time it didn't feel quite so okay, not because I feared Naftali, but because I wanted Sol's company, wanted him to listen to my concerns and reassure me. What I said was, "But if you're driving up there tonight, we should eat early. I don't like the idea of you on the road after midnight."

Sol had just begun to fashion a meal out of whatever he could scrounge from the depths of the fridge and the freezer, when the phone rang. I picked it up. "Bel, turn on Channel 8." It was Ma. She hung up before I had a chance to ask her what the urgency was behind her cryptic message. I walked into the living room and turned on the TV. It was already tuned to Channel 8. Fortunately I was standing in front of the sofa when the sound and picture came on because the damning words

in her class it only bitches get de A,
she hate stuntin niggaz so maybe she gay

blazed across the screen and were being read aloud by the commentator, Jackie Pendleton. I collapsed onto the sofa and called to Sol.

"What is it, love? I'm trying to defrost this chicken in the microwave." Sol took his cooking very seriously since he retired and we'd remodeled our kitchen.

"Screw the chicken. Please look at this. Oh my God, I think I'm going to be sick," I said, unable to project my voice over the rising tide of nausea. Sol crossed the open kitchen to the living room area, wiping his hands on a towel he carried. "Look. It's that website, the critique. It's on cable, on the evening news. Everybody in the world is going to know what a lousy prof I am. And kids into hip-hop around here will figure out who wrote it. Then when the word gets out about the extent of Naftali's injuries, they're going to think I'm a lot worse than that. And they'll be right." I hung my head and bawled.

I had no appetite for the chicken cacciatore and pasta that Sol had crafted out of the dribs and drabs of stuff we had on hand. I was pushing a chicken thigh around on my plate when the phone rang. I let Sol pick it up. It was Ma again. When Sol hung up, he was smiling. "Your remarkable mother says it's a good thing that Jackie Pendleton has exposed the site and slammed it for being a repository of vengeful and ungrammatical diatribes against competent and caring faculty. I swear, Bel, your mother could spin an obituary into a birth announcement."

Calls continued to punctuate our meal. After he hung up from a chat with Illuminada, Sol summarized. "She didn't say why, but Illuminada thinks it's good that Jackie did some research and interviewed Sarita Singh. I guess we didn't catch that part."

"Oh don't worry. That show will be rebroadcast all week at different times. Nobody in this county who's alive and breathing will be able to avoid seeing it," I said, tossing another wad of wet Kleenex onto the pile beside my placemat.

My sarcasm was lost on Sol who, it seemed, had resumed worrying about my safety. "The thing is that the guy who wrote that rap is a wounded vet, possibly armed. And this publicity may inspire him to, you know, to do something even worse. I'd like to know how you plan to protect yourself from him. Dammit, I wish I weren't leaving tonight."

The image of the empty black sweatshirt sleeve dangling from Naftali's shoulder had made a permanent home in my head, so it was easy to speak to Sol's concern. "He's armed, all right, Sol. One-armed. What can he do to me?" Even the recollection of Naftali's angry expression didn't inspire fear as much as sympathy, maybe even empathy. I found myself rubbing my shoulder every time I flashed on the young man's injury.

Betty called while Sol was doing the dishes. As he listened, Sol's eyes darkened and his murmured interjections sounded grave. When he hung up, he left the sink and took a seat across from me at the table. "Betty figures Woodman is going to go over the edge when he hears about this show. There's nothing like having the college's faculty bad-mouthed on TV to rile the Trustees and hurt recruitment yabba dabba dabba." Sol gestured with his fingers and thumb to indicate the enraged yapping I might expect to hear from the college's president.

I lowered my head to my arms at the table and began to weep again. When I could speak, I said, "I don't blame Woodman. Not only have I ruined this kid's life, but now I've hurt the college. Who wants to matriculate at a school with boring sexist and racist profs?"

When the phone rang again, Sol said, "Maybe I'll just let the machine take this call. We've had enough drama for one night."

I shook my head. Ever since my children had grown old enough to leave home for a play date or a party, I'd been unable to hear the phone ring without picking it up. And now that Rebecca and Mark were theoretically adults but Ma and Sofia were so fragile, I still felt the same way. "No, answer it, please. It might be Ma. Something might be wrong."

With a resigned shrug, Sol picked up the phone. In a moment he returned it to its cradle. "Nobody there," he said. "Not even a telemarketer. I sure hope that kid isn't going to start making intimidating phone calls." For the third time that evening, Sol's eyes darkened. When the phone rang a second later, he said, "Let the machine take this one, please, Bel. If it's a prankster, I don't want to encourage him. If it's one of the kids, we can pick up." I nodded, and we sat there in silence until we heard our answering machine's deliberately innocuous message, one recorded years ago by my son, Mark, who had returned to the nest for a brief respite from the demands of adult life. "You have reached 201-555-4493. We are unable to take your call now. Please leave your name and number and one of us will get back to you."

"Hi, Bel, it's Sarah. Boy, I guess you pissed off one of our local gangsta rappas. What's the scoop? I know there's a huge story lurking in between those lousy lines. Get back to me. I'm home tonight." It was good to hear Sarah's voice, even though I suspected she was annoyed with me for not having told her about *pickur-profs.com* when it was still a scoop. In return for a few favors, I'd given my old friend the heads-up on the story behind the story of the murder of RECC President Altagracia Garcia. That scoop had finally earned Sarah the promotion to managing editor she had long deserved. Ever since, she'd counted on me to be a kind of informal liaison between RECC and the *Jersey City Herald*. "Do you want to call her back?" Sol had begun loading the dishwasher while we listened to Sarah's message. "Sarah's always got an insightful take on things."

"Are you kidding? If I tell Sarah about Naftali, she'll want to do a story on him as a returning war hero, and that will make everything worse," I replied, annoyed that Sol hadn't figured this out for himself.

"I know that," Sol answered. "But Naftali's going to be news regardless, and wouldn't you just as soon Sarah write the story as somebody else? Maybe she can spin it so it doesn't make you look like a witch."

"She's a journalist, not a magician, Sol," I said. "Besides, seeing how things worked out, I am a witch."

"I hate the thought of leaving you alone after this bombshell. I think I'll call Alexis and . . ." Sol reached for the phone.

Putting my hand on his arm to stop him, I said, "Don't even think about it. Get your stuff together and go. I'll be fine. I've got so many papers to read I won't even notice you're gone. But call me when you get there so I know you made it." It wasn't long before Sol was out the door carrying the small overnight bag that he kept packed for his frequent overnight trips upstate. He was a shoo-in for this year's Grandfather of the Year Award.

I tried to concentrate on the speech outlines my students had submitted, but I was distracted by images of Naftali. First I imagined him as I remembered him, young, rebellious, and whole. He hadn't been a very conscientious student, but he was bright and articulate, and he'd shown a certain presence, what the kids call attitude, that might carry him far. By contrast, the post-Iraq Naftali I'd glimpsed that afternoon had appeared old beyond his years, his rebellion mutated into rage, and his missing arm an unbearable loss. It was nearly eleven when, finally finished with my work, I turned on the TV.

Sure enough, Jackie Pendleton's show *Hudson Happenings* was rebroadcast as part of the late news. Knowing Sol would want to see the whole thing, I taped it from beginning to end while I watched. This time I caught Jackie's interview with Sarita Singh. Sarita replied to Jackie's queries about *pickurprofs.com* in the same cool tone she had used when speaking with Illuminada and me. When Sally asked her how she knew students benefited from the information made available on the site, Sarita read verbatim endorsements that grateful students had sent her via e-mail. " 'Thanks to *pickurprofs.com* I got professors who are willing to give extra help.' " " '*Pickurprofs.com* helped me to not take classes with profs who are known for their boringness.' " " 'My GPA is going way up this semester. I stayed away from profs that other students said were hard graders or gave too much work. No more probation for me.' "

I wasn't the only RECC faculty member whose reviews Sally aired. She cited a few scathing critiques of several of my colleagues. She also read some positive ones, including a string of flattering superlatives about my teaching posted by grateful students. But, as I told Sol when he called, Naftali's lengthy and bleep-filled cri de coeur stood out from the others just as its angry, injured author had known it would.

Chapter 9

**Returning Vet Wounded in Iraq
Takes on Prof Who Put Him There**

**Local Hip-Hop War Hero
Raps for Revenge**

Spc. Naftali Thompson, whose arm was blown off
last winter by a roadside bomb in Iraq, returned to
Jersey City to a warm welcome from area veterans,
as well as from the local hip-hop community. Thompson, an aspiring rapper who performed as Nas-T before enlisting in the military, has long been part of
the Hudson County hip-hop scene. At a welcome-
home party last night at the Jersey City VFW Head-
quarters, VFW President Major Lance McFee turned
the mike over to Thompson amid cheers and salutes.
The young vet proved he hasn't lost his touch by
treating assembled family and friends to a hard-
driving beef about a RECC professor named Bel Barrett whose antipathy to black men drove him to

enlist. He also previewed another percussive beef called "Roadkill" about the risks facing convoys of GIs traveling in Iraq. (Read an interview in next Sunday's feature section in which Thompson tells *Herald* editor Sarah Woolf about his tour of duty, the explosion, his medical ordeal, and his future.)

I had opened the morning paper with trepidation after a sleepless night. I'd lain awake reliving Naftali's performance or lack thereof in my speech class and wondering how I might have responded to him differently. Should I have tried to reschedule the two conferences he missed? Given him yet another chance to make up his speech? I'd successfully persuaded countless students with far less ability than Naftali to retake courses, get counseling, do whatever it took to stay in school. Where had I gone wrong with Naftali? I was still pondering this question when I spotted the article. Just then Sol called, and I read it to him, my voice grainy with fatigue, dulled by despair. When I finished, he said, "It's Sol's Law. Just when you think things can't get any worse, they do." Anxiety made his usually deep voice sound a bit thin and reedy.

I recalled his drawn face and the lines around his eyes when he'd left the night before. I shouldn't have read him the article. What had I been thinking? I had to reassure him that I was okay and that I was going to get through this ever-worsening nightmare. "Sol, you know as well as I do that I'd have gladly sacrificed my hard-earned professional reputation if I could have spared Naftali the injury he's suffered." Sol was silent, probably wondering where the hell I was going with this line of thought. "And you know I'd gladly give up the same reputation if I thought it would spare River Edge Community College's reputation."

"Yeah, I know, love" was all he said in response.

"As the last best hope for higher education for thousands of poor urban students, RECC doesn't need bad publicity." There was no affirming response from Sol this time, so I continued to speechify. "But I can't change any of this. So I'm just going to go to school and teach my classes. I'll deal with my own remorse and everybody else's reaction as best I can. That's all I can do."

When Sol again said, "I know, love," I realized that although I had meant my words to reassure him, I had also needed reassuring. I was talking myself into going to work. Sol's next words were: "I told Alexis I'd be leaving tonight. She promised me Xhi would be back by seven to look after his Maya. I love you. Take care of yourself."

When I reached my office, I saw that Wendy had left a chocolate croissant on my desk, something she hadn't done since the day years ago, during the investigation of Vinny Vallone's murder, when I told her I thought Sol had dumped me for another woman. Sighing, I assumed that my thoughtful officemate had either caught the news on TV or read the article in the *Herald*. Not surprisingly, there was a message on my machine from Betty summoning me to President Woodman's office after my first two classes. There was also a message from Marietta Malfetta, a reporter on the *RECC Rag*, the college's student newspaper. That was no surprise either.

What was surprising, though, was that my classes

went smoothly. I had decided not to bring up the matter at all with my 8 A.M. ESL group. Attendance was low, as it often was in that early morning session, and the few students who straggled in seemed oblivious to their professor's new notoriety. Those students were less likely than my more English proficient students to understand the nuances of Naftali's rap, even if they had seen it on TV.

In my 9 A.M. Cultures and Values class, where attendance was also down, a few students had caught the news on TV. Angered by Naftali's post, they vowed to write critiques in defense of me to contradict his attack on my teaching ability. I didn't encourage them, but I didn't discourage them either. I assigned *pickurprofs.com* as a journal topic because in this group we had often considered the impact of changes in technology on contemporary culture. We agreed that after everybody had had a chance to see the site and reflect on it, we would incorporate *pickurprofs.com* and the media barrage it had generated into our ongoing discussion.

After class I returned to my office to wait until it was time for my appointment with the president. As I typed up a few exam questions, I thought I heard a knock at the door, but when I swung my chair around and peered out, there was no one there. Feeling edgy, I decided to leave the office and arrive a few minutes early for my audience with Woodman. Most students and faculty used the elevators, so the stairwell was deserted. I flashed back to the time I followed a suspect up these same stairs when I was investigating the killing of a colleague.

Then, forcing myself to focus on the present, I heard

footsteps behind me. The hairs on my arms prickled and I climbed the stairs faster. The footsteps sounded closer together and louder. Was Naftali following me? Shivering, I recalled the hostility I'd seen in his eyes during our brief encounter at Good Deal. Not satisfied with insulting me on-line and savaging my professional reputation, had the angry and bitter young man decided to track me down in person and . . . and . . . ?

Before I allowed myself to contemplate what Naftali might do to me should he get me alone, I moved to foil him. When I reached the next landing, I fled the stairwell and took refuge in the ladies' room a few steps down the corridor. I ran into a stall and locked it, relieved to have eluded an enraged adversary. But my adrenaline surged again when the door slammed and footsteps echoed in the room. He had followed me into the ladies' room! Instinctively, I raised my feet, hoping to buy time while I fumbled in my purse for something I could use to defend myself.

That's when I heard the accusatory voice of a breathless young woman: "Professor Barrett! I know you're in there! I'm Marietta Malfetta, with the *RECC Rag*." My pursuer was a reporter from the student newspaper! I felt my muscles relax as I lowered my feet and zipped shut my purse. "I know you're in here, Professor. You haven't returned my calls, so I decided to try to catch up with you today. What do you have to say about the posting about you on *pickurprofs.com*?"

I was torn between admiration for this fledgling paparazzo's persistence and fury at her *chutzpah*. I wanted to utter a haughty "No comment" and flounce off like a celebrity, but instead I flushed the toilet so she'd think I'd actually used it. Then I emerged from my stall, saying sweetly, "Sorry, Ms. Malfetta. I have an appointment with the president in a few moments. I'll contact you when I'm ready to speak to the press." I washed my hands, smoothed down my hair, and left.

In a few moments I was perched on the edge of a chair in the anteroom leading to President Woodman's office. I noted the grim set of Betty's jaw as she sat at her desk talking into a headset and typing rapidly. "One sec, Bel. I'll let him know you're here" was all she said to me after she ended her phone conversation. She stood and walked over to the door to Woodman's office and peered in. I imagined the inquiring look on her face and his solemn nod in response. She signaled me to enter and gave my arm a hard squeeze when I edged by her in the doorway.

I was no stranger to Ron Woodman's fourteenth-floor office or "suite" as he referred to it. President Woodman had relied on my penchant for sleuthing to extricate the college from several other situations that would have resulted in disastrous publicity. His inner sanctum was as I remembered it. The only carpeted area in the chronically underfunded college, it was also the only room to boast a spectacular view of Manhattan's scarred skyline. This vista competed for the visitor's attention with the gilt-framed portraits of members of RECC's Board of Trustees glowering down at the president from behind his massive and highly polished desk. These trustees were an assortment of mostly political appointments in a town where politics has long been synonymous with patronage. RECC provided lucrative consulting and administrative work for the friends and relatives of the trustees, so these trustees didn't want the college to go under. Neither did I.

I entered the office with an apology on my lips, but before I could utter a single word of it, President Woodman rose, and, in lieu of a greeting, waved the morning paper in my face. "How could you do this to us, Bel? How could you betray the college this way? There's going to be an interview with this war hero you failed in Sunday's paper. Maybe even a wrongful discrimination suit." It had not escaped me that Sarah Woolf had gotten the drop on Naftali's story without my help. But there was no time to consider what my old friend, a longtime peace activist, would make of the young veteran's troubling saga because my boss was literally tearing his hair out in front of me. I watched, mesmerized, as, with his free hand, he yanked at a brownish-gray tuft of the wispy wool that circled his bald pate like dark fringe on a pink pillow. The poor man was hysterical. But my sympathy atrophied along with my apology as he continued to rant and flash the paper under my nose. "The college will never survive all this negative publicity. We have to shut down that website. The Board is having an emergency meeting tonight. I've got to have a plan."

Clearly the antianxiety meds that Betty had gotten Ron Woodman to seek and take after 9/11 were not kicking in. They did not seem to be insulating him at all from the panic brought on by the present situation. Moving out of range of the still-flapping newspaper, I spoke in what I hoped was the measured tone of an attendant in a psych ward. "Ron, stop waving that paper and listen to me." To my relief, he lowered the arm that had been brandishing the newspaper. "We can't shut down the website. This is a free country, remember? We prize freedom of speech here." The skin of his neck began to turn reddish purple, and the color crept upward until the man's entire face was a flushed testimony to his frustration and fear. "A RECC alumna started *pickurprofs.com,* and it's actually not a bad idea. She's quite the entrepreneur. She wants to extend the site to serve all the community colleges in New Jersey." I watched as he tried to take in this concept and then to calculate how *pickurprofs.com*'s expansion might affect RECC's current predicament. "What we want to do is to get the webmistress to monitor the site and filter out biased remarks as well as comments that are not related to a professor's teaching. That's got to be part of any plan we put forward."

For a moment, I thought RECC's beleaguered leader looked relieved to have even a piece of a plan articulated for him. "But what about the TV show? And this?" He picked up the paper and was about to resume waving it at me.

"Ron, if you shove that newspaper in my face one more time, I'm going to walk out of here." I spoke quietly and turned toward the door. When I saw him lower the paper again, I stopped walking and, instead, seated myself in one of the chairs across from his desk. "Ron, please sit down. Let's try to talk calmly about this mess." Not unlike a child given a time-out, Ron Woodman retreated to the large chair behind his desk.

Satisfied, I tried to refocus the conversation. "First of all, before we problem-solve, let's get a little perspective. The real tragedy here is that this young man, Naftali Thompson, a RECC dropout, has lost an arm fighting for his . . . for our country." Woodman looked amazed, as if I had just revealed a long-hidden mystery of the universe. While he digested my statement of the obvious, I persisted. "Unfortunately, he blames me and the low grade he earned in my class for the choice he made to drop out of RECC to enlist in the military. He also blames me for his injury." I paused, impressed by how rational I sounded.

Encouraged by the argument I was making, I went on. "It's equally unfortunate that because Naftali was enrolled at RECC and I teach at RECC, the college *is* getting a lot of bad publicity." Woodman nodded, an indication that he understood. I hurried on, eager to make one more point before his notoriously limited attention span ran out. "Ron, you and I have worked together for a long time, and because of that it's important to me that you understand how miserable I am about all of this. I want you to know that I'll gladly do whatever I can to help improve things. But I'm not sure what I can do."

"You can retire," he said. The words slid off his forked tongue so fast and so easily that I knew Ron Woodman had had a plan all along. That's why he hadn't let me walk out, had made a pretense of listening to me. The wimpy wuss was going to force me to resign, to fire me if necessary to placate the Board and the press. As I stood there in stunned silence, assorted headlines began streaming through my head, one after another. RACIST RECC PROF AXED was the first; RECC FACULTY PURGED OF RACIST PROF another; RAPPER RIDS RECC OF RACIST PROF came third; and WEBSITE PURGES RECC OF BIASED PROF was fourth. After RECC BOARD ACCEPTS RESIGNATION OF RACIST PROF, they flashed through my mind so rapidly that I grew dizzy trying to read them. Blinking back tears of hurt and rage, I turned and left the room.

I rushed past Betty's desk, relieved that she had abandoned her post for the moment, probably to visit the ladies room or use the Xerox machine. I didn't want to see anyone until I could pull myself together and process Woodman's devastating suggestion. And I couldn't do that until the headlines trumpeting the end of my career stopped streaking through my brain. I made it back to my office without running into anyone and shut the door behind me, my head still filled with flying banners of newsprint.

A glance at the clock told me that my third class of the morning was to begin in a few minutes. The prospect of the upcoming session of Speech served to slow down the printing press in my head just enough for me to remember that my students were scheduled to rehearse informative talks with partners. These partners would then provide feedback, including suggestions for improvement. If I could keep my head clear, I ought to be able to handle that. I spent the last few minutes before the class collating speech outlines to return and xeroxing handouts of concise tips on body language and delivery.

When I got to the classroom, a few students were already there, but most of them were not. Remembering that attendance had been poor all morning, I expressed some concern as to what had happened to the other twenty or so students. Were they all absent? Had I been so upset that I'd forgotten it was some religious or school holiday? Many RECC students were hard-pressed to find child care for their kids when local public schools were closed. Or perhaps the missing students all had the same class before this one, and it had run over, maybe for a test. No one there seemed to know. With a shrug I divided the six students who had shown up into three sets of partners and advised them as to how I expected them to rehearse. I wanted them to time their partner's speeches and offered to lend my watch to the one couple who didn't have a watch between them.

Just as I was unbuckling mine, the rest of the class trooped in. "Sorry, Professor," said Darius Putee, the first one to cross the threshold. The pudgy young man was out of breath, so his words came out in spurts. "The subway wasn't running." I felt a moment of pure panic. I flashed back to September 11, 2001, when the PATH trains stopped running. "I already missed my Spanish class." Darius, who was calmly opening his book bag, did not look or sound as if we were experiencing another terrorist siege. Before I could ask what had caused the delay, he continued, his nasal voice matter-of-fact, as if recounting a routine disruption. "Some dude got run over last night. They had to get the body off the tracks."

"Yeah, man," said Shariah Valparise, her usually lively voice subdued. "A cop I know was at the station. He tol' me it was Nas-T. You know, that rapper on the news who just got back from Iraq."

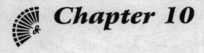 **Chapter 10**

To: JewelCorona@juno.com
From: Bbarrett@circle.com
Re: URGENT Union Matter
Date: 04/30/04 10:15:04

Jewel,

Need to talk with my trusty union rep ASAP. I'm in my office all afternoon tomorrow. Stop in if you have a second. If not, please call me at home.

Thanks,
Bel

I had e-mailed Jewel Corona right after my chat with Ron Woodman. She arrived minutes after I had heard Shariah's report of Naftali's death. After considering Shariah's news for about two seconds, I found it simply unbearable to contemplate, so I decided it must be a rumor. In other words, I denied Shariah's account altogether. After all, I reminded myself, there were other rappers in Jersey City and other veterans. The cop who told Shariah that the body on the subway tracks was Nas-T's might have gotten only a partial ID and made up the rest. Or Shariah herself, not the world's keenest listener, might have misunderstood. For Naftali to have survived an exploding bomb in Iraq only to fall off a subway platform in Jersey City seemed absurd to me. And the more probable scenario, the one in which the injured young vet was depressed and threw himself off the platform in front of a train, was too dreadful to even consider. I was relieved when Jewel's arrival in my office interrupted my brooding.

Eons ago in the eighties, when Wendy and I had banded together secretly with a few other intrepid colleagues to start a faculty union, a forbidden action at patronage-ridden River Edge Community College, I'd been naïve. I never dreamed that *I* would ever need a union to save *my* job. Rather, I'd thought of unionizing as enabling all RECC profs to bargain collectively for tenure, smaller class sizes, functional offices, and salaries comparable to those of faculty at other New Jersey community colleges. And our union had worked that way for twenty years. So Ron Woodman's clear intention to placate the Board by getting rid of me had been, to say the very least, a nasty jolt.

Jewel Corona made no effort to hide her own shock when she arrived at my office, and I told her Woodman was seeking my resignation. As our longtime union rep, Jewel had been around the block with President Woodman a few times, but she was still incredulous. "Bel, you've got to be kidding me! Even Woodhead would never ask *you* to resign. You're the bright light on the faculty! You've been Prof of the Year how many times? You teach the Faculty Development Seminar, for God's sake. You've mentored so many of us. I mean, you're the Mother of All Mentors. And, besides, Bel, how many times did you save Woodhead's sorry ass with your incredible detective work?" Jewel smiled. Her smile was as bright as her checked pants and white jacket were drab. But even the regulation uniform of her first profession did not dim the woman's red-headed radiance or disguise her voluptuous curves. A dazzled older man in Jewel's Baking II class once described her as "a red hot-hot mama in a chef's hat." "What happened, Bel?" Jewel asked, her smile replaced by a frown that drew the sprinkling of freckles on her brow into a cluster.

"Do you know about the website *pickurprofs.com*?" I asked, sighing at the prospect of having to explain Sarita Singh's brainchild yet again.

I was relieved when Jewel nodded. "Yes. Dean Cholent told me I got a really nasty write-up on that site. In fact, he referred to it during my performance review. So I checked out the site. The student who posted the nasty evaluation of me griped that I was willing to help everyone but her and . . . get this, Bel. She said that my car was too nice for a college professor!" Jewel shrugged at the absurdity of both allegations. "I'm pretty sure I know who she is because she's the only student who failed last semester. That kid was all thumbs. She couldn't fry an egg. I think she's taking uppers." Jewel's frown returned. "So I've put *pickurprofs.com* on the agenda for our next union meeting. I haven't logged on to it since then, but I saw enough to know that if our department chairs are going to use the site to evaluate our teaching ability, it should be monitored to avoid extraneous comments. The way it is now, it's a magnet for abuse."

"I agree," I said. "But the webmistress isn't very co-operative. I'll tell you about her later. For now, just check this out." I handed Jewel the printout of Naftali's rap. She glanced at it and said, "Yes, I caught this on TV. It was on *Hudson Happenings* this morning. It's nasty, but who would take this tripe seriously?" Jewel smoothed out the printout on Wendy's desk. "I mean, certainly no one who knows you would pay any atten-tion to this."

"That's what you think. That's also what I had hoped. Silly me." I could hear the bitterness in my voice. "But Woodman is totally freaked out over the publicity it's gotten. The Board is having an emer-gency meeting later today. To make matters worse, you probably know that my detractor is a vet who's lost an arm." Jewel nodded. "He's a war hero. I mean, he was. I mean . . ." I'd confused Jewel with my sudden shift of verb tense, so once again, her freckles were conven-ing as her brow contracted. I took a deep breath and tried to explain. "Oh, Jewel, I just heard that the poor kid is dead."

"Oh no. Was his wound fatal?" Jewel's shoulders slumped and her eyes widened.

"No. He lost an arm. That was bad enough. But as you know, he came home recently. Well"—I gulped air before I continued—"I heard from my students that he was run over by a PATH train early this morning. I don't even know for sure if that's true." The strain of having taught three classes on no sleep and my despair over the events of the past few days had lowered my voice and slowed my speech so that my words came out in a hoarse drone. "Now I really don't know what to do."

"I'm glad you contacted me, Bel," said Jewel, shaking her head as if to dislodge the image evoked by my report of Naftali's death. "Regardless of what has happened to this poor boy,Woodman should not be threatening you by suggesting that you resign. You're not a sacrificial lamb he can just throw to the damn Board to appease them." Energized by my plight, she spoke with conviction, her voice strong and her diction crisp. I reminded myself that we had elected Jewel union rep several times because of the zeal and skill with which she championed faculty rights. "Has he sent you anything in writing?" My union rep was all business now, like me, drawn to the task of saving my job and repelled by even the thought of Naftali's death. If Naftali were really dead, neither she nor I could bring him back, but Jewel could do something to help me keep my job.

While we were talking, the office phone rang several times. I didn't want to talk to anyone else. Whoever was calling might bring news that would pierce the cocoon of denial I was trying to spin around myself. She or he might tell me that Shariah's "rumor" was fact, that the corpse on the subway tracks that morning was, indeed, Naftali's. Praying that the caller was not a relative in desperate need of immediate help that only I could provide, I forced myself to let the damn phone ring until the machine picked up. But I soon realized I was in a classic no-win situation: Damned if I did and damned if I didn't. At each ring anxiety tightened my shoulders and knotted my stomach. I felt as if I'd invented a new form of torture, listening to a ringing phone without picking it up.

Jewel said, "I'll get on this, Bel, and get back to you about what the next step is. But before I go, you said you had something to tell me about the webmistress of *pickurprofs.com*?" Even in my misery, it was refreshing to talk with someone who still had her short-term memory. I had already forgotten that I'd promised to tell Jewel about Sarita Singh.

"Yes, you're right. Here it is in a nutshell." I took a deep breath to fortify myself to tell this story yet again, as well as to make the effort being succinct required. "Sarita Singh is an RECC graduate who's at State now. Illuminada Guttierez, an adjunct at RECC, and I met with Sarita. We suggested that she monitor the posts to eliminate sexism and racism and to exclude factors unrelated to a prof's teaching ability."

"Like what kind of car she drives," said Jewel.

"Yes or like whether she's Puerto Rican," I added. "Anyway, Sarita said the site was very popular with students because it performs a real service. In fact, she plans to expand it to include all the other New Jersey community colleges. And, while she didn't say *pickurprofs.com* wouldn't benefit from monitoring, she has no time to do it. She's smart and very self-confident."

"Thanks, Bel. I'll try to get over there to talk with her before the next meeting. Maybe I'll even invite her to address the union. Meanwhile, why don't you go home and get some rest? You look like you just catered a three-course meal for a few hundred guests all by yourself. And don't worry about Woodman. By the time I finish with him, he'll be begging you to stay on."

The instant Jewel left, I listened to my messages.

Ma had called, but she was hardly in distress herself. Rather, she told me not to worry because I was a wonderful teacher. Sol said he would be home a little earlier than he'd expected. Sarah Woolf wanted to interview me about "Nas-T as a student." Betty hoped I was okay after my chat with Woodman. And Illuminada had called twice, saying only, "*Chiquita*, get back to me on my cell ASAP." And neither of my kids had called, so I could only assume that they had managed to survive without being able to reach me for the past half hour.

I forced myself to return Illuminada's calls, but while her number was ringing, Wendy came into the office, so I hung up. Wendy's puckish features were drawn, and her eyes made straight for my face. "Bel, I'm so sorry."

Assuming that she had learned through the notorious RECC grapevine that Woodman was trying to can me, I tossed her a flip reply. "Whatever for? Getting hassled by Woodman is practically a distinction around here. Besides, our union is behind me. I just talked to Jewel."

With her eyes still glued to my face, Wendy said, "What are you talking about?"

"I'm telling you that your ill-concealed dream of having this entire office to yourself could become reality. Woodman's trying to can me." Surprise widened her eyes and jutted her chin forward. I realized that Wendy had not yet heard about Woodman's scheme. "What are *you* talking about?" I asked.

Wendy sat down, lowering her books and papers to the desk in front of her. "You don't know?"

"Know what?" I said, but I did know. The hairs on

my arms stiffened as I braced myself for her next words.

"They found your rapper's body on the PATH tracks this morning." If Wendy noticed that I cringed at her word choice, she gave no sign. "That's why so many students were coming in late. Didn't you notice? Didn't anybody tell you? Everybody's saying he jumped in front of a train. Oh, Bel, I'm so sorry." Her eyes still fixed on mine, Wendy reached out to touch my arm.

The gentle pressure of her hand on my arm had the force of a knife thrust. "I did hear, but I've been hoping it wasn't true." I paused. "That poor kid." Tears I'd fought back welled and spilled. "Doesn't he have a sister?" Before Wendy could answer, I went on. "She must feel so bad. She said in that article that she raised him. He was her baby." My head was down on my desk, my tears blurring the dates on the blotter that served as a calendar. "He must have been suffering from post-traumatic stress disorder, like Sol after 9/11. Imagine getting blown up and losing an arm. Imagine what that must have been like." My words were muffled by my own arms as they cushioned my head, so Wendy probably had trouble understanding them.

But I could tell by the way she answered that she got the idea. "Bel, this is awful, but it's not your fault." Wendy sounded angry. "We've all got former students over there now, either from the regular army or the reserves. The poor kid probably did suffer from PTSD, but not because of you. You can't take responsibility for his suicide. That's crazy." As if that settled the matter, Wendy shoved a wad of Kleenex into one of my hands and said, "So pull yourself together and tell me what's going on with Woodman. He can't be trying to can you."

After blowing my nose and wiping my eyes, I sat up. "Well, he can—and he is. He's freaked over the bad PR the college is getting because of this whole mess and so is the Board. Even before he could have known about Naftali's death, he asked me to retire. We know what that means."

Wendy's jaw dropped. "He can't do that. Wait until the Faculty Senate hears about this. We'll stand behind you. After all, as I said before, this could have happened to any of us. You're not the only one getting slammed on that website. I think I already told you I've put *pickurprofs.com* on the agenda for the next Faculty Senate meeting." Wendy touched my arm again. "Now, why don't you go home? You look like you've eaten a poisoned apple and lost your glass slipper both on the same day."

Chapter 11

Depressed Vet Killed by PATH Train

Family, Fans Mourn Rapper

Port Authority Engineer Horace Sims spotted the man lying on the tracks seconds after the subway train rounded the curve leading to the Grove Street terminal in Jersey City early this morning. "It was too late," the distraught Sims said. "No way I could stop the train in time." Medical examiner Dr. Carlotta Guevera pronounced the man dead. Police identified the body as that of twenty-one-year-old Spc. Naftali Thompson of Jersey City, recently returned from military duty in Iraq.

Train service between Jersey City and Hoboken and Jersey City and New York was delayed while police removed the corpse. Admirers of Thompson's rap music, which he performed locally under the name of Nas-T, have brought flowers, poems, and photos to the subway platform near where his body was found. "Naftali was my baby," said Thompson's sister, Olivia Durango. "He was like a son to me. I raised him. He was a good boy."

"Sybil, you can't take responsibility for the whole world. You didn't make this poor kid do badly in your class, you didn't make him enlist, you didn't make him lose an arm, and you certainly didn't make him jump in front of a subway train," said Ma, shoving a plate into the dishwasher with extra force as if to underline her point. "It's like I'm always saying, you think you're responsible for everybody." Echoing Sol and Wendy, Ma had been going on at me like this ever since she'd read about Naftali's death. "Remember when Harold Goldstein, that kid you used to tutor in French, got caught cheating on the final exam?" I almost managed a smile. Ma had been getting a lot of mileage out of poor Harold lately. But I felt lousy, so my face remained glum. When I didn't answer right away, Ma insisted. "Remember, Sybil?" I nodded, trying to focus on the long-gone event she was recalling. "Well, you thought it was your fault he cheated because you hadn't tutored him enough, remember?" The flatware in the basket jangled as she slammed it into its place on the bottom rack of the dishwasher. I nodded again. Ma stood, looking smug, as if she thought she could reason away my despair. I knew enough to let her think she had succeeded because I didn't want to add making her worry to my list of sins. I was only dimly aware that I was assuming responsibility for her state of mind too.

While Ma loaded the dishwasher and I unloaded the groceries, Sofia lugged at least a week's worth of newspapers to the recycling basket at the top of the basement stairs and dumped them in. Ma banged the dishwasher door shut and wiped her hands on her apron, a gesture I recalled from my childhood. When Sofia returned, slightly out of breath and looking flustered, the two women began to hurriedly shelve the cans and boxes I had put on the counter. "Hey, are you two expecting company?" I asked, suddenly aware that their almost frantic domestic activity was unusual.

Suddenly both women smiled, and Sofia said, "Sort of. It's Paul's day. He's due any minute."

"Paul?" I asked.

"The man from the cleaning service, remember? Today's his day." The look Ma gave me made it clear that she did not understand how I could have forgotten something so important.

"Oh right," I said, suddenly recognizing their flurried straightening up as the classic effort of two conscientious homemakers to clean before the cleaner arrives. I was glad that their concern for me hadn't interfered with their domestic rituals. "I hope this guy appreciates the trouble you take to make his work easier."

"He does. He says we're his favorite clients. He really is the nicest young man. He reminds me of Mark," said Ma. Comparing anyone to her precious grandson was Ma's highest compliment.

"I don't know where he is," said Sofia. "It's just three. He's usually so punctual."

"Well, I'll get out of your way," I said, hugging both women. "I have to run anyway. I'll take the empty carton with me unless you need it." Slipping into my sandals in the vestibule, I left. As I walked down the steps,

I was glad to see a young man approaching Ma and Sofia's house. He wore a spotless white T-shirt, jeans, and had a blue headscarf tied pirate-style so as to completely cover his hair. His bright eyes looked out from behind oval-shaped lenses of titanium-framed glasses, and his ready smile was a flash of white teeth. His visit would certainly prove a welcome distraction from Ma's concern for me.

When I got home, it was clear that Sol had been thinking of ways to distract me. "Bel, do you want to rent *Something's Gotta Give*? It'll cheer you up." He began talking the minute he heard my footsteps on the stairs. "Your union is not going to let you get canned. Woodman hasn't even sent you anything in writing. He's probably rethinking his knee-jerk reaction to the PR generated by *pickurprofs.com*. And you had nothing to do with that poor kid's suicide." Sol was folding laundry when I entered our bedroom. "Like you told me after 9/11, you've got to move on."

"What I told you was you've got to see a shrink," I said without a trace of a smile. "I didn't expect you to just magically forget what you'd seen and feel better." I picked up a towel and began to fold it. "I'm trying to process this whole mess in my own way and on my own schedule."

"Well, maybe *you* should see a shrink," said my soul mate, the love of my life, my best friend, my husband of just over a year. His deep rich voice was low and honeyed. It dawned on me then that, after monitoring my misery all week, Sol had finally concluded that I had a screw loose. And I'd just provided him with the opening he needed to share this insight. "Come on, love, you have to admit it is a little narcissistic to think that this young man's whole life and death revolved around what you did or didn't do in your damn speech class." Sol was about to toss a tangle of socks into a drawer without even turning them right-side out, let alone pairing them.

"So now *you're* diagnosing *me*? Why should I pay a shrink when I have you to spout psychobabble at me for free?" I put the folded towel down on the bed and left the room before I said something even sharper, something I'd regret. What I did call over my shoulder was: "Betty and Illuminada are coming over tonight. They're bringing leftovers for a potluck dinner. You're welcome to join us."

"Are Raoul and Vic coming too or is this an evening of girl talk?" Sol probably had a glint in his eye when he used the expression "girl talk." On a good day, it was guaranteed to inspire me to lecture at length about how politically incorrect the phrase was, but this wasn't a good day.

"Raoul is meeting with a client and Vic has some kind of respiratory infection. I suggest you join us for dinner, and then, if we go on too long about makeup and clothes, you can just disappear." I stuck my head back into the bedroom to deliver this invitation.

"Well, love, that's an offer I can't resist," Sol answered. I interpreted the man's refusal to be piqued by my bitchiness as a sign of how worried about me he really was. "What leftovers are we contributing?"

"Beats me. Why don't you see what we have? I think there's enough take-out Chinese in the fridge from last night." The phone rang, and I ran downstairs and picked it up, effectively ending our conversation.

"Sarah Woolf, girl reporter here." Although I was

delighted to hear the voice of my old friend, for a fleeting moment I wondered if the managing editor of the *Jersey City Herald* was returning my call out of friendship or in pursuit of the inside track on a story. "Hi, Sarah, does this mean our exciting game of telephone tag is finally over?" I settled into a corner of the living room sofa. I was eager to talk to Sarah about her interview with Naftali on the off chance that, maybe, just maybe, he'd said something to her that would make me feel less responsible for his death.

"I don't have much time, but I'm worried about how all this PR from Nas-T and that website is sitting with your president. I bet he's hassling you." Good old Sarah. She'd called out of concern, not to sniff out a scoop. Sarah knew all about Woodman's aversion to negative publicity about RECC. "I had no idea you were even involved until I caught the news on TV, and then it was too late to pull that article. But don't worry, Bel, I've edited the interview we're running Sunday."

"Well, it's too late. Woodman wants me to resign," I said. I heard a soft gasp.

"You're kidding, right?" But Sarah's voice was matter-of-fact, as if she already knew the answer to her question.

"No. I've gone to the union for advice. Sarah, this is off the record, right?" It felt strange to be asking Sarah this, but I needed to be sure. After all, she was a journalist.

"Of course. Oh, Bel, I'm so sorry this has come down on you. You sound terrible. Is there anything I can do?" I resisted asking her to pull the interview with Naftali. Anyway, there was little more the poor kid could do to hurt me now. He'd said it all in that rap, his legacy to me.

"No, I don't think so. I'm feeling down because I gave that kid a D, so he couldn't transfer the credit, so he enlisted, and then he got hurt. He must have been depressed, and so he . . ." I'd explained myself so many times over the past few days that when I listed yet again the sequence of events leading up to Naftali's suicide, they sounded singsong, like the oft-repeated refrain in a children's rhyme.

I was relieved when Sarah interrupted me. "Bel Barrett, you are too much. He didn't enlist because of his grades or your class or anything like that. At least that's not what he told me."

"What did he tell you, Sarah?" I asked, almost afraid to hope that Sarah's reply would actually offer me a reprieve from my self-inflicted guilt and remorse.

"Naftali told me he enlisted so he could rap about the war and the soldiers in Iraq. He wanted to make a name for himself as the only hip-hop performer rapping about the war firsthand. He had actually written a few raps while he was over there and was planning to turn them into a demo. I think he even had a producer lined up to talk to, some guy in Newark. Bel, you had as much to do with that kid's suicide as the man in the moon." Sarah sounded so certain.

Even so, I was afraid to believe her, afraid my old friend might just be trying to make me feel better. "So what were you going to edit out of the interview?" I asked.

"I asked him if his speech prof was really as bad as he made her out to be in his beef, and he said, and I quote, 'Barrett one stone cold bitch. She cold enough to fight in Iraq herself.' " Sarah paused to let these words sink in.

"That's hardly a ringing endorsement. He was very angry at me," I said. "I know because I ran into him, and he didn't speak to me. He just glared. But it is interesting that he had planned to enlist anyway. I guess he just didn't figure on getting blown up and losing his arm." I was digesting the idea that Naftali could have hated me and yet enlisted for other reasons.

"Like many young men, the kid probably thought he was immortal. Remember when Mark was skateboarding in lower Manhattan near the Tunnel entrance? He thought he was invincible." I winced at the recollection of sleepless nights filled with visions of Mark flattened by a truck speeding into the Holland Tunnel. I'd tried to talk him out of skateboarding. Had Naftali's sister tried to talk her brother out of enlisting?

By the time Sarah and I finished talking, I felt slightly better. Naftali had planned to enlist all along. Maybe his low grade in Speech had accelerated his decision, but it was not the primary factor. I was upstairs telling Sol what Sarah had told me when Betty and Illuminada rang the doorbell. "So maybe now, love, you'll listen when I tell you you're not the center of everybody's universe," said Sol as we went downstairs to greet our guests together.

The dinner menu was definitely potluck. Everybody had brought leftovers and, to our amusement, everybody's leftovers consisted of take-out Chinese food. "I haven't had a chance to cook all week, and Raoul is eating with his client," Illuminada explained. "Even my mother didn't feel like cooking this week."

"Me either. I bought Vic a couple of quarts of won-

ton soup, and I've been eating all this other stuff for
days," Betty said, plunking down several cartons on
the kitchen counter. Sol and I added our eggplant with
garlic sauce and moo shu chicken to the collection and
began to arrange the cartons in the microwave. I put a
pot of water on for tea.

"So, *chiquita,* how does it feel to be asked to resign
after over two decades of devoted service?" Illuminada's tone was flip, but her eyes looked troubled. She
and I had not managed to connect on the phone all
week and had been communicating via cryptic e-mail
messages. I was sure that she and Betty had decided to
come over to commiserate about Woodman's desire to
can me and to talk me out of my guilt over Naftali's
suicide.

"I felt so bad watching you walk into Woodman's
office the other day. I knew he was upset, but I had no
idea he was going to ask for your resignation," Betty
said, shaking her head. She spoke with a sparerib in
her hand.

"At least the fool hasn't put it in writing yet," said Illuminada, pragmatic as always.

"The prospect of getting canned is pretty awful, but
to tell you the truth, what I've really been focused on
all week is the suicide of that poor boy," I said.

"My bride had actually convinced herself that she
was responsible for that kid's suicide," said Sol, shaking his head. "She's been walking around in a self-
imposed hair shirt all week." Betty and Illuminada
nodded. Sol wasn't telling them anything they didn't
know. I could see my two friends gearing up to talk me
out of my guilt.

To put them at ease on that subject and avoid yet another lecture, I said, "But I just talked to Sarah Woolf. She interviewed Naftali for the *Herald*'s feature section before he died. Naftali told her he had planned to enlist all along. He wanted to rap about the war, wanted to see it firsthand. He thought that would make him stand out from all the other wannabe rappers and make it easier for him to get a demo out there." Now it was my turn to shake my head at the price the young man had paid for his daring and ambition. "I guess he just never figured on getting hurt."

We all started at the sound of the doorbell. Sol was the first to lower his fork and get up to answer it. "Maybe Raoul got done early and decided to join us," I said.

"Not likely," said Illuminada. "He's with really a high-maintenance client. This dude needs a lot of hand-holding before during and after tax season. I don't see how Raoul stands it, but he does." She smiled indulgently at the thought of her handsome husband's patience.

We heard Sol talking at the doorway, and then he turned and entered the room, flashing me a puzzled look. "Bel," he said, "these people want to talk to you. They're from County Homicide." Sol's surprise at the intrusion made his statement sound like a question. I experienced a reflexive flash of maternal panic until I reminded myself that Mark was in Mexico and Rebecca in Seattle. Then I remembered Ma. Had something happened to her?

"My mother?" I said, picturing her mugged, her skeletal limbs akimbo in a pool of blood on the street. "Is she all right?"

"We're not here about your mother, Professor," said

the taller of the two men, the one who walked first into the room, holding his badge in front of him as if it were a cross that he hoped would ward off a vampire. He nodded at Illuminada, whom he clearly recognized, and then returned his glance to me. "Professor Barrett, I'm Detective Oliver Fergeson from Hudson County Homicide." His eyes scanned the table, taking in the cartons of Chinese food. "Sorry to interrupt your dinner party. This here is Detective Jack Rago." He nodded to the shorter man with him, who was also extending his badge. "Could we talk to you alone for a minute, Professor?" He looked around at Sol, Illuminada, and Betty. Without a word, the two women got up and walked over to stand beside Sol.

"Will you be long?" Sol asked.

"No. We've just got a couple of questions to ask the professor here." Detective Fergeson sat down in the chair opposite me that Sol had vacated, and Detective Rago seated himself in Betty's place on my right. The first floor of our house was really one room, an open living-dining-room-kitchen area, so there was nothing for Sol to do but lead Betty and Illuminada up the steps to the bedroom floor. I pictured them huddled on the landing, ears trained to catch the conversation below.

"What's this all about?" I asked as I watched my three dinner companions climb the stairs.

"We're the ones asking the questions tonight, Professor. Where were you on the night of Thursday, April 29, between midnight and 2 A.M.?

"You mean last night?" I asked. Both men nodded solemnly. That was a no-brainer. "I was here. In bed," I said. "Why?"

Detective Rago ignored my question and asked another one of his own. "Is there anyone who can verify that?"

"My husband. No, wait a minute," I said. "He was baby-sitting for his granddaughter in upstate New York. I was here alone. But why does it matter?" Suddenly my stomach tightened.

"You knew this young man?" Detective Fergeson flashed the headshot of Naftali that had accompanied the article about his death in the newspaper. "He was a student of yours?"

"Yes. Yes," I said. "But then he enlisted in the service and lost an arm and . . ." I hesitated. "He jumped in front of a train."

"That's not what his family thinks. His sister ordered an autopsy. He sustained a fatal blow to the head before he hit the tracks. He bad-mouthed you on-line and on TV. We heard you might lose your job on account of what he said." The detective took a deep breath and continued. "Without an alibi, Professor, you're our number-one suspect. Mind if we take a look around?"

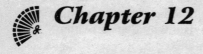

Chapter 12

Halpern Argument Prevails

Jury Acquits Suitcase Strangler

After Defense Attorney Richard Halpern's summa-
tion, jury members took only a few hours to vote to
acquit Hydar Wali, the Egyptian immigrant accused
of strangling his wife, Janet, in the couple's bed. The
prosecution had argued that Wali strangled her, dismembered her corpse with a butcher's knife, stuffed
her body parts in a suitcase, and stowed it in a closet
in the couple's Weehawken apartment. The closet
door was cemented shut, plastered, and painted.
Drawn to the unit when neighbors complained of the
stench, authorities soon uncovered the remains of
the woman whom, the prosecution asserted, Wali
had married in order to obtain a green card. Detectives located a butcher knife in a Dumpster in the
neighborhood . . .

Dick Halpern was about to become my new best friend. Only a nanosecond after Detectives Rago and Fergeson finally left our house, Sol, Betty, and Illuminada were downstairs. I was right. They had been eavesdropping from the landing. Sol spoke first. "Bel, you need a lawyer. You didn't even ask if they had a search warrant before you let them loose in here. I'm calling Sue Carlyle." His face was ashen, and the hand he extended to pick up the phone was less than steady, but his voice was decisive.

Illuminada placed her hand firmly on his outstretched arm. "Sol, wait." I was so relieved. As usual Sol's concern was exaggerated. It was simply inconceivable to me that Naftali's enraged rap had morphed into a murder rap with my name on it. Sooner or later the cops would find Naftali's real killer and this latest nightmare would go away. And as for now, Illuminada would set Sol straight, and he'd listen to her. "Sue Carlyle's a divorce diva, right?" Sol and I both nodded. Sue had handled Sol's divorce. I wasn't quite sure where Illuminada was going with this question.

Her next words clarified her intentions. "Sol, Bel needs an ace criminal lawyer. I suggest you call Dick Halpern." Sol didn't react at the mention of this name, so Illuminada produced a dog-eared copy of a newspaper article and handed it to him. While he read it, she summarized it for me and Betty. "Years ago Dick Halpern defended that Egyptian immigrant who married an American to get a green card. Then he strangled her, dismembered her, packed the pieces in a suitcase, and sealed it up in a closet, remember?" As he read and Illuminada talked, Sol's white face gradually darkened to a shade of yellowish green. Betty closed her eyes and shuddered.

Once Illuminada had forced us to revisit this grisly scenario, she pressed her real point. "Dick actually got that animal off, claiming that because the wife outweighed the husband by fifteen pounds, he couldn't possibly have overpowered her. The jury bought it. And Dick's gotten reduced sentences and acquittals for a lot of other stone killers. Dick Halpern's the best criminal lawyer in the state, maybe in the country. I have his business card on me, but I keep this article handy too, in case a client of mine needs convincing. It's better than a résumé. Dick's pricey, but he's worth every penny."

The notion that my husband and friends felt I needed the same legal defense as the ghoul Illuminada had just described upset me almost as much as the fact that the detectives considered me a suspect. "Don't you think they're going to find out who really killed that poor boy?" I asked. "If you ask me, which you didn't, you're getting way ahead of yourselves here."

Ignoring me, Illuminada pulled a business card out of her card case and handed it to Sol. "Keep it. I have others. Phone Dick tonight and leave a message. I'll call him tomorrow and reinforce it. He's busy, but I've helped him out a few times, and he's grateful. He'll get back to you, and he'll take Bel's case."

"I am not crazy about being left out of the discussion here," I said in the voice I used when I reprimanded a student for claiming to have lost a completed assignment to a computer glitch, the modern equivalent of claiming one's homework was devoured by a hungry canine. I was used to Betty's managerial style, but nothing had really prepared me for the simultaneous emergence of Sol and Illuminada's inner despots. "If I think I need a lawyer, I'm perfectly capable of calling one myself."

"Nobody's saying you're not capable," said Betty. "But, girlfriend, listen to me. You're in denial. You have no alibi and a strong motive. Why should those two dudes pound the pavement looking for another suspect? They think they've solved the murder. They're going to focus on implicating you." She spoke gently, as if she was talking to someone very old and fragile and just a bit demented to boot. Often quick to snap and fond of sarcasm, Betty had never talked to me that way before. It scared me.

"Betty's right. The only reason Fergeson and Rago didn't cuff you, read you your rights, and drag you off to prison a few minutes ago is that, as yet, they have no eyewitnesses or forensic evidence linking you to Naftali's murder," said Illuminada.

"That's why they went pawing through our drawers and closets. They probably did have a search warrant." Sol had not been happy to have his messy sock drawer inspected and his meticulously organized kitchen cabinets invaded. "When a bloody cudgel failed to turn up under our bed, and no empty pill vial materialized in our garbage, those two clowns actually looked disappointed."

"Sol's right, *chiquita.* Don't be fooled by the polite smiles those *hombres* flashed when they took off their rubber gloves and left." Illuminada stretched her mouth into a not bad imitation of the men's pseudo grins. But her face was grave when she resumed speaking. "They'll be back. And they'll try very hard to get evidence enough to justify an indictment. I'm surprised they're not tapping your phone." She paused and took a sip from the wineglass Sol had just filled. Silently he made his way around the table, filling the other three glasses as Illuminada continued. "*Chiquita,* they've never forgiven you for what you did to their honcho, Chief Detective Ralph Falco. You got their hero put away for being on the take and an accessory to two murders, remember?" I nodded at the recollection of an earlier sleuthing triumph. "So you better believe they're going to work their sorry buns off to hang this kid's killing on you." Her voice had become so low and severe that it was almost a growl.

Pulling his chair next to mine, Sol sat down, and we all sipped in silence for a minute or two. Then fueled by a little wine, a lot of adrenaline, and years of yoga instruction, I pulled my tense shoulders down, lifted my heavy heart, and breathed deeply until I could feel the air filling my belly. I'm not sure if my merlot or my prana was responsible, but when I spoke, my own voice was calm and assured. "Well, I'll just have to out sleuth them to save myself." I saw Betty and Illuminada exchange glances. "After all, let's say the RECC Faculty Senate vouches for my professional competence. And suppose Sarah Woolf deletes Naftali's latest negative comment about me from her interview. Then maybe the union can save my job. But being bad-mouthed or even canned won't make any difference if I end up behind bars on a murder rap, will it?"

"No, it won't," said Sol. He ran his fingers through his thinning hair, a sure sign that he was anxious. I was relieved by his next words. "Where will you start? How can I help?"

"Yeah, what can we do?" Betty's eyes flashed and she took out her Palm Pilot, ready to record our strategy as she had so many times before. Her note taking had often made the difference between our carrying out a plan effectively or forgetting we had made it.

Although I had anticipated these questions, I wasn't prepared to answer them fully just then. But I had a few ideas. "Okay. Illuminada's always saying that homicide begins at home, so I want to check out Naftali's family first. If I recall correctly, I read in the paper that his sister is a beautician who reads palms as a sideline, so for starters, I'm going to get a haircut and have my fortune told." Illuminada nodded, pleased, no doubt, that I was taking her advice.

"Is that legal? Reading palms?" Betty asked. "It screams scam to me."

"Fortune-telling is legal in New Jersey," said Illuminada. "New York, Connecticut, and Pennsylvania have outlawed it, but here in the Garden State, we're more broadminded, and the occult lives."

"It falls under the label of New Age," I added. "It's both legal and profitable. That's why you see signs all over advertising psychics."

"Come to think of it, you're right. But still, I assume you'll go undercover," said Betty. "After all, once Naftali's rap about you went public, your name probably became a household word among his relatives."

"I'll be Martha Salem," I said. Facing prison, I could at last fully identify with Martha Stewart, another midlife woman from New Jersey, as well as with those poor women once accused of witchery in Massachusetts. And because I suddenly craved one of the mentholated cigarettes I had long ago foresworn, Martha Salem struck me as the perfect alias.

"Wait a minute, Bel," Betty's brow was furrowed. "Naftali went on about how you hate blacks. Wasn't he black? Maybe his sister just does black hair, you know, dreads and cornrows and straightening. You'll look pretty stupid showing up with that Jewish mop-top you've got. It's frizzy, but it won't pass." Her smile was the first I'd seen that evening. Illuminada was smiling too, and I knew she was impressed that Betty had thought to raise this issue. We all knew that going undercover was tricky enough without surprises. "Do you want me to go for the haircut?"

"Actually, Naftali wasn't exactly what I'd call black." I winced at the inadequacy of my words. "I mean, he was a whole lot lighter than you, sort of a café au lait color. And he only spoke Black English when he rapped. The rest of the time his English was pretty standard." I'd encouraged many urban students to be bidialectical, but occasionally some, like Naftali, came to RECC already fluent in both standard American or British English and another, less academically viable dialect. "But you're right. And I don't know the address of her salon, but that probably won't tell me what kind of hair she does anyway. I'll ask when I call for an appointment. And if she won't do my hair, she'll just have to read my palm." I held out my hand.

"I'd pay money to be a fly on the wall for that," said Illuminada, adding yet another welcome touch of levity to our conversation. My nearly pathological aversion to anything that smacked of what I sneeringly called "New Age crap" was well known.

"Then after that I'll figure out some way to talk to

Naftali's friends. Maybe he had a rival who was jealous of his success. I can probably pose as a reporter and interview them. Wannabe rappers ought to welcome a little free publicity." The prospect of sleuthing my way out of this mess had buoyed my flagging spirits, and I drained my wineglass.

"Sounds like a plan," said Illuminada. "I'll get you the autopsy report and any police reports I can." Illuminada had a lot of grateful former clients in law enforcement. She was always willing to use these resources to supplement our unofficial investigative efforts. I reached over to squeeze her arm by way of a thank-you. "*Chiquita,* you'd last about five minutes in the county lockup," she snapped, hoping, I knew, to forestall any more emotional expressions of gratitude on my part. "I'm going to head home. I'm beat."

Always the first to leave, Illuminada stood. Betty followed. As we closed the door behind our friends, Sol said, "Go on up. I'll be right behind you as soon as I call Dick Halpern. You can sleuth yourself silly if you want, love, but you still need a good lawyer."

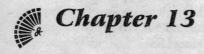 # Chapter 13

UNISEX HAIRSTYLING BY OLIVIA DURANGO
CUTS! PERMS! COLORING!

Olivia Durango, Palmist
Is he or she Mr. or Ms. Right? Should I quit my job?
Is it time for plastic surgery? Will I ever be rich?
The answers are in your hands.

El salon de Belleza Unisexo de Olivia Durango
¡Cortes! ¡Permanentes! y ¡Tintura de Cabello!

Olivia Durango lee su mano.
¿Es él o ella mi pajera perfecta?
¿Debo renunciar a mi trabajo?
¿Llegó la hora de una cirugía plástica? Será
un momento afortunado para operarme?)
¿Seré rico?
Las respuestas están en sus manos.

The question I wanted to ask Olivia Durango was quite unlike any of those on the small black and white sign in her front window. I'd already found Mr. Right, was about to lose my job, needed no surgery, and would never be rich as long as I was forking out almost a week's pay for every hour Dick Halpern, Esq. was in my employ. What I wanted to ask Olivia was: "Do you have any idea who might have murdered your brother?" But because I was undercover, as Martha Salem, I'd have to learn the answer to that question indirectly.

Fortunately for me, Olivia Durango was listed in the Yellow Pages under both BEAUTY SALONS and PALMISTS. And even more fortunately, her salon had turned out to be only a few blocks from RECC. She lived and worked on the ground floor of a well-kept three-family building on a busy through street in a once largely residential neighborhood. Parking was competitive and metered, but lots of commuters walked by on their way to the nearby subway and bus terminal. They would note her sign, which looked much like the ones in the windows of the many doctors, dentists, and chiropractors who had offices in the area.

While I stood on the sidewalk in front of Olivia Durango's house studying her sign, the door opened and a short burly man in a brown uniform with KINNEY embroidered on the shirt pocket came out. I assumed he was another client, who had just had his dark wavy hair coiffed, but I changed my mind when I noticed that his skin was the same café au lait color as Naftali's. His nose and mouth were broader versions of the dead rapper's, so that the older man's face looked like a blurred version of Naftali's. That's why in spite of the fact that the man on the pavement was just slightly taller and much fleshier than the dead man, I knew he had to be Olivia and Naftali's brother, Marcus. As he passed me without nodding, I noted that while Naftali's eyes had burned, his brother's gaze was glassy and distant.

Glad to have had an unexpected glimpse of Marcus, I climbed the few steps to the porch, rang the bell, and waited. In seconds the door opened to reveal a petite woman with skin and eyes the color of her brothers'. She was holding a comb in one hand and a blow-dryer in the other and wearing pegged black slacks and a neat white tunic with lots of pockets. "Olivia Durango," she said, tilting her head slightly. "And you are?" Olivia's voice surprised me. It was deep and resonant, a large sound for such a diminutive figure to produce.

"Martha Salem," I said. "I called this morning about getting my hair cut."

"Oh yes. You're the one who wanted to know if I did white folks' hair." Olivia smiled, but this cheerful facial expression seemed out of place on her sad face, with its circled dark eyes, seamed brow, and drawn cheeks. It was the face of a woman much older than she probably was. Her own bottle black hair was cut short and blunt except in front, where a long straight shock made a diagonal stripe across her forehead.

I smiled in return and followed her as she ushered me quickly and wordlessly through a tidy and simply furnished living room and dining room. It was hard to picture the hyperkinetic, pierced, and tattooed Naftali in his low-riding jeans and baggy sweatshirt growing up in these staid quarters, even though I thought I glimpsed a photo of him on a side table. Before I had a chance to look at it closely, we had reached the kitchen at the rear of the house.

A cozy space had been carved out of a corner of this room, a space just big enough to accommodate the sink, rotating chair, and mirror that comprise a beautician's work station. A blonde matronly looking woman in a brightly colored coverall occupied the chair. She was holding up a hand mirror and surveying the back of her head. Nearby was the kitchen table where, I speculated, Olivia read palms. It apparently doubled as a waiting room, for she said, "Have a seat, please, Martha," and gestured toward one of the chairs around the table. "We're almost done here."

I settled in for a wait, using the time to observe Olivia. I'm embarrassed to confess that I'd expected a palmist to dress like my fantasy of a Romanian Gypsy in a turban and a long swirling skirt of green and gold and purple. But in her simple black and white outfit and black sandals, Naftali's sister looked as if she had just stepped out of an Eileen Fisher ad.

If Olivia Durango was no Gypsy, neither was her kitchen the Gypsy's tent I'd pictured. There were no candles, no crystals, no incense, and no drapes of crimson velvet. Instead the rectangular wooden table in front of me was enameled in gleaming white, as were the six matching chairs around it. White appliances, white cabinets, and crisp white café curtains bracketing the one large window ringed the room. Only a lush philodendron on the windowsill over the kitchen sink, black and white linoleum flooring, and gray-speckled laminate on the countertops provided contrast. The kitchen was so neat and clean as to appear unused.

Before the client ahead of me left, she handed Olivia some folded bills, saying, "Thank you, Olivia. And remember, you and your family are in my prayers." In response to this effort at condolence, Olivia nodded and brushed her hand across her eyes. The woman continued. "Don't bother walking me to the door. I can find my way out. And I'll let you know if he calls." I assumed that Olivia had read this client's palm earlier and predicted that a phone call from a certain someone was imminent. Olivia nodded in response. The woman left the kitchen, and, in a moment, we heard the front door close behind her.

Squaring her shoulders, Olivia motioned me to the chair in front of the sink. While I watched, she swept snippets of blonde hair off the floor behind this chair. I noticed some marks on her little toe. Could she have a tattoo there? That was surely a novel and tiny canvass for a tattoo artist. Before I could inquire, she said, "So, Martha, what kind of haircut do you want?" Did I detect an undertone of mockery in her deep voice? Why would she make fun of a new client? A quick glance at her face told me nothing. Olivia took her place behind me, and in the mirror I could see her holding a strand of my kinky graying hair between her thumb and index finger and fanning it out, first on one side of my head and then on the other.

By the time I answered, she had run her fingers through the fringe on my forehead and turned on the water in the sink. "No more bangs, please," I said decisively. "I'm sick of bangs. I'd like my hair to frame my face all the way around. Can you make it have a soft look?" I fluffed out my curls in an effort to illustrate. I'd not given much thought to actually having my hair cut, so the decision to lose my too curly bangs was spontaneous.

Olivia nodded, wrested from my lap the book bag I still clutched, set it on the floor in the corner, and tied the bright coverall around my neck. It was made of hot pink oilcloth printed with sprawling blue and orange flowers, the kind of fabric and design you used to see in tablecloths dating from the fifties. The oilcloth was slightly stiff, but it provided a welcome splash of color in the pristine workspace. "What great colors! Wherever did you get this?" I asked.

"My brother's ex-girlfriend, Ariel, made it for me. It was a tablecloth she found someplace, but she made it into a smock. That girl is one for bright colors. She made a headband for Naftali that was so orange he said it glowed in the dark." Olivia choked up before she finished her sentence. Was she distressed because her brother and the handy Ariel were no longer together or because the memory of Naftali was so painful? "She's the creative type." Olivia sighed.

In the hope of learning more, I said, "My daughter's like that. She beaded this chain for my eyeglasses. It's so practical."

"Yes, it is." Then Olivia added softly, almost to herself, "Ariel was good for my brother. Marcus tends toward the serious side, and she could always lighten him up." Suddenly Olivia changed the subject slightly. "Martha, Ariel's apartment hunting now. If you hear of anything, a studio, a room . . ."

"It's so hard to find places around here, but I'll keep my ear to the ground," I promised. Olivia lowered my head into the sink and held the spray close to my scalp.

"Thanks. Warm enough?" I grunted an affirmative. Then, having enlisted my help, Olivia reintroduced the coverall into our conversation. "It doesn't bother you that the oilcloth's a little stiff?" Her deep voice made even our small talk sound significant. I detected faint vestiges of a West Indian accent in the lilt of her speech. I assumed that her parents were born in the Caribbean, but that they raised her here.

"No, not at all. It's so cheerful. I came in from work feeling totally miserable, and the colors and the flowers gave me a lift." What was really making me feel better was Olivia massaging my scalp as she applied shampoo.

"I'm sorry you're miserable. Trouble at work?" The question might have been innocent, but I assumed she was hoping to impress me with her clairvoyance so as to get me to ask her to read my palm later. I suspected that most of her palmistry clients were women who came in for cuts, perms, or coloring and ended up having readings as well. When I'd spoken to Olivia on the phone earlier to make the appointment, I'd mentioned that I couldn't get out of work until at least five, so her assumption that my mind was still on the job was not really evidence of exceptional intuitive ability.

"Yeah, I've got to get out of there." I scowled, and then, before she could interject anything, I added, "It must be wonderful to be your own boss." It was important that I get her to talk about herself rather than let her draw me out. Fortunately I was used to helping students discover and express their ideas, so I had no doubt I could elicit information from her.

As she rinsed my hair, Olivia sighed and said, "Yes and no. I really have no time off. It's like owning a restaurant."

"I guess that can be a problem, especially if you have kids," I said. "Do you have little ones?" I had gotten to the subject of my visit faster than I'd hoped.

The hands that were toweling my hair stilled abruptly, but Olivia didn't speak right away. I didn't either, aware that an interjection of mine might cut off her train of thought and the flow of information. When she did answer me, she tossed aside the towel and began to comb out my hair. "I have no kids. But I raised my baby brother, Naftali. Our other brother, Marcus and me, we raised him together." Her hand stilled for a second, the comb frozen in midair just above my head. "Naftali was a lot younger than me, fifteen years. He could've been my son."

" 'Could've been?' Did something happen to him?" I asked, feeling slightly guilty about duping this newly bereaved woman into making revelations to an imposter. But several thoughts served to banish my reservations. The first was that I didn't want to go to jail. The second was that in a few minutes I'd be crossing Olivia's palm with silver in return for letting her probe my own paw in search of revelations. And finally, I figured Olivia probably wanted to know who really killed Naftali as badly as I did. After all, it was she who had initiated the official murder investigation.

"He died," she said, spitting out the two words as if they burned her mouth. If I'd been hoping for more, I was going to have to work harder for it. In the mirror I saw her brush her hand across her eyes again, and then, scissors flashing, she began to snip my hair.

"I'm so sorry," I said, and I meant it.

While I was trying to devise an evocative follow-up to that highly original response, Olivia rubbed one eye with the heel of her free hand as if she could press her welling tears back into her tear ducts. In a moment she said, "Yeah, it's so unfair, crazy really." She resumed snipping. The activity seemed to soothe her, and she continued to talk. "Marcus and I begged him not to enlist, but Jude . . . Jude thought the army would be the making of him." I wanted to ask who Jude was but was leery of interrupting her. Maybe the woman really was a mind reader because she sensed my curiosity and said, "I met Jude a few years ago and we got along good, so he came to live here with me and Naftali. They didn't always see eye to eye. Jude was glad when Naftali enlisted. Said the military would straighten him out."

A bitter edge had crept into her voice. "My brother made it through a couple of months in Iraq and then . . . he got blown up." She articulated the first part of this sentence slowly and paused. The last part literally exploded out of her mouth, so that there was no escaping the stark horror of the blast of which she spoke. "He survived, but he lost an arm." I gasped but did not speak, still unwilling to interrupt her. At the thought of Naftali's missing arm, I found myself once again rubbing my shoulder. "Yeah, so he had a lot of surgery, months of physical and occupational therapy." Olivia sighed. "While he was in the hospital, Jude and my brother Marcus, they soundproofed and rewired his room, so when he came home it would be almost like a studio. They worked like dogs, taking everything out and tearing up walls. They wanted to surprise him, take his mind off his injury." Olivia paused. "So finally he came home and was trying to get back on his feet, you know, make a new life for himself."

Olivia sighed again, a long, low moan. "He was a very gifted rap artist with big ideas, a big future. He had a following here." Her voice lifted with pride as she described Naftali's talent and bright prospects. "So what happened?" Yet again I remained silent, sensing that this was a rhetorical question. "Last week somebody knocked him out and pushed him onto the subway tracks in front of a train. It was in the paper." Suddenly Olivia sounded tired as she spoke. She had undoubtedly repeated this part of the story many times.

"Oh no! He was a wounded veteran. He fought for our country. Who would do that?" Although my surprise was feigned, my horror and my question were not.

She shrugged and stepped back, automatically surveying her handiwork. "We don't know for sure. But Naftali . . . that was his name, Naftali . . ." Her tongue caressed the syllables. "Our mother named him after her father. Anyway, Naftali, he wasn't always careful what he said." Here she shook her head, very much the older sister recalling advice that had been ignored. "Like I told you, he was a rapper." Again pride animated her voice for a minute, but when she continued, her tone was dismissive. "He dissed one of the professors he had when he was at the community college and . . ."

I started at the sound of a door slamming. A bearded, balding, dark-skinned man entered the kitchen carrying a blue thermos. Suddenly the room seemed even whiter, brighter. He walked to the sink, emptied the thermos, rinsed it, and left it upended on the drain board. When he turned, he nodded perfunctorily at me and smiled at Olivia. He was clearly used to finding strangers in the kitchen. "Hey, Liv," he said, approaching her from behind and massaging her shoulders.

In the mirror, I thought I saw her recoil slightly at his touch before she shrugged him off. "Martha, Jude," Olivia said by way of introduction. Jude favored me with another nod and left the room. In a few seconds the drone of the TV in the living room hummed, a kind of white noise in the background of our conversation.

"How's that, Martha? Short enough?" Olivia asked. "If I take off any more, it'll be too severe. Here, have a look."

I held up the hand mirror and made a show of studying my hair. "Wow! It's really short," I exclaimed. There was now just a half inch of fuzz where my bangs had been and the frame of hair around my face was a narrow one. The effect was not altogether unflattering, but it would take some getting used to.

"It's short because you didn't really need a haircut, did you, Martha?" Olivia asked, putting one hand on her hip and cocking her head at me. Her pose and her tone, both mockingly accusatory and chastising, had suddenly shifted. "That's not what you really came to see Olivia for, is it?" One of her dark eyebrows jumped up as she posed this question.

At these words, my heartbeat suddenly threatened to deafen me. If Olivia knew why I had come, she must have known who I was. How had I given myself away? Had she recognized me from Naftali's descriptions? Did she really think I had murdered her brother? Beneath her calm and neatly groomed exterior, did she yearn for revenge? Was she about to grab her scissors and stab me to death? Had she waited for the husky

Jude to come home before letting me know she recognized me? Before Jude's arrival, she'd implied that I was a suspect. But perhaps she had another possible suspect in mind as well. With my cover blown, I might never know. Damn.

I struggled to retain some semblance of composure, but it was hard because suddenly I was in the throes of one of those retro hot flashes triggered by a rush of adrenaline. It was also hard to focus on what Olivia was saying as she calmly brushed hairs off my neck while I sat there, bracing myself to fight for my life. But I strained to hear her over the throbbing of my heart. "So don't worry, Martha. Olivia won't tell. Your secret is safe with Olivia." Olivia's accent was now more pronounced, her deep voice had lowered to a conspiratorial murmur, and she had begun to speak of herself in the third person. Maybe the woman was a Gypsy after all.

"Lots of Olivia's clients, you know, they want to have their palms read, but they're like you, Martha. They're afraid to say so, afraid their friends will mock them, afraid their husbands or wives will not approve." When I heard this, I realized that my cover was still good. Olivia had assumed that getting my hair cut was just an excuse to get my palm read! I exhaled with relief, released my tensed muscles, and relaxed back in the chair. She was half-right. I had certainly gotten the buzz cut under false pretenses. But she was wrong to assume I was just another clandestine palmistry client, another troubled soul, embarrassed to be found seeking solace in a fortune-teller instead of turning to a shrink, a priest, or a pill.

"My clients don't know it, but their husbands and

wives, they visit Olivia too." She was undoing the Vel-
cro tabs at my neck as she spoke. Just as earlier she had
motioned to me to sit in the rotating chair to have my
hair cut, she motioned to me to join her at the kitchen
table. I did. The bad news was that our conversation
about Naftali's death had been interrupted. The good
news was that Olivia's aggressive sales tactics made it
unnecessary for me to even find an excuse to stay for a
reading so I could continue to draw her out. A ray of
late afternoon sun fell across her lined face and onto
the white table. It was in the center of that splotch of
sunlight that she placed both her small hands, palms
up, an unmistakable invitation that I wouldn't refuse. I
placed my two now cold and clammy upturned hands
in hers.

 ***Chapter 14***

". . . I think I aced the interview with the recruiter from
Omaha General today! Their starting salary is way cool.
Attached are new photos of Abbie J from the time I took
her to visit Cindy and Ted in Wenatchee . . ."

These lines from Rebecca's latest e-mail message
leapt out at me from the printout when I reread it on
the train after my meeting with Olivia Durango. That's
when my skepticism began to give ground to wonder at
how eerily close to the mark Olivia's palm reading had
been. She had begun by holding my upturned hands in
hers with her eyes shut. Neither of us spoke. In the sudden silence, I was conscious again of the faint drone of
the TV coming from the living room.

After a second or two, Olivia opened her eyes and
began slowly palpating my palms and fingers. She
twisted my wedding band. Her brow furrowed when
her fingers brushed the side of the middle finger of my
right hand where I have a callus. It's been there for
years, a rough-textured testimony to the hours I spend,

pen in hand, writing comments in the margins of student papers. Olivia lingered over it for a moment and then grasped my thumbs and flexed them back and forth.

Next she turned my hands palm down and ran her fingers over my knuckles, my raggedy cuticles, my short uneven nails. Her own nails were short too, but neatly trimmed and gleaming with clear polish. Gently Olivia pinched the skin just below my knuckles and then studied the resulting pleats as they gradually flattened back into the web of tiny lines and blue blood vessels crisscrossing the sun-damaged backs of my hands.

Just when I began to despair of ever again engaging her in conversation, she said, "Your hands tell Olivia you're tired and worried." Well, no extrasensory perception was required to make that pronouncement. I'd come in after work whining about needing to leave my job. My chewed cuticles and less than elastic skin could only corroborate what she already knew. "You came about your work situation, but your hand tells Olivia that your real problem is with a family member." I tensed. What the hell was she blithering about? The kids were fine, Sol was fine, and Ma was holding her own. I tried to keep my face from registering my skepticism, but I needn't have bothered. Olivia wasn't interested in reading my facial expression. She was hunched over my palm again, turning it this way and that so as to catch the waning sunlight. "It's your daughter." I'd mentioned Rebecca earlier when I'd bragged about the chain for my reading glasses she'd made me, so Olivia's mention of her was unremarkable.

How the hell was I going to get her to talk about her own family while she was poring over my palm and making up stuff about mine? I wanted to get the reading over with in the hope that I could once again get her to talk about Naftali. "Yes, I do. She's grown," I added, as if the fact that Rebecca had reached adulthood somehow exempted her from playing a part in this bizarre ritual.

Olivia massaged the mound beneath the little finger of my right hand with her thumb as she spoke. "The line here, which represents your daughter, is crossed with many tiny lines, see?" She stopped massaging my hand and pointed to the spot she had been rubbing. To placate her and, I hoped, end the session, I put on my reading glasses. Then I made a pretense of focusing on the spot on my hand she pointed to. Even wearing my glasses, I was barely able to discern the minuscule lines going every which way. While I squinted at my hand, Olivia continued. "Although you're usually a good communicator, Martha, you're not listening to your daughter. She's troubled, but Olivia sees here that you're too distracted to draw her out." Again, I struggled to keep my face from betraying my impatience. Slowly she pushed her chair away from the table, stood, reached behind her, and switched on a light. "That's all for now, Martha. It's enough for you to take in on your first visit."

I was unprepared for the light that suddenly flooded the kitchen, as well as for Olivia's remark about this being my "first visit." Blinking and taking off my reading glasses, I nodded. Clearly by ending the session abruptly, Olivia hoped to lure me back, and I was glad. Her transparent tactic gave me the excuse I needed to return and continue to pump her about Naftali's life and death. Realizing that I could come back and try again made it easier for me to leave. And it was time for me to go because the light that had taken me by surprise had apparently sent a signal to Jude. He lumbered in from the next room with the expectant air of a man in need of a meal. "Yes, I'll have to think about my daughter," I said. "I just have to think about what you told me. I'll have to talk with her. I'll come back after that. Thank you. And how much do I owe you for the haircut and the reading?"

"The haircut is twenty dollars, and the reading today, well, I didn't really finish, so make it twenty dollars too," Olivia answered. She had resumed using the first person, and the West Indian lilt had almost disappeared from her speech. Her tone was no longer conspiratorial but matter-of-fact. I didn't mind paying for the haircut, but it was hard for me to part with twenty dollars to pay for what I considered to be a lot of mumbo jumbo. I handed her the money anyway, and, like the client before me, saw myself out.

On my way through the living room, I paused to look at the photograph of Naftali. His face was animated, and he stood with his feet wide apart on a stage of some sort. His hair was almost completely hidden under a backward baseball cap, and he wore baggy jeans and a sleeveless leather vest. In one many-ringed hand he clutched a microphone. With the other ornately tattooed arm outstretched, he pointed imperiously at someone in the crowd of onlookers. He was handsomer than I remembered him. At the sight of the young man standing there, alive and whole, I felt compelled to rub my own shoulder again, perhaps this time in anticipation of his loss. I only stopped when I got outside and began to walk to the PATH station a couple of blocks away.

On the train before I reread Rebecca's e-mail, I reflected on my visit with Olivia. Was there something she had said or done or something in the house that might shed light on Naftali's death? Her brief reference to Jude's desire to dispatch Naftali to the military hinted at a back story worth learning. That remark combined with the way Olivia had seemed to almost cringe at Jude's touch made me want to know more about him and his relationship with the dead boy. Jude and Olivia were living together, but I didn't know if they were actually married. Either way, Naftali would have been more like a stepson than a brother-in-law to the older man. Illuminada just might be right. After so many years as a private investigator, she had a very dim view of the American family. As she liked to put it, "When looking into a violent crime, the search for suspects begins at home." There could very possibly be something in the Durango family dynamic that had resulted in Naftali's death.

I disembarked at Grove Street to wait for the train to New York, where I had planned to meet Sol for dinner. As I stood on the platform, I pictured Naftali's lifeless one-armed body landing on the tracks. This image recurred several times, so that I was relieved when my train finally came and I got on. Once seated, I forced myself to continue to review my visit with Olivia while it was still fresh in my mind. It occurred to me that Olivia would have been surprised if she'd known that while she had been translating the lines in my hand to read that I was not listening to my daughter, I had been interpreting her body language to read that her partner was a killer.

At the thought of Rebecca, I smiled. Olivia's statement that Rebecca was in pain was a joke. Olivia had no way of knowing that, just then, my family was the only part of my world that was not falling apart. She couldn't have known that Rebecca was on the way to landing a dream job and was thrilled. To reassure myself, I pulled out her last e-mail message and the photos of Abbie J. It was a rare day when I didn't have at least one of these printouts stuffed into my purse to savor at my leisure or, on occasion, to share with Ma or with friends. It was only when I reread this one that I felt my stomach churn. Had I been so caught up in the escalating drama of my own skewed affairs that I had failed to read between the lines of these messages? Could Olivia have been right?

And why was Rebecca even applying for a position in Nebraska? Keith had a good job working as a concierge cum super at an upscale residential hotel in downtown Seattle. The position came with an apartment and a more than living wage. It was highly unlikely that he'd find a similar situation in Omaha. And why had Rebecca taken Abbie J to visit friends in Wenatchee alone? Where was Keith? Rebecca and Keith had always waited for a weekend when they could both get away and made that trek over the Cascades with Abbie J together. Were they separating? Divorcing? Whatever was going on, clearly Rebecca's relationship with Keith was in big trouble. And, equally clearly, her relationship with me was too. Why else wouldn't she have told me that she and Keith were on the outs? How long had they been having problems? And how the hell had Olivia Durango figured this out by looking at the lines in my hand?

Chapter 15

To: Bbarrett@circle.com
From: Lbarrett@squarepeg.com
RE: Like mother like daughter
Date: 05/13/04 16:08:23

The acorn doesn't fall far from the tree, does it, Bel? First Rebecca sends me a two-line e-mail bailing on Cissie's thirty-fifth birthday bash because she has an interview in Omaha that weekend. That's in Nebraska, right? She didn't mention Keith at all. And he's not in any of the photos of Abbie J either. I called right away and left a message, but so far she hasn't gotten back to me. It looks like Rebecca is dumping Keith just the way you dumped me.

I wasn't keen on their marriage to begin with, I admit, but now that boy's making good money. He put up with her going to grad school, even though she has a child. Thanks to him, they live in a comfortable apartment. He's been a good provider for her and Abbie J. You better talk some sense into that daughter of yours. And don't tell me it'll all work out for the best in the long run like you kept telling me when you trashed our marriage. After you kicked me out, I spent three of the most miserable weeks of my life until I finally met Cissie. Get back to me on this.

Lenny
LBarrett CPA

I always printed out e-mail from Lenny to share with Sol and a few close friends, because his messages were so totally, well, Lenny. That is to say they were infuriating, narcissistic, and, often, unintentionally hilarious. Periodically they appeared on my computer screen, virtual reminders that if women are from Venus, Lenny is from hunger. But this one actually echoed the guilt-induced recriminations that had plagued me since Olivia Durango had made me realize that Rebecca and Keith's marriage was in jeopardy. Because I'd divorced her father, maybe I really had been a poor role model for Rebecca.

Like Lenny, I hadn't been able to reach Rebecca the evening before and so had passed another sleepless night. I had entertained myself with visions of my daughter as the quintessential divorced mother, struggling to begin a career and find an apartment, child care, and friends in faraway Nebraska. As the endless night went on, I pictured Abbie J reacting to her parents' separation by pulling out clumps of her hair and developing problems in school. Perhaps she'd regress and begin bed-wetting again. These behaviors would, of course, spiral to nail biting and then to scarification and eating disorders. And if she survived these adolescent scourges, it would only be to abuse alcohol and drugs as she continued her pitiful efforts to come to terms with the pain of her parents' divorce. When these scenarios became too oppressive, I contemplated myself behind bars for the murder of Naftali Thompson.

When I shared these dismal predictions with Sol, he held me tight and, of course, declared the one about Abbie J both unrealistic and premature. Then he tried to debunk it with humor. "Love, you know Abbie J's much too vain about that gorgeous red hair of hers to ever pull it out."

I didn't even smile. Instead I snapped, "Sol, Mark pulled out clumps of his hair when Lenny and I separated. The kid made himself a little bald spot right over one ear. And do you know why?" I was pointing at the side of my head and trying to keep from shouting at Sol. After all, it wasn't his fault that I hadn't been able to reach Rebecca. "That was his way of punishing himself. Kids often think it's their fault when their parents divorce. You know that." I grabbed my book bag, stuffed with blue books and term papers, and headed for the door. I planned to spend the whole day in my office going over student work and assigning final grades. Maybe this familiar end-of-semester push would distract me from both my daughter's problems and my own.

"I know, Bel," Sol said, shaking his head. "But remember, Mark's got more than his share of hair now, and he turned out fine. I'm sure you'll feel better after you've heard Rebecca's explanation. Don't work too hard today, love." The big hug he gave me at the door was, I knew, intended to bolster my spirits, and it did. I would work hard, so hard that I would become completely absorbed in the words and ideas in the papers and exams I was reading. These words and ideas would eclipse my own dark musings.

Wendy would be there too. I wanted to share Lenny's latest diatribe with Wendy and hear her joke away Rebecca's unhappy marriage, let alone the fact that it was my fault. For years, at the end of each semester Wendy and I had made a ritual of spending a day together in the office reading our students' work with time out to order in and scarf down sandwiches.

But I knew something was wrong when I saw Wendy standing in the hall outside our office. As soon as she saw me coming, she said, "Bel, you will not believe what is going on in there." She jerked her head in the direction of the door to our shared sanctuary. Anxiety made her voice sharp, and it echoed in the empty corridor. "They were inside before I got here. The custodian let them in." I must have looked both puzzled and indignant because Wendy rushed on to explain. "Don't blame maintenance. These guys actually have a search warrant." The import of what Wendy was saying suddenly hit me. The detectives from Hudson County Homicide must be searching our office. "They're going through everything: files, desk drawers, even the books in the bookcase. The short one took the damn desk lamps apart, would you believe? And he spent a long time on your computer. He read your e-mail. Bel, he even poured out your M&M's. See for yourself."

I peered into the office through the pane of glass that comprised the top half of the door. Detective Rago was rooting in the trash can under my desk, his small, even features twisted with distaste. Detective Fergeson was reshelving the books piled haphazardly on the floor. M&M's polka-dotted my desk blotter. I didn't know whether to scream or sob. Stifling both these responses, I opened the door and stuck my head inside. "Good morning, detectives. When do you expect to be finished? Professor O'Connor and I have a lot of exams to read today." I tried to sound serious but respectful, so that they wouldn't guess how upset I was by the sight of their rubber-gloved hands touching our things and invading our privacy, not to mention that of our students.

"Give us another five minutes, Professor Barrett. Detective Rago is replacing those books. Sorry for the inconvenience, but we have a little paperwork of our own to do," said Detective Fergeson. He didn't bother to keep the sarcasm out of his voice, so his response, although politely worded, resonated with insolence and menace. I watched him peel off his gloves, one finger at a time, and deposit them in the wastebasket, his features pursed into a mask of self-righteous fastidiousness. It was the expression of a man who has just been handling used condoms at a rape scene rather than rifling through a basket of empty M&M's bags and half-eaten sandwiches in a college professor's wastebasket. I was near tears when the two men finally left. Sol had been right to engage an attorney, and I was glad Dick Halpern had agreed to take me on.

The minute Wendy and I entered our office and closed the door behind us, she said, "What the hell is going on, Bel? What have you done?"

"Nothing. Trust me." The eyebrows she raised were eloquent testimony to her skepticism, but she opened her book bag. "I'll explain at lunch," I promised. Wendy nodded and, after restoring order, we began to work in compatible silence. Sure enough, before too long my students' words and ideas crowded out thoughts of the intrusive detectives, an angry dead rapper, my pending prison sentence, and even my troubled daughter and granddaughter. It was not that I no longer cared about my personal problems, but rather that working somehow enabled me to give myself permission to table them for a while. This had always been true. Teaching has a strong and deeply rooted claim on my psyche.

Hours later, when I was rereading the essay of a particularly weak composition student and despairing because I had not managed to convey to her how to support her opinions, I heard Wendy's chair squeak as she pushed it away from her desk. Stretching, she said, "So how about a sandwich? I'm ready. Want to call or should I?" After Wendy placed our order, she said, "So what's with these detectives, Bel? What are they looking for? Did you break into the M&M's factory again?"

Wendy's smile and attempt at humor faded when I answered. "No. It seems that Naftali Thompson was hit on the head and then pushed onto the tracks. I'm surprised it hasn't made the papers yet."

"So what does that have to do with you?" Wendy, looking more and more troubled, reached for her purse to get the money to pay for our lunch. "It's my turn, remember?"

"Thanks," I said. "What it has to do with me is that those detectives are from County Homicide, and they think I killed that poor boy."

Wendy paled and then suddenly leapt to her feet, saying loudly, "That's ridiculous. Come on, Bel, let's wait for our sandwiches outside. It's so beautiful." Now it was my turn to be puzzled. RECC's setting is indisputably urban, and the college is grossly under-funded. It boasts no landscaped quad, and there is no picnic-friendly park nearby. The press of students, clients of the adjacent unemployment office, junkies, and occasional dealers, not to mention the aggressive pigeons, do not make the immediate environs conducive to alfresco dining. But Wendy's pixie features were distorted with anxiety, so I stood, grabbed my purse, and followed her. As soon as we were out of the office, she whispered, "I think they tapped our phone. Maybe they wired the whole office."

"Why do you say that? Did you see them do it?" Spooked by her speculation, I whispered my questions. Then, collecting myself, I said in a normal voice, "Let's eat in an empty classroom. We can talk there and then come back to the office to finish our work." I shuddered at the thought of Fergeson and Rago eaves-dropping on our conversation. In a few moments we spotted the delivery girl with our sandwiches and headed her off in the hall. Wendy paid her and, forti-fied with tuna and tea, we entered the nearest empty classroom and closed the door.

Wendy seated herself in the swivel chair behind the teacher's desk, and I took a seat in the front row. Wendy continued her explanation. "Okay, so as I was saying, when I called out for lunch, I heard something funny on the phone line, a little static, a little buzz. I didn't think anything of it then, but if you're serious, we can't take any chances. I don't know how long those two were in our office before I got there, but for all I know, they had time to wire the whole place."

I might have accused her of watching too much TV, but we were in New Jersey, where electronic surveil-

lance has become a cherished folk tradition. Illuminada had expressed surprise that my home phone
wasn't already tapped. "Well, they're wasting their
time because I'm not teaching summer school, and by
the time I get back in the fall, this whole mess will be
resolved. I hope it doesn't bother you too much. You're
not teaching summer school either, are you?"

"No," she said with a sigh. "So tell me why on earth
they think you overpowered this guy and pushed him
off the platform. You couldn't overpower a flea, let
alone a young man."

"I'd feel better if you had said I wouldn't do anything like that, rather than that I'm not capable,
Wendy," I said, trying to smile.

"Well, of course you wouldn't," Wendy said. "But
why on earth do they think you would kill him?" Then
her face darkened. "Is it that they think you were upset
by that rap he posted? My God, they can't think that
you'd kill a boy because you were upset by his rap!"

"Well, yes, they can and they do. They figure that
since Naftali ruined my professional reputation and
probably cost me my job, I have a strong motive. And
it doesn't help that I have no alibi. Sol was in upstate
New York baby-sitting the night it happened, so there's
no one to verify that I was home in bed. But, Wendy,
there's more." I could tell by Wendy's silence that she
was still having trouble believing that anyone could
mistake me for a murderer.

Wendy sat in the teacher's swivel chair in the empty
classroom, her untouched sandwich clutched in her
hand, her face pale. She began to rotate her chair back
and forth. "So tell me. What else?"

"I think Rebecca and Keith are separating. Rebecca

and Abbie J are moving to Omaha, Nebraska. Abbie J is tearing clumps of her hair out. And I found out about it from a damn fortune-teller and my idiot first husband." I handed her the printout of Lenny's e-mail. It took me the rest of our lunch hour to fill Wendy in.

Wendy's response was well-intentioned but hardly helpful. "Listen, Bel, let's forget the fortune-teller, okay? Let's not even go there." Wendy shared the antipathy to the paranormal that I'd always felt until I had literally placed myself in the hands of Olivia Durango. "As for Lenny, since when have you started seeing the world through his beady little eyes? And why don't you wait until you talk to your daughter before you give her the lead in your own private intergenerational soap opera? You're just so upset and sleep deprived you can't see that everything's going to be fine."

Wendy hesitated, as if hearing the hollowness of her words. "Anyway, you know what we always say, when the kids were little, they had little problems, and we could often solve them. But when they get bigger, they have big problems, and we can't do a damn thing about most of them." Wendy made quotation marks with her fingers and chanted in a singsong rhythm to illustrate that she knew what she was saying was a cliché. With her dream husband, perfect kids, and picture-book grandkids, Wendy could hardly be expected to understand. To hear Wendy tell it, her daughter's biggest problem was balancing her fulfilling and lucrative job with the demands of her blissful, stimulating, and erotically exciting personal life.

Not for the first time I reminded myself that Wendy couldn't help it if her kids were well adjusted. I pretended to be reassured so we could return to our bugged office and resume reading papers. I was eager once again to lose myself in my work. For the first time in years, I dreaded the end of the semester, when I wouldn't have any papers or classes to distract me from my own problems. Once back in our office, we got to work. All afternoon, anybody listening would have heard only the rustling of papers and the occasional request to "Please pass the M&M's."

Chapter 16

Veteran's Death Declared Homicide

RECC Prof Suspected

"My brother did not kill himself," said Olivia Durango, sister of Naftali Thompson, whose body was found on the tracks of the Grove Street PATH Station after being hit by an oncoming train. Investigators had initially assumed that the young rapper, recently returned from Iraq, where he had lost an arm in an explosion, had jumped to his death. "We thought we were looking at post-traumatic stress," said Detective Frank O'Leary of the Jersey City Police Department. "But the dead man's sister pushed for an autopsy."

Detective Oliver Fergeson of the Hudson County Homicide Squad told reporters, "That kid was dead before he ever hit the tracks. Someone hit him over the head and then shoved him off the platform. We've got a real promising lead." According to an unnamed source at County Homicide, detectives are investigating a professor at River Edge Community College whom Thompson had disparaged in a rap. RECC President Ron Woodman did not return calls to his office for comment.

The *Jersey City Herald* published this article on the morning of the last day of the semester at RECC. This was the day I returned papers and portfolios and conferred with students about their progress. I always brought in donut holes and juice for them to snack on while they waited their turns. Those who had missed a lot of classes or skipped the final or failed to turn in work did not usually attend. This meant that I got to spend a rewarding few hours affirming those students who had done well or, at least, passed. And they got to thank me, often with cards and poignant notes.

But on the day this article appeared in the paper, only a few students in each class showed up. During conferences, the few who did come seemed stilted and awkward. A young composition student I'd enjoyed working with did not make eye contact with me. An older woman, the star of my Cultures and Values class, brought her husband with her. He sat at her elbow, his eyes following my every move. The students who didn't show placed stamped, self-addressed envelopes in my mailbox with formally worded requests that I mail them their papers. For most of the day I sat alone in the classroom, staring at the box of untouched donut holes and a full bottle of juice.

The only thing that sustained me was the prospect of meeting with Jude Lafayette. I'd arranged this encounter after Wendy and I had found Detectives Fergeson and Rago turning our office inside out in search of evidence that would put me in jail for murder. Their visit and Wendy's speculation that our phone was tapped and our office wired were very disturbing, but they had galvanized me into action again. As soon as I got home, I made two quick phone calls. One was to Illuminada, who had learned that Jude Lafayette worked at Newark Airport, where he loaded and unloaded baggage for Continental Airlines. With that information scrawled on a Post-it, I called Sarah Woolf at the *Jersey City Herald*. Sarah agreed to set up an interview for me with Jude, and she got right on it. She told his boss that we were doing a piece for the paper as part of a series on morale among newly security-conscious airport workers and wanted to talk with a few baggage handlers. Sarah planned to accompany me in the guise of photographer, a role she had played when we had used this ploy before. She offered to drive us to the airport. "I'll pick you up at 11 A.M. sharp at home."

"I'll be disguised," I reminded her. "I've met Jude Lafayette. He came home when I was getting my hair cut by Naftali's sister, Olivia Durango. Jude lives with her, and her salon is in their kitchen."

"Sounds like you're already on the case," Sarah said.

"Well, I did check out Olivia. And Jude walked in twice while I was there, so I need to look completely different." It was only when I heard myself say this that I remembered what I had to do to morph into someone else before meeting Jude again. "Now that I think about it, why don't you pick me up at Vallone and Sons?"

"Good idea," Sarah said. She knew that Vic Vallone, funeral director and love of Betty's life, was an expert in cosmetic transformation and costuming. Vic usually worked his magic on dead people, rendering them more attractive than most of them had been in life. That's why Vallone and Sons boasted a collection of wigs, clothing, makeup, and costume jewelry that would have done a small repertory theater company proud. My third phone call had been to make sure that Vic was free to do a quick makeover on me.

"You're a genius," I called over my shoulder to Vic as I got into Sarah's car the next day.

"Bel, you look great!" Sarah glanced at the new blonde me before she pulled out of the parking lot into traffic. "You should wear lipstick more often. It takes years off. And you've been blonded! I love that platinum hair on you." She tactfully avoided mentioning the circles under my eyes, and I avoided commenting on the fact that unlike the young towheaded socialites who shopped at Bergdorf's, I did not normally use the word "blonde" as a verb.

Instead I said, "This is the same wig I wore to that fake audition to trap the guy who stabbed the Sinatra impersonator, remember?" Sarah nodded. "Vic thought it was a good fit then, and he still had it, so he suggested I use it again. I'm just lucky he hasn't buried anybody in it yet."

Sarah smiled. "I like the peddle pushers. Do you get to keep them?" Her tone was approving. I wore new khaki Capri pants and a black silk pullover.

"Thanks. The clothes are mine actually. I bought them just before everything fell apart," I said, trying not to whine. "You don't look so bad yourself, Sarah. A little tired, maybe." The smudges under her eyes vied with mine, but Sarah wasn't suspected of murder, so I didn't have to be tactful. Tired or not, she skillfully guided the car through the traffic on the New Jersey Turnpike. "Working hard?"

"Yes, but that's not what I'm heartsick and bone-tired over. It's this damn war," Sarah's voice was low, the doleful whisper of one in mourning. "It's so much worse than even I had imagined. It's really got me down." Sarah, who could trace her peacenik credentials back to Vietnam, had marched and lobbied and otherwise protested against our invasion of Afghanistan and then Iraq. Hearing the defeat in her voice made me realize that facing an indictment for murder had, for the moment, distracted me from the horrors of the war.

"I know," I said. "It's awful. When I saw Naftali with one arm missing, the cruelty of it, the human cost, really came home to me. I wonder how many Naftalis there are now, and how many dead or wounded Iraqis." Picturing legions of maimed young people and corpses, we drove in silence for a few minutes.

Then Sarah shook her head as if to dislodge the images of carnage. In an abrupt, almost welcome return to my bizarre predicament and the purpose of our trip, she said, "Okay, Bel, so what do you want to find out from this guy we're going to see today?"

"I'd like to size him up, see what he's about, if he seems capable of murdering somebody. It's a long shot, but I'll try to get him to talk about Naftali. Olivia inferred that Jude had some negative feelings about her youngest brother. If that's true, Jude may have had a motive for murdering him." Sarah didn't respond, so I continued. "Also, I'd like to get him to talk a little about Naftali's family."

When she did answer, Sarah's initial response was not encouraging. "That's a tall order. It'll be hard to get Jude to talk about that family in the context of an interview about his work. But if anybody can do it, you can. You can worm personal information out of a rock, Bel, I swear."

I was relieved to hear Sarah's vote of confidence, especially after she had laid out the challenges I faced. "That's nice of you to say, but it's a little exaggerated. I'm having trouble getting any story at all out of my own daughter about her marital problems. I can't even get her on the phone." I couldn't seem to keep my concern for Rebecca, Keith, and Abbie J out of my mind for more than a few minutes. And whenever this worry wedged its way back into my consciousness, I needed to talk about it.

We had exited the Turnpike into the big and busy airport, so Sarah sounded slightly distracted when she answered. "You mean Rebecca won't take your calls?"

The possibility that Rebecca was screening her calls to avoid speaking to me about her troubles with Keith had crossed my mind when, again, I'd failed to reach her the night before. Sol had advised me not to take it personally because, as he had put it, phone screening was a generational habit. "Alexis often doesn't take calls from me, and she only calls me when she needs me to baby-sit," he added to illustrate his point. "I don't let it get to me. She's busy."

Maybe he was right. But it was hard for me to understand because I so rarely screen calls. Ever since Rebecca had been old enough to be anywhere without me, I'd never heard a phone ring without imagining her, and later Mark, at the other end wanting or needing something. After they got their driver's licenses, the jangle of the phone immediately translated in my overanxious mind to a cop phoning me from the ER. And my worries had not been without basis. Over the years I'd had my share of phone calls from hospitals and police stations. My conditioned response had not changed just because we were all older. And speaking of older, for the last few years, I had been worrying about Ma too. Every now and then she phoned in for help. Not too long ago Sofia had called to say that Ma had had another dizzy spell while putting a new plastic bag in the kitchen trash can. I was still on call 24/7.

But now that Sarah had brought it up, I remembered that Rebecca and Keith took no calls at all when they read to Abbie J, watched TV, shared a "family meal," showered, had sex, or just didn't feel like talking. And the rest of the time, they screened their calls. Keith said they did it to avoid telemarketers, but maybe he wasn't telling me the whole story.

When I finally answered Sarah's question, my voice was muffled by my effort to hold back tears. "Could be she's not picking up when she sees it's me. They have that lousy caller ID. All I can tell you is that Rebecca and I still haven't been able to connect on the phone." The implications of this were too painful to contemplate for very long. I did not want to believe that Rebecca, with whom I had always thought I was so close, was avoiding talking to me about something as important as the breakup of her marriage. Once again, I began to deny a truth I couldn't face. "Between her job and the damn three-hour time difference, it's not easy to get through." I didn't have to mention the anguish this delay was causing me or the fact that I hadn't really been sleeping at all since the twin specters of Rebecca's divorce and my own incarceration had begun to haunt me, but I didn't have to. Sarah knew.

"You okay?" She reached over and patted my arm.

"Yeah," I muttered, taking a breath so deep as to be audible. "I'm okay, just miserable and worried." I tried to sound reassuring when I added, "But I'll do what I have to do."

"I figured," she said. "So get out one of those stupid little notes you've wallpapered your car with and write down where we're parking." I welcomed the task, as well as the return of Sarah's usual flippancy. She had pulled the car into an empty slot, and, without comment, I jotted down its location on a Post-it and stuck the tiny purple flag in my purse. It was a given that, otherwise, neither of us would remember the two-digit code.

Once out of the car, Sarah shouldered the camera she used. I knew she had a small tape recorder in her purse, and I had one too. If we failed, it would not be for lack of equipment. We strode through the airport, flashing the press passes Sarah had provided. She had arranged for us to jump the line at security and, after retrieving our equipment, purses, and shoes from the tray, we made straight for Continental's VIP area. It was here that Jude's supervisor had agreed to bring Jude and two other baggage handlers from Jersey City.

But once we had entered that privileged enclosure filled with suits on cell phones lounging in upholstered armchairs, only two men came forward to greet us. One, a sandy-haired young white man in shirtsleeves and khakis, was obviously the supervisor. The other, to my immense relief, was Jude, wearing a neon-bright lime green vest over a navy blue T-shirt with jeans. What looked like giant black earmuffs on a headband hung loosely from a cord around his neck. I was again relieved, this time to see that, thanks to Vic's efforts, Jude gave no sign of recognizing me.

The man in khakis approached us. "Ms. Wolf? Cal Hopper here. Sorry to tell you, ma'am, but there was a storm in Chicago held everything up, so we got a big backlog out there now, and I can't spare anyone else." His leisurely southern drawl seemed as out of place in the hurly-burly of Newark Airport as a mint julep at a keg party. He looked at his watch and frowned. "But I brung the job description you asked for and Jude Lafayette here." Cal handed Sarah a sheet of paper and nodded at Jude. "My man, Jude here, he's been with the airline for over five years, longer than anybody else workin' here. Longer'n me even. He's been here since before 9/11 even." Cal shook his head, clearly impressed by Jude's stability in an unstable world where five years in one job was a long time and few things had remained the same after 9/11. "What my man, Jude, don't know about handlin' luggage ain't worth knowin.' " Jude smiled, seemingly pleased by the praise. Or maybe he was just glad to have a respite from heaving bags. Cal looked at his watch again.

"This is Melissa Dworkin, a *Herald* feature writer." Sarah nodded at me as she spoke, and I smiled at both men. There was still no glimmer of recognition in the glance Jude gave me, and his polite nod merely acknowledged the introduction of a stranger. So far so good. "She's going to interview Jude, and I'm going to take a few pictures," Sarah added. Cal brushed back his hair and tugged at his collar. "Cal, to save time why don't you show me around out there while Melissa does the interview? That way I can get a few shots of you and the other men at work." Sarah jerked her head in the direction of the busy runway and tarmac visible through the ceiling-high window. "Besides, if I'm with someone who has clout, I won't get hassled by security." Sarah hadn't gotten to be managing editor of the *Jersey City Herald* without learning how to stroke her way through closed doors. After she left with Cal, Jude and I were the only two people in the room without laptops and carry-ons.

"Thanks for agreeing to see me, Jude," I said, scouting the area for adjacent empty chairs.

He nodded. "No problem. I could use a break." He executed a couple of shoulder rolls and reached up to knead his neck.

"Why don't we sit over here?" I pointed to two empty armchairs facing the windows with a small table between them.

"No problem," he said. Normally this ubiquitous response, often a blatant lie uttered reflexively by students when asked if they understood something, irked the hell out of me. But Jude's affability seemed sincere, especially as he sank into the soft chair.

"And do you mind if I tape our conversation? That way I won't have to take notes," I asked. I was in no mood to take notes.

"No problem," he replied once again, settling deeper into the chair.

I got my tape recorder out, set it on the table between us, and turned it on. "I don't know if Cal told you that I'm writing a series on morale among airport workers." Jude nodded. "I'll read your job description, so I don't have to ask you things that are covered in that. Instead, I have a few other topics I'd like you to talk about, okay?" Jude nodded. Before he could assure me that this posed no problem for him, I hit him with the first question, one designed to make him comfortable speaking to me, not to elicit a useful response. "So tell me, Jude, how did you learn about this job? Do you remember?"

He frowned, scratched his head, and then replied. "I was outta work, and my ol' lady's kid brother tol' me 'bout it." Jude's answer came as a surprise to me. Was he actually going to introduce the subject of Naftali himself? That was too much to hope. As if he too were surprised by his answer, Jude rubbed his head as he continued. "He knowed somebody had a cousin workin' here. Said they was hirin'. I thought maybe I was too old, but . . ." Jude glanced down at his prominent biceps. "I been here ever since. Keep me in shape."

"It certainly does," I said, not averse to using a little flattery myself. Jude looked to be in better than good shape. I judged him to be in his late thirties, a few years younger than Olivia. "I bet your girlfriend's son felt good that he had managed to steer you to a job that worked out so well for you."

Jude's laugh was another surprise. It erupted in a snort loud enough to cause a woman to look up from her laptop and glance in our direction. I kept quiet for a minute, hoping he would explain. When he didn't, I said, "What's so funny?"

"That Naftali, he happy whenever anybody got a job long, as it don't be him. Long as I know'd him, he didn't mind his sister workin' two jobs, his brother jockeyin' cars day and night, me haulin' bags, long as he didn't have to do nothin' hisself." Jude shook his head again as if still marveling at Naftali's indolence. "Tha's what funny." But there was more bitterness than amusement in his tone. "His sister and brother, them two like a mama and a daddy to that boy. Nothin' too good for him. They even got his name tattooed on their toes when he enlisted." Jude shook his head and rolled his eyes in disbelief. "Hell, I was sorry Naftali got hurt. That's why I helped Marcus fix up his damn room. But that don't change nothin'. Them two done spoil that boy useless."

We had digressed from the alleged topic of the interview, and although I really wanted to ask more about Naftali, I knew I had to refocus the conversation or risk arousing Jude's suspicions. "Well, if he provided you with a job lead, that's something," I said. "Now, Jude, tell me, if you will, how do you feel about being a luggage handler, especially after 9/11? Do you like it or are you worried about a terrorist attack here? Do you recommend the work to others?"

Again Jude surprised me by ignoring the first three parts of my question and focusing on the last part. "I tell Naftali to come work here while he goin' to college. A couple a young dudes here, they in college. But he don' wanna punch a clock, lif' dem bags." I sensed that Jude was enjoying telling tales about Naftali and wanted to continue. He paused for only a moment and then went on speaking slowly and emphatically. "Dat kid jus wanna hang out in clubs hopin' some big shot gonna hear him rap and make him famous like Biggie Smalls." I couldn't tell whether it was derision or admiration that animated his voice when he pronounced the name of a man so notorious that even a hip-hop virgin like me recognized it. But there was no mistaking the contempt in Jude's tone when he continued. "Only thing Naftali do like a real rapper was get hisself killed."

"Oh no. I'm so sorry." I said, widening my eyes as if surprised to learn of Naftali's death. "Is he the one I read about in the paper? Wasn't he a veteran? That's tragic." It was only polite to offer condolences. I hesitated, curious as to what response this normal civility would elicit.

Jude lowered his eyes for a fraction of a second before he replied, "No problem," illustrating yet again just why I found this overused phrase entirely unequal to the tasks assigned to it in most conversations. It occurred to me that even though Naftali's death hadn't posed a problem for Jude, it was certainly wreaking havoc in my life. But suddenly things were looking a bit brighter. Jude seemed obsessed with the dead Naftali, and his monomaniacal responses were nothing short of music to my waiting ears. The interview was going better than I had dared to hope.

Once again, in the interest of preserving my credibility as a reporter, I fed him a question that, I was sure, would have led another luggage handler to a different response. "Jude, is your work compatible with family life?" He looked a little puzzled, so I reworded the question. "You have to work some weekends, right?" He nodded. "And some evenings?" He nodded once more. "And the work is hard, right? And now there's always the worry about terrorists." He nodded a third time. "So how does your family feel about that?"

Jude snorted again, not as loud as before. When he

responded, he spoke slowly, as if trying to explicate the intricacies of quantum physics to a toddler. "I bring home a check reg'lar, no problem. My ol' lady, she like that check. And her brothers, they like it too, 'specially when Naftali was still comin' up." He paused, as if recalling a time long ago. His voice was softer when he went on. "My ol' lady, she work alla time too, like I say. She do hair and she read hands all day most days, even Sunday." He extended a beefy hand of his own, palm up, to illustrate. "Her and Marcus, her other brother, they slave to take care 'a that damn Naftali." His eyes clouded for a moment, and then he shook his head and scowled. His disapproving expression was echoed by the annoyance in his voice. "Now he dead, they still slavin' to pay up fer his fun'l. Them two, they laid that boy out like he a king, I tell you. And they ain't neither one a them over him yet." He hesitated, and then smiled, as if pleased with his answer to my question. Or was he pleased that Naftali was dead? The smile vanished before I could interpret it. When Jude spoke again, his voice was stern, his bearded chin jutted forward. "I haul them bags to keep a roof on us. No terrorist gonna change that. My fam'ly, they like that a lot."

I nodded, acknowledging that I understood what he was working so hard to get across to me. "Jude, I have another question. Do you enjoy your coworkers? Do you have lunch with them? Do you get together with them outside of work?"

His eyes flashed before he spoke, leading me to believe that I had finally tapped into a part of his life that he could not relate to Naftali. I was wrong. "They all listen to that same damn noise like Naftali."

"Oh," I said. "You mean hip-hop?"

"Whatever," he said, his voice impatient. "I wear these on the tarmac to keep down the sound of the planes." He tapped the earpieces around his neck. "Why I wanna hear more noise when I eat? I eat my meal in the food court where they ain't no loud music. Got me a MP3 player and a headset in my locker. That way I get a little Motown with my food. I hear that damn rap at home when Naftali practice. Now it be quiet there too." Jude lowered his head. Was he finally expressing some regret at the death of Naftali? His next words came out on the breath of a sigh. "It peaceful."

 *Chapter 17*

To: Bel Barrett@circle.com
From: Hdunleavy@juno.com
Re: Parenting Adult Children Together
Date: 05/21/04 11:17:56

Screened Out Mom,

So your Gen-X daughter won't take your calls. Stop whining and look at the bright side. At least she won't be breaking your heart with detailed rundowns of all those
problems you can't solve. When Bethany stopped picking
up or returning my calls, I asked myself some hard questions. Do I really need to know what went wrong between
her and the latest loser she's living with? Do I want to for-
feit a night's sleep after gritting my teeth through a blow-
by-blow account of the run-in she had with her supervisor?
Will it improve my quality of life to know how and why
she's just flubbed another job interview, audition, or
exam? Totaled her car? Pissed off my only sister? Decided
to take a year off from temping to "find herself"? Will I rest

any easier in my own bed after hearing about the most recent burglary/fire in her building or mugging in the slum
where she's opted to live? Bel, eventually your daughter
will get it all together, and then, maybe, she'll call you!
Meanwhile, get a life of your own.

Screened out and surviving,
Hettie

In the past whenever personal problems kept me
awake, I'd indulged my habit of soliciting a solution
from on-line support groups. So it was with a sense of
relief that once again, while Sol tossed fitfully, I had
gotten out of bed, pulled a sweatshirt on over my
nightgown, and booted up my PC. I went at once to
one of my bookmarked sites, a support group called
Parents of Adult Children Together. PACT.org had seen
me through other family crises, so I was confident that,
at the very least, my cry for help would not go unheard.
And it worked. After I read Hettie's reply, I felt a little
better about not hearing from Rebecca.

By the next evening, though, I really wanted to un-
load my concern about Rebecca on Betty and Illuminada. But I had other even more pressing matters to
share with them first as we sat around the coffee table
in Betty's living room. They hadn't come to hear about
my dysfunctional family, but to help me avoid a murder rap. So I recapped the relevant portions of my visit
to Olivia Durango and played the tape of my interview
with Jude Lafayette.

Betty, who held a deviled egg in her hand, was the
first to react. "It's a damn good thing you taped your
conversation with Jude, Bel. Otherwise I never would

have believed how he just rolled over and gave up all that stuff about Naftali." Having offered this opinion, she raised the egg to her mouth and took a big bite. Betty had begun her own version of the Atkins Diet since I'd seen her last, and she appeared to be enjoying it. "I was in the kitchen when you explained what his girlfriend said that made you suspect him."

"While Olivia was cutting my hair, she mentioned that Jude had thought going into the military would be good for Naftali, make a man of him. She sounded just a little bitter. If Jude thought Naftali needed a military makeover, I figured he and the kid had a history of some kind of conflict. And that had to affect Jude's relationship with Olivia." I paused, realizing that I had forgotten one other detail when I'd recounted my visit with Olivia. "Also, when Jude came home, he made an affectionate gesture, as if to massage her neck, and Olivia seemed to pull back. At least that's how it looked to me." Betty nodded and consumed the rest of her deviled egg. "Anyway, didn't you think that on this tape, Jude seemed obsessed with Naftali?" I didn't wait for a response before elaborating. "No matter what I asked him, when he answered, it was all about Naftali. You're right," I said to Betty. "It was almost too smooth."

"Remember when Jude says something about the family's toe tattoos? Well, a cop who saw the body told me that Naftali was wearing sandals when he died and he had *OLIVIA* tattooed on one of his little toes and *MARCUS* on the other. The cops thought these tats were gang-related until they realized that Olivia and Marcus are the names of his siblings." Illuminada sighed at the quirkiness of this latest manifestation of family loyalty.

"That explains the marks I'd noticed on Olivia Durango's little toe. I spotted something there and thought it might be a tattoo, but I didn't have a good opening to ask her about it," I said. "It is weird, but it's also touching in a way."

"When I start tattooing Randy's name on my toes, you've got my permission to commit me," said Betty.

"Wait until he enlists and gets deployed to Iraq," Illuminada snapped. The look on Betty's face as she contemplated the unthinkable was not unlike that on the faces of the Congressmen accosted by Michael Moore in *Fahrenheit 9/11* when Moore suggested that they sign their own kids up for military service in Iraq. Seeing that she had made her point, Illuminada continued. "But if Olivia and Marcus really doted on Naftali, this was probably the first chance for poor Jude to say anything negative about the kid, especially after he was injured. *Chiquitas,* you two know how awkward it can be living with stepkids," said Illuminada, always quick to remind us of the potential for conflict in any kind of family.

But she was right this time. Vic had a daughter who occasionally bunked with her father and Betty as did Betty's son, Randy. And between us Sol and I had three kids with whom we had each struggled to forge good step-relationships. When Mark had lived with us for a short time a few years ago, it had been hard for Sol to witness what he called my "spoiling" of my grown son. As if to reward herself for having reminded us of the challenges inherent in blended families, Illuminada grabbed a handful of unbuttered popcorn. Betty had thoughtfully provided it for both Illuminada and me. We were not averse to ingesting more than an occasional carb but could no longer clog our already crowded arteries with extra eggs and butter. Illuminada, a popcorn junkie from way back, grimaced when her tongue made contact with the naked bland kernels. "This Jude dude seems a very likely suspect to me," she said, chewing determinedly. "He clearly harbors a lot of resentment against Naftali."

"But if Jude killed Naftali, would he be so upfront with his negative feelings about his victim?" Betty's question was one which had occurred to me.

"Maybe he's not too bright and doesn't realize that he should keep his thoughts to himself." Illuminada paused a moment, trying to think of another rationale to explain Jude's candor. "Or, try this. Maybe his resentment of Naftali has never been a secret. You said Olivia seemed aware of it." I nodded. "So maybe he figures that for him to change tunes now would be suspicious. Maybe he's counting on an alibi to place him beyond suspicion." Illuminada looked pleased with this conclusion and, with a shrug, reached for another fistful of popcorn. "And maybe this foul stuff will grow on me," she added, half to herself.

"So we need to find out if he has an alibi," I said. "I'm not sure how to do that yet, but I'll figure something out."

"Although I have to agree that he's an attractive suspect, you haven't really talked to any of the other family members besides him and Olivia," said Betty, picking up another egg. "You better get a hold of that brother, the one who helped Olivia spoil Naftali." Betty's use of the imperative often grated, but this directive didn't really bother me. Her concern for me took the bite out of her bark, and, besides, she was right.

"Okay, I'll talk to the other brother, Marcus, and I'll even go back to Olivia again. Maybe I can get her to tell me if Jude had an alibi." I sighed at the prospect of submitting to another palm reading. "But remember, Naftali was barely out of his teens. His peers were probably as much an influence on him as his family. I really need to talk with some of his friends. And he must have had a girlfriend." I was thinking out loud.

"*Chiquita,* how the hell are you going to get Naftali's hip-hopping friends to talk to you?" There was no mistaking the sarcasm in Illuminada's next words. "You haven't been credible as a groupie since the Beatles got here. And you don't know squat about rap music or hip-hop."

"I know. I know." I didn't take offense after my friend as much as said I was too old and ignorant to get young rap enthusiasts to talk to me. Like Betty's directive, Illuminada's scathing outburst was prompted by concern, and knowing that took the sting out of her skepticism. "I've already figured this out." Anxiety about my future may have sharpened my friends' tongues, but it had also jump-started my survival mechanism, my wits. "On the way home from Newark Airport I spoke to Sarah about doing a piece on the hip-hop scene in Jersey City as a follow-up to her interview with Naftali. It can be a kind of memorial with commentary on him by his friends and even his rivals. I'm willing to bet my last bag of M&M's that those wannabe rappers are all publicity hounds and that they'll gladly talk to a reporter, no matter how old or uncool she is."

In spite of my bravado, I knew I might have trouble connecting with young rap artists. What little I knew about rap I'd learned from headlines about shootings, op-ed rants about obscene and misogynistic lyrics, and an occasional student paper on "hip-hop culture." The angry men in baggy jeans shouting rhymes about bitches, guns, and money in slang I could barely decipher offended me. Even the touted film *8 Mile* had not made me a rap or hip-hop fan. I could see how the rhymes were descendants of the dozens and reggae and, like these, important means of self-expression. But I cringed at the way so many rap lyrics demeaned women and glorified violence. And Naftali's crude rap about me hadn't raised my opinion of the genre.

Grilling Naftali's cohorts certainly would challenge my celebrated interviewing skills, skills which had been honed in a classroom setting with students who, for the most part, wanted to please their prof. Interviewing undercover to track down a killer was different. But my meeting with Olivia had yielded a lead. And my session with Jude had been unexpectedly productive. In fact, since I'd begun sleuthing, I'd convinced quite a few people to give up information to me. For sure, connecting with the hip-hop set would be tough, but I knew I could make contact. I had to. "Sarah's really freaked over this whole thing, so she's eager to help. She's putting me in touch with the guy who books local talent for that club downtown that stages concerts. He's an old friend of hers. I'm going to start with him. I'm hoping he'll give me other names."

"Good," said Illuminada, "because I really don't want to have to visit you in jail. Speaking of jail, take these damn reports before I walk out of here and forget to give them to you. I haven't read the police report yet, so I made a copy for myself too." She handed me two manila envelopes: one labeled AUTOPSY REPORT and the other POLICE REPORT.

"How's your mother taking the fact that you're a murder suspect? What odds does she give that you'll beat the rap?" Illuminada's tone was light, but I knew that her question was motivated by concern. Ma's anxiety and fragility were as much a part of her persona as her spunk and her tendency to bet on anything that moved.

"She was doing great until the other day when those damn detectives, Fergeson and Rago, showed up at her house and began poking around and asking questions. That really upset her and Sofia too. Ma actually called Rabbi Ornstein-Klein and went to talk to her." It was chilling to think of Ma and Sofia being subjected to the prying eyes and intrusive gloved fingers of the detectives. "Those bastards really frightened her."

"Did they have a search warrant?" asked Illuminada, whose eyes had flashed when I mentioned the detectives' visit.

"No, but they said they could get one if necessary, so Sofia told them not to bother. She said that she and my mother had nothing to hide." I wasn't hungry, but out of habit I reached for a handful of popcorn. I was used to fighting frustration with food, and at that moment even food that tasted like Styrofoam mailing pellets was better than no food.

"Sol must be pretty unhinged too. I can't see him enjoying conjugal visits with you behind bars." Betty was trying for a laugh, but her one-liner landed in our midst with a heavy *thud* and threatened to end our conversation. My friends knew that, like Ron Woodman, Sol had suffered from post-traumatic stress after witnessing the attacks on the World Trade Center. They also knew that even before 9/11 Sol hadn't always been comfortable with my sleuthing. But sleuthing to exonerate somebody else, as I'd done in the past, was an option. Sleuthing to save my own neck was a prerequisite for survival. After a few seconds of rather grim silence, Betty shifted our focus. "That reminds me of our other two lovebirds. Illuminada, have you any news?"

"No, *chiquita,* I was hoping you did. I called Lourdes last night, and Raoul tried to reach her too. We still want to take her and Randy to a concert or a show for her birthday next month, and we need her to give us some dates, but she hasn't gotten back to either one of us yet."

"Join the club," I said, welcoming the company my misery craved. I opened my purse to look for the printout of Lenny's e-mail message. "I didn't tell you this yet, but Rebecca and Keith's marriage is in big trouble." I didn't have to look up to know that my friends' faces registered surprise. "And I can't get her to return my phone calls, so I don't even know why. I think she's started screening my calls."

"Doesn't that just drive you nuts?" asked Betty. She pushed the plate of deviled eggs away. "Sometimes I'll call Randy and get his machine. I know he's home. But I leave a message asking him to call me by that evening and two or three days later, after I've tried him again at all hours, he might just get back to me. And he might not."

"Yes, but you call Randy a lot," I said. It was true. Betty, who had been known to micromanage the lives of relative strangers, still called Randy to remind him to pick up his dry cleaning, to alert him to sudden weather changes, and to suggest activities, books, and DVDs he might enjoy. Even though my observation was true, and I wasn't making it for the first time, I regretted having repeated it when I saw Betty's eyes cloud with tears.

"So what? He's my only kid, and I like to stay close. I just like to hear his voice." Betty's words were defensive, but her tone was apologetic, as if she were trying to forestall an argument.

"So listen to his recorded message and then hang up," snapped Illuminada. Now Betty's eyes widened at the sharpness of our friend's retort. Betty had expected Illuminada to offer sympathy, not a sarcastic suggestion. But Illuminada's pragmatism shouldn't have come as a surprise. "I'm serious, *chiquita,* don't call the poor kid and tell him what to do all the time. My mother does that with me in person, and it makes me crazy. *Díos mío,* the best thing about having Milagros Santiago living upstairs from us is that she doesn't phone very often!"

As much to give Betty a chance to recover from Illuminada's suggestion that Randy might perceive his mom's calls a nuisance as to refocus their attention on my more pressing family problem, I said, "Check this out. It's Lenny's latest." I handed the wrinkled printout to Betty. Illuminada leaned over and read it with her.

"So, Bel, is this why you think Rebecca and Keith are separating?" Betty asked, sliding the printout back across the coffee table to me. "Lenny could be wrong, you know. He usually is."

I sighed again and let it all out, talking rapidly. "Not this time. The last I heard from Rebecca, she had had a great interview at Omaha General, but I know Keith wouldn't be able to get a job there like the one he has in Seattle. So why would she be interviewing there? Besides," I added sheepishly, "Olivia Durango read my palm and said that Rebecca had problems, but that I was too distracted to draw her out." I saw the chins of my two friends drop open simultaneously, and I raised my hand to silence their protests at the notion that I was now taking seriously the prognostications of a palmist.

"And don't tell me she'll explain everything over the phone, because it's not just Lenny's calls she doesn't take. She doesn't pick up when I call either, and she hasn't gotten back to me. She hasn't even answered my e-mail." I shrugged and took back the printout and crumpled it in my fist. "I always thought Rebecca and I were so close." I was near tears, and both Betty and Illuminada knew it. The fact that I was fighting a murder charge tempered their response to my perception that, in her hour of need, Rebecca had shut me out of her life. Betty blew me a kiss across the coffee table between us. Illuminada, not known for displays of affection, reached over from her seat on the other end of the sofa and squeezed my arm. That did it. I began to sob.

Chapter 18

To: Bbarrett@circle.com
From: AyeshaJ@earthink.com
Re: Screened Out Grandma
Date: 05/02/04 07:45:21

Screened Out,

We empathize with you. Our only child, André, and his
wife, Keisha, began screening our calls after the birth of
our grandson, Monty. Charles and I just wanted to know
how they were managing, so we phoned them a couple of
times a day to ask about how the latching was going and
how long little Monty was sleeping and to check, you
know, Monty's output in his diapers or to see if he had a
rash or gas. After about the third or fourth day when we
called, neither André nor Keisha picked up or got back to
us, and we were really worried. They weren't answering
our e-mails either. Charles and I are both retired, so we
got into the car and drove twelve hours to Cincinnati. Were
those two surprised to see us! Thank goodness little Monty

was fine, just not sleeping a whole lot. But now André and Keisha call us back the same day. Good luck.

Sharlene

Sharlene's message greeted me when I logged on after returning from Betty's, but her implied advice didn't do a lot for me. With a murder charge threatening, I was in no position to travel three thousand miles across the country because my daughter did not return my calls. But maybe I could persuade Sol that we should head west as soon as I could figure out who really killed Naftali Thompson. I spent the rest of the weekend Googling hip-hop sites.

By Monday names like OutKast, 50 Cent, Lil Kim, Jay-Z, and Ludacris spun around in my head, but I still didn't have much understanding of their wide appeal. Even so, when Sarah called to tell me that she had arranged for me to talk with Doug Equivera that very afternoon, I was glad that I'd made some effort to educate myself. "Doug's the guy who books musicians at the Rap Room, that big club and concert venue in Jersey City," she'd reminded me, sounding as pleased as if she'd just arranged for me to have an audience with the Dalai Lama. "I've known him for years. He knew Naftali, and he knows the local hip-hop scene. You'll like Doug. He's very chatty, and he can give you other names. Wear the wig. Doug's first two wives were blond."

The Rap Room was in an old warehouse between Hoboken and the Holland Tunnel not far from the light rail tracks or, for that matter, from the subway station where Naftali's body had been found. Until about

twenty years ago this area had been an industrial
wasteland on the margins of Jersey City. But luxury
high rises had materialized along the Hudson River
and equally upscale office buildings, hotels, and
restaurants now circled a mall and the PATH station.
Many of those offices were home to firms displaced by
the destruction of the World Trade Center. Realtors and
developers had recently dubbed the long-forgotten Jersey side of the Hudson "the Gold Coast," but, as the
saying goes, "All that glitters is not gold." In between
the gated condo complexes and office towers a few forgotten housing projects, soot-grimed trestles, and deserted, rubbish-strewn cul de sacs remained, grim
ghosts of a grittier time. They lent the area that special
no-man's-land quality peculiar to former body drops
and the landscape paintings of a few perverse urban
artists.

Sarah couldn't go with me, so I drove there myself,
aware of the unseasonable chill in the air and the dark
threatening clouds. Against the slate-colored sky, the
Rap Room loomed large and surprisingly bright. The
club was in a former factory with the boxlike shape of
a Wal-Mart's with high ceilings. Every inch of the
massive exterior was splashed with colorful graffiti, so
the whole building resembled a giant Manhattan subway car, circa 1983. There were only a few other vehicles in the vast lot, so I parked near the front, locked
my Toyota, and made for what looked like the entrance. I pushed the button beside it and waited.

In a moment the door swung open, and I peered into
the darkness. "Welcome to the Rap Room." The husky
voice seemed to gurgle up from somewhere around my
knees. I looked down to find a gray-haired black man

in a wheelchair gazing up at me from beneath the brim of a straw boater perched jauntily atop his head. "You must be Sarah Woolf's connect, Melissa Dworkin. Doug Equivera. Welcome to my world." The heartiness of his greeting was muted only by the liquid hoarseness of his voice. I bent down and gripped his outstretched hand.

We made an awkward tableau there in the doorway, and when I stood up, I felt a twinge of annoyance. Sarah hadn't mentioned anything about Doug using a wheelchair or, for that matter, about his being Latino. I'd expected a man who booked rappers into a hip-hop club to be an able-bodied African-American, spouting urban slang and four-letter epithets. Instead Doug was physically challenged, had at least one Spanish-speaking ancestor, and greeted me in entirely proper if somewhat hip-hop-inflected Standard English.

Disgusted with my biased and un-PC preconceptions, I was revising them to fit reality when Doug said, "C'mon in. Any friend of Wolfgirl's is a friend of mine. We used to work together." I smiled at his nickname for Sarah. I'd never heard it before. He must have known her for a long time, back when she was a lean and hungry girl reporter sniffing after the telling details that had turned her stories into award-winning exposés.

I followed him in and heard the metal door clang shut behind us. There were tiny lights along the floor, like those in airplane aisles to guide passengers to the emergency exits. We followed these twinkling dots until we came to a half-open door. Doug pushed it and waved me ahead of him into a sudden blaze of light and color. I blinked. When my eyes had adjusted, I saw that we were in a windowless room. Three walls were Fisher-Price red and plastered with posters and photos of performers. The other wall was royal blue like the carpet, and the ceiling was yellow and crisscrossed with track lighting. The office reminded me of a room made entirely of giant blocks or Legos. In contrast with the *Romper Room* color scheme, the furniture was strictly corporate and featured a desk and computer stand of blond wood and some soft black leather chairs. In one corner was a blond wood table.

The strident, percussive rasp of an angry rapper reverberated off the walls. I struggled to prevent myself from putting my fingers in my ears to stave off deafness. But my host saw me flinch and wheeled himself behind his desk where he pushed a button on the console next to it, silencing the loud voice. I nodded my appreciation. "Have a seat. Want some coffee? Tea?" Doug's voice was a lot like Louis Armstrong's, an amiable and grainy gurgle, soothing after the ear-shattering noise.

Feeling like a tourist exhausted by alien and unexpected sights and sounds, I sank into one of the cushy leather chairs and glanced around. There was no sign of coffee makings. "Is tea a lot of trouble?" I asked.

"No. I usually order in something for myself right about now." Doug propelled his chair out from behind the desk and positioned it across from mine. He pulled a cell phone from his belt and pushed a button. "What do you take in it? Want a sandwich or something? This place I'm calling makes dynamite burgers."

"Just black tea for me, thanks," I said. "I'm easy." While Doug communicated our order, I took a good look at him. His sienna-shaded skin was mostly clean-shaven, the better to showcase a generous graying mustache and goatee. The goatee was embellished by a dime-sized tuft of hairs sprouting just above it and beneath his lower lip. In contrast with this extravagance of facial fur, the silver hair on Doug's head, barely visible beneath his hat, was closely cropped. He didn't wear glasses, but his eyelids appeared swollen, narrowing his eyes into a permanent squint. He wore a blue and white striped long-sleeved shirt with a red and white polka-dotted scarf knotted at the neck. His jeans were set off by a belt of brown embossed leather. The leather band on his right wrist matched the belt. His soft and sensible brown oxfords, the kind my dad had worn on occasion, were out of sync with his otherwise casually modish look. I recognized the diamond stud the size of an M&M that he wore in one ear as an example of "bling," a word that my students had taught me awhile back meant pricey and glittering jewelry to hip-hoppers. That glitzy globe was the only thing about Doug that fit my preconceived notion of a hip-hop booking agent.

After I'd given Doug a quick once-over, I stood and inspected the photos. Not all of them were of rappers. There were several featuring break dancers and one or two of graffiti-covered subway cars. A picture of a triumphant Mike Tyson was paired, incongruously, I thought, with one of the legendary bluesman Robert Johnson. I was so absorbed in trying to find a link among the disparate images that I almost missed the picture of Naftali. It was a headshot on a poster, the image of a ghost, the face partially shrouded by the hood of a black sweatshirt. I started at the sight of it and, recovering, examined it closely. In one hand Naftali

clutched a hand mike that did not even begin to ob-
scure the enormous silver cross suspended from a
heavy chain around his neck. The eyes of the dead boy
bored into mine, and that gaze from the grave, like the
siren of a distant ambulance, brought pain, war, and
death into Doug's cheerful office. I shivered. Beneath
the photo were the words HIP-HOP ACADEMY WANTS YOU
and a Web address. I would have to ask Doug about the
poster. As soon as I heard him complete his call, I returned to the chair and said, "Thank you, and thanks
too for agreeing to talk to me."

"Glad to do it. Good to talk to somebody over thirty
for a change." Doug's lips stretched into what he no
doubt intended as a smile of complicity. I ignored his
not so subtle reference to my age. Now it was his turn
to check me out, and he did. His eyes lingered on my
borrowed blonde hair and traveled down to my ample
bust, dwelling there not long enough to be insulting,
but long enough to bring a blush to my cheeks. I was
relieved when he said, "Wolfgirl saved my ass a few
times when I was at the *Herald*." I made no mention of
his appreciative glance and focused instead on his reference to the newspaper and Sarah. "Oh? You used to
work at the *Herald*?"

"Yeah, didn't Sarah tell you? I was a freelance
music critic for the *Herald* and a few other Jersey papers in the early eighties, just when hip-hop was starting to really happen." Suddenly Doug's voice seemed
huskier than usual and a faraway look dimmed the
gleam in his eyes. "I went to block parties, clubs, and
concerts all over Manhattan and the Bronx. I ran my
tail off following the flow, scoping the sound, and I
was beginning to get a name." He shook his head be-

fore continuing. "I did a few magazine pieces too." Doug sighed, and shut his eyes for a moment as if to obliterate an unpleasant memory. I didn't speak, willing him to continue. "But then one night on the way back from the Bronx to my crib in Jersey City, I got blindsided by a drunk driver, and when I woke up in the hospital . . ." He paused at this critical moment in what was obviously an often-told tale.

When he felt that I had waited long enough for the end of his sentence, he went on. "I couldn't move." He paused again, anticipating my intake of breath. After he heard it, he added, "But I'm lucky. I got back the use of everything but my legs." I was marveling at Doug's seeming lack of bitterness. If I had lost the ability to walk, I would hardly have described myself as lucky. I would have seethed with anger and resentment. He grinned and said, "And then I sued the pants off the son of a bitch."

Chapter 19

The Rap Room Hip-Hop Academy

A hip-hop and cultural arts program that provides Jersey City youth instruction in hip-hop writing and music production, as well as the rudiments of business, the Rap Room Hip-Hop Academy is funded by the Jersey City Council on the Arts in cooperation with the Rap Room. An after-school program, the Academy works with high school and college students ages 14–20 who have been recommended by teachers, counselors, or clergy members. Classes meet four times a week at the Rap Room, where students write lyrics and work on beats and rhythms that they will eventually record in the club's sound studio. Here students get hands-on experience with all aspects of pre- and post-production recording . . .

It wasn't until he had finished describing the aftermath of his accident that I really understood the genesis of the Rap Room Academy. I was relieved when Doug acknowledged that he had sued the drunk driver who had crippled him, hardly a frivolous litigation. "I can understand suing," I said. "Is that why you gave up journalism?"

"Yeah," Doug dragged out his one-syllable response into a sigh that his huskiness made sound like the last wet wheeze of a pneumonia patient. Here was a man who had probably spent half a lifetime inhaling and had finally quit. There wasn't so much as a hint of cigarette smoke in his office. "It was too much trying to make all those gigs in the chair." He tapped the arms of his wheelchair and looked up. "But the silver lining was that I bought into this place with the real paper I made from the lawsuit."

This was another factoid Sarah had left out when she'd given me her hurried description of Doug. "Oh, I didn't realize you owned the Rap Room. I thought you just worked here booking acts."

"There are three of us co-investors, but I manage the club, book the acts, and do the marketing. And I dreamed up the Rap Room Hip-Hop Academy." He nodded to the poster I'd been eyeing. "I'm the only owner who's on-site. Hell, man, I practically live here." Doug smiled. His use of the word "man" grated on me, but I decided not to call him on it. "We're starting to show a profit this year. We're getting bigger names, drawing bigger crowds. We've even got TV coverage of tomorrow night's concert." Just as I was about to ask him about the Hip-Hop Academy, the doorbell rang. Doug wheeled himself over to his desk and pushed a button. In a moment a sweaty young man came in with his bike in tow carrying our take-out order. Doug paid him and waved him away with a casual, "Thanks, Jésus."

I sipped my tea. Doug picked up his burger and attacked it with gusto. Sarah was right. I did like Doug. And he was chatty. "What's the Rap Room Hip-Hop Academy?" I asked, hoping to catch him between bites.

Doug put down the burger and carefully wiped his hands. He reached around behind him and took an electric orange folder from a stack of them on his desk. "Here, take it home. Maybe you can work it into a feature, the one you're doing about Naftali or another one down the line." I had just opened the folder and glanced inside when a young white man strode through the door. I didn't recall hearing a knock. From his baggy jeans and black sleeveless T-shirt to his shoulder-length dreads, this rude intruder personified a white version of the rapper I'd expected. Even I recognized an Eminem clone when I saw one. I glimpsed the edges of tattoos sticking out from under his T-shirt, and bangles and chains ringed his arms. A large gold peanut dangled from a heavy chain around his neck. He wore black high-tops that I recognized as the kind Mark used to wear skateboarding in the eighties. His black eyes glinted, and a beak-shaped nose and receding chin lent his face a hawkish sharpness. He was attractive in a predatory sort of way. And at first glance he looked vaguely familiar. I wondered if, like Naftali, he too had passed through my classroom at RECC.

"Sup, man, wha's wid the juice? Forgot to pay the damn bill again? C'mon, Doug, I can't do shit wid dem kids widout no power." His lips faked a smile made bright or grotesque, depending on how you felt about the glittering gold caps on several of his front teeth. An occasional student of mine had boasted dental jewelry, so I was not totally unaccustomed to it, but P-Nutz's dentist definitely had the Midas touch. The gold in P-Nutz's mouth rivaled that in Fort Knox, and I had to stop myself from staring at his gilded teeth. Didn't food get trapped in the interface between gold and gum? Between bling and bicuspid? Wasn't his million-dollar metal mouth a pricey plaque magnet?

While I was concerning myself with P-Nutz's oral hygiene, he noticed me. After checking me out for a second or two, he turned to Doug and said, "Didn't know you was busy, man." But there was no trace of contrition in his tone, no hint of real deference to the much older man in the wheelchair.

Ignoring P-Nutz's peremptory manner, Doug said cordially, "P-Nutz, this is Melissa Dworkin. She writes for the *Jersey City Herald*." Only after registering this did P-Nutz deign to glance my way. "Melissa, I'd like you to meet P-Nutz, an up-and-coming local rapper. He teaches at the Academy." P-Nutz preened, puffing up his chest. "P-Nutz, Melissa's here to do a memorial piece about Nas-T." P-Nutz's fourteen-carat grin froze on his face for a moment and then faded. He raised his right hand to his left shoulder and rubbed it, the same gesture I'd made whenever I thought about Naftali and his lost arm. I felt the stirrings of empathy for P-Nutz.

"Nas-T and P-Nutz used to battle together when they were just kids really," said Doug. "You dudes went way back, right?" P-Nutz nodded. His eyes glittered, and I was touched by his effort to contain his tears and mask his grief over the death of his friend.

"I'm so sorry about what happened to Nas-T," I said.

Then I remembered that I was a reporter, professionally obligated to relentlessly stalk and grill the recently bereaved. "P-Nutz, if you're going to be around in about an hour, I'd like to get a quote from you about Nas-T." When I addressed him directly, P-Nutz stopped rubbing his shoulder. It was then that I noticed that the word DREAM was tattooed there in deep purple ink. Recalling the Everly Brothers' "All I Have to Do Is Dream," I assumed P-Nutz had put his own updated spin on the golden oldie. He nodded and turned once more to Doug. "The lights, man."

Doug nodded. "I hear you. It's probably just a blown fuse again like it was last time. I showed you how to fix that, didn't I?" P-Nutz raised his eyebrows. "Are you telling me you don't do fuses?" Doug's good-natured chuckle bubbled up from somewhere below his throat. I marveled at his patience with P-Nutz's prima donna posturing and air of entitlement. "Excuse me for a second, Melissa, while I go and show this playa how to flip a switch. He can run a hundred thousand dollars' worth of audio gear, but he can't or won't flip a circuit-breaker switch."

"Take your time. I'll look this over while you're gone." I nodded at the orange folder Doug had given me just before P-Nutz made his appearance. When Doug wheeled back into the office a few minutes later, I was reading the description of courses in spinning, mixing, lyrics, promotion, and contracts. I greeted Doug with a rhetorical question. "You teach kids how to become hip-hop performers here?"

"Yup. I wrote a grant to get money from the Jersey City Council on the Arts to pay a couple of local DJs and MCs to work after school. The Rap Room provides the space and the equipment. We've got a sound studio and two practice rooms. We charge hardly anything, but applicants need recommendations to get in. The kids love it, their parents love it, and the performers love it. It's my way to give back to the community. And it helps to keep neighborhood folks from complaining when a concert audience gets a little out of hand once in a while," Doug added with a barely discernible wink. "It's a win-win deal. P-Nutz teaches at the Academy. Naftali took classes here and taught." Doug's smile was rueful. "The kid started here as Naftali and by the time he graduated he was Nas-T. In fact, he was IM Kra-Z's teacher, and, damn, if my man Nas-T didn't do such a good job that IM just signed with a Newark producer."

I stored away the fact that Naftali had taught Derek and that the student had, perhaps, outstripped his mentor, but I didn't refer to it when I spoke next. Instead I pumped Doug about Naftali. "You've anticipated one question I wanted to ask you."

"Ask away," Doug said, opening his hands as if to welcome my questions.

"I was curious about how you came to know Naftali." I took out my tape recorder. "Do you mind?"

"No problem," Doug said. "Naftali Thompson was the youngest kid to show up to study at the Academy right after I got it started. He was a fourteen-year-old hip-hop head. His sister, I guess it was, brought him over one day and enrolled him with the blessing of his high school guidance counselor. That kid took every course we had for a couple of years. Spinning, mixing, writing lyrics, you name it. He never missed a class, but his specialty was free-styling." Doug and I both

shook our heads, he marveling at Nas-T's studious-
ness, I recalling the many speech classes Naftali had
skipped.

"I'm sorry, Doug. I'm not a music maven. I usually
cover education and feature stuff. But Sarah really
wanted this to be a human interest article, so she figured I could handle it. Now I'm in over my head," I
said. "Spinning is what DJs do to records, right?"
Doug nodded. "But mixing? What's that?" I'd seldom
met a man who didn't relish explaining things to a
woman, so I figured it would be easy to get Doug to
give me a crash course in hip-hop lingo. I was right.

"In the eighties, DJs spinning records in discos got
a hold of a little piece of technology that enabled them
to shift music from one turntable to the next without
stopping to change records." I nodded to show that I
understood. I was grateful that he hadn't laughed at my
question. "It was called a mixer."

"So you're saying that hip-hop grew out of disco?"
I was pleased that the explanation might be this simple.

"Disco and a lot of other things. You remember how
every group had its own disco? Gays, rich folks,
blacks, working-class whites?" I nodded, although I
was almost as ignorant about the disco scene as I was
about hip-hop. I was beginning to feel really out of it.
"Well, the Caribbean communities in New York began
to adapt the 'dub' style of the DJs from Jamaica who
played in people's yards. It was less about melody and
more about a pounding bass." Doug crumpled the
paper that had held his hamburger. He turned his attention to his coffee.

"So that explains why there's no tune to rap," I said.
Doug nodded again. I knew that as a former journalist

he would be very suspicious if I let too much time go by without pressing him for the story I was supposed to be after. "So, Doug, tell me about Naftali. If he was so interested in hip-hop, why did he enlist in the service? And was he part of a group or did he perform solo? Did he really have a shot at making it big? What did he teach here? And do you know . . ."

Doug raised his hands, as if to shield himself from the barrage of questions. "Hold it, Brenda Starr, one at a time." He put down his coffee cup before he spoke. "For Naftali it was all about the lyrics, the hook. That kid just loved to freestyle." I must have looked puzzled because Doug added, "That's when you extemporize the lyrics to minimal musical accompaniment. And the kid loved to battle. Know what his sister told me the first day she brought him here?" Without waiting for my blank stare, Doug answered his own question. "She swore that when Naftali was a baby, he cried in rhyme." Doug grinned at the memory of this detail. "P-Nutz, he writes his lyrics out before he performs, but not Nas-T. He made them up like he thought he was Coltrane playing a riff or a preacher trying to scare off the devil. His rhymes weren't always the best, but he had a lot of them."

I sipped my tea, again saddened by the thought of Naftali's early death. Doug's voice was low when he continued, so I knew he too was moved. "The kid said he was enlisting so he could rap about war firsthand, tell the real story. He was sure there was going to be another war and, you know, he figured he could interest a producer if he kind of embedded himself in the military. He figured he'd get in on the action and then rap about it." Doug shook his head. "I tried to talk him out of it, but he didn't want to hear it. That sorry dude figured he was going to be the Iraq War's hip-hop Ernie Pyle, only he didn't even know who Ernie Pyle was." Doug shook his head again, perhaps at Naftali's youthful bravado, perhaps at his ignorance.

"Off the record, the kid failed a couple of courses at community college and blew off his chance to transfer to State anytime soon. On top of that, he was using up his financial aid with nothing to show for it. College was always his sister's idea anyway. His sister's man thought a few years in the military would do the kid good." Doug shook his head one more time. "That dude had the off-the-wall idea that Naftali should get a job." Doug's sarcastic tone and stress on the "J"-word made it clear that Naftali had found this rather sensible suggestion outlandish. "But no, Nas-T wouldn't listen to him either. Nas-T just wanted to make it big as a rapper, and he figured the war would work for him."

Doug paused. Perhaps he was thinking that an arm was a heavy price for a young man to pay for failing a few courses and trying to avoid a sluggish job market. In a moment he continued. "On the record, Nas-T used to be in a group with P-Nutz, but that was backinthe-day. They had their last big collabo in the limelight a year or so ago the night they opened for Joe Budden when he played the Rap Room." When I furrowed my brow at the unfamiliar name, Doug quickly explained. "Joe's a Jersey City homey who got signed by Def Jam a while back." He pointed to a poster featuring a lean and somber young black man wearing a ski cap and sporting a trim mustache leaning against a chain-link fence. "Def Jam is a big hip-hop producer. So Joe's a supahero to all the wannabe rappers in Jersey City now. Naftali worshipped him."

I nodded, trying to assimilate all that Doug was saying. "Do you have a quote about him, about Naftali, I mean? A quote I can use?"

Doug thought for a few seconds and then said simply, "Naftali loved rhyming and he loved hip-hop. He enjoyed teaching kids how to write lyrics. Everybody here missed him when he left for the service. We still miss him." I noticed that Doug had paid tribute to Naftali's enthusiasm rather than to his talent.

"You know, Doug, Naftali's sister doesn't think his death was a suicide. Do you think it might be one of those gangsta rap killings?" Even I knew that there had been a spate of shootings of rap artists by rival rappers, and I wondered if Naftali had gotten caught up in that deadly game.

Doug's narrow eyes narrowed further as he gave me a stern look. When he spoke his tone was reproving. "Yo, Melissa, a young black male in Jersey City doesn't have to be a gangsta rapper to get himself killed." My stomach tightened defensively at his not-so-subtle reminder that drug dealers, gangs, and guns still ravaged the streets of Jersey City's impoverished ghettos. "Naftali wasn't important enough or successful enough yet to provoke a rival rapper." Doug emitted a liquid sigh. "As far as I can tell, the only one who might have wanted to see him dead is some big old white lady, an English prof at the community college. I heard she got fired because he dissed her, and his beef with her made the evening news. Word is the cops are talking to her." Doug now made a series of phlegm-filled noises. Still smarting from his rebuke, I didn't realize for a moment that he was chuckling. Apparently the idea of an aging and avenging white female academic was laughable to him. I wished that Detectives Rago and Fergeson shared his sense of the absurd. Then Doug's chuckle evolved into a spasm of coughing that wracked his whole body and shook his wheel chair. His hat fell to the floor. I picked it up and held it in my lap.

When Doug finally stopped coughing, I said, "Are you okay?" It seemed like a silly question because he suddenly seemed frail and vulnerable in a way that he hadn't before he had coughed.

"For now," he answered cryptically. I handed him his hat, and he put it on and smiled. "But I've got a group auditioning in about ten minutes, so I've got to get ready." It was as if his coughing fit had reminded him of the passage of time and, once reminded, he had to rush. "If there's anything else I can do here, holla." He pulled a business card out of his shirt pocket and handed it to me. Then he reached behind him to pick up something else from his desktop. "And here, take a couple of tickets to tomorrow night's concert. P-Nutz and some other kids from the Academy are opening for two Middle Eastern rappers doing a gig to promote peace. Give me a break," he said in the world weary tone of a cynic who has given up on peace in his lifetime. "Damn, I almost forgot, I've got to talk with the cops about jacking up security." His shoulders slumped as if deflated by the contradictions inherent in trying to make anything to do with the Middle East secure.

Then his face brightened and he straightened in his chair. "But definitely check out the concert. So why don't you go and get P-Nutz to give you that quote?" He looked at his watch. "He's had enough time to come up with something by now. He's in a room straight down the hall on your left. And don't forget, tell Wolfgirl to stop by. Tell her, 'Long time no see.' "

Chapter 20

My Nigga

my nigga Nas-T u rapped hard n black
before u went to dam i-rak
u made up raps and spit em fast
u coulda been da bomb like Cris or OutKast
had a stretch humma and pimped in style
wore gucci leatha and a bling-bling smile
why u do it bro?
what u leave us fo'?
u left yr homeys and yr Dream behind
to make up rhymes behin enemy lines
you got blown up got blown away
and u come back not wantin' to pray
why u do it bro?
what u leave us fo'?
when u come back u aint got no hand
no medals neitha no bitch no band
u jus anotha messed-up soldier
a one-armed nigga wid a chip on yr shoulda

why u do it bro?
what u leave us fo'?

P-Nutz did not give me the rap he had written about Naftali until he finished working with a gangling girl-child with skin the color of milk chocolate. Her tentative smile had that old familiar pre-bling brightness long provided by braces. She wore jeans that were tight enough to reveal the knobs on her knees and a scoop-necked T-shirt that she had somehow managed to make taut over her still-budding breasts. Her long hair fell in a single braid down her back into the pronounced hollow between her bony shoulder blades. She was seated at a table with a few aspiring young male rappers, all hunched over lined paper and scribbling away like medieval monks. There were no PCs, but lots of high-tech audio gear lined the walls. The kids probably practiced mixing and spinning there, as well as rhyming.

"LaShawn, ya gotta write it like ya feel it. That's your sister got the virus, man. Put in some heart." This injunction from her mentor or the thought of her sister's illness apparently distressed LaShawn, and her braces disappeared behind a trembling lower lip. At the sight of this age-old harbinger of the weeps, P-Nutz's jaw tightened and a fleeting frown compressed his own sharp features. He straightened up and said, "Here, girl. Check out how Lil 'Kim and 50 Cent do." He handed LaShawn a headset and an MP3 player. She took them silently and tuned in, a millennial believer literally hearing voices.

P-Nutz did not introduce me to the kids, some of whom had looked up from their labors when I came in.

Instead he reached into his pocket and produced his rap about Naftali, scrawled in longhand on the same lined paper his students were using. "This here's my quote about Nas-T," he said, his free hand reflexively rubbing his monogrammed shoulder. "You wanna hear it wid beats, make it back here tomorrow night." I could tell that this self-serving invitation was the closest P-Nutz planned to come to being polite. "We're openin' for some foreign dudes. But for me tomorrow night's all about my man, Nas-T. And here's my photo." Seeing no irony in following his profession of loyalty to his dead friend with flagrant self-promotion, P-Nutz stopped rubbing his shoulder and handed me the rap and a glossy black and white headshot featuring his aquiline profile against the backdrop of what appeared to be prison bars.

"Thanks, P-Nutz. I'll try to come." I spoke quickly because I was aware of the young people around us growing restless, probably wanting their teacher's attention. "And thanks for the quote too."

It wasn't hard to persuade Sol to go with me to the concert. He said, "I've never really gone out with a blonde. I'm curious. Do you have more fun?" In spite of his attempt at lightness, I knew that my Scarlatti-loving husband was not looking forward to an evening of unintelligible harangues barked over an amplified percussive beat. He surprised me, though, when he said, "I'm curious about the Middle East rappers." Grateful for his company, I didn't protest when he added, "But I'm bringing earplugs, just in case. I don't want to lose what's left of my hearing at the Rap Room. Not even for you, love."

In addition to my blonde wig, I wore jeans and an

old River City Fair T-shirt. This shirt was a relic of by-gone summer festivals in Hoboken and seemed some-how appropriate for my debut hip-hop concert. We arrived early and parked easily. Noting the number of police cars, I wondered if they were there in the event of a fight in the audience or to protect the same audi-ence from terrorists who might choose to strike at a concert focusing on peace in the Middle East. We passed through a metal detector that I hadn't noticed on my previous visit. My first response to the sight of this device was to wonder if P-Nutz's golden grinders set it off. I didn't know whether to be annoyed at the inconvenience or relieved that some effort was being made to weed out potential troublemakers, including terrorists. I eyed the crowd with suspicion. Many of them had probably arrived by PATH from Manhattan and, given the Middle Eastern focus of the concert, there was also a large contingent from Brooklyn. A cluster of young people stood near us, speaking rapidly in Russian. "Jersey City's Russian Jews," Sol said, re-minding me of the presence of one of the region's newer immigrant groups.

We joined the diverse growing crowd of mostly young people in the club's cavernous concert space. After half an hour of milling around, my legs began to ache. I remembered how I'd stood for hours to hear the Stones or the Dead. But years of standing in front of the classroom had taken their toll on my anatomy. There were no seats in the huge room, so it was painfully clear that sitting down anytime soon was not an option. I glanced at Sol, hoping for an empathetic nod or a word or two of commiseration.

But to my amusement, Sol's eyes were riveted on a

group of young women just ahead of us and to the right, very close to the stage. There were black girls, white girls, brown girls, and one or two girls with Asian eyes, all showing more cleavage, butt, and thigh than he'd seen in a lifetime. They were poured into tight, low-riding pants or miniskirts and skimpy tube or tank tops. The hearts, dragons, flags, and roses tattooed on their bare shoulders and arms made an intriguing text, a text that cried out to be interpreted. Recognizing several students, current and former, I reached up and patted my wig to make sure it was in place. I poked Sol, and when he turned to me, I crossed one index finger over the other a few times in what I meant as a playful "Shame on you" gesture. Caught in the act of ogling, he had the good sense to wink.

Mostly to take my mind off my aching legs and feet and the fact that my husband was leering at the bevy of young beauties before him, I too began to observe the girls. It wasn't long before I focused on one, the one standing closest to the stage. A simple black tube dress that was not much longer than a wide sash accentuated her cocoa-colored skin and slender curves. Even in her platform sandals she wasn't much more than five feet tall, but she had an air of almost regal self-possession that added inches to her height. Her long black hair was pulled severely back from her face into a high ponytail that fanned out behind her head like the hair of a Barbie doll styled by an aggressive seven-year-old.

Both Sol and I snapped to attention when an ear-searing drum roll exploded all around us. Sol reached into his pocket for his ear plugs just as P-Nutz, without further introduction, swaggered onto the stage. He was dressed much as he had been the day before. Holding a mike, he pranced and strutted in front of two DJs spinning discordant military beats that might have been the rhythms of "Sgt. Pepper's Lonely Hearts Club Band." Still in motion, P-Nutz shouted out his poignant paean to Naftali. He kept the mike close to his mouth, but even though I was already familiar with the lyrics, I could barely make them out over the pounding music. The rest of the audience had no such trouble and joined in each chorus, singing and swaying to the beat. Before long the whole room was mourning Naftali in what seemed like a heartfelt outcry. P-Nutz ran off the stage to thunderous stomping and cheers. As soon as he had gone, the young women in front of us left too.

It was nearly midnight. I motioned to Sol to remove his earplugs. "I'm going to say hello to Doug and thank him for the tickets. Maybe I can catch P-Nutz and tell him how good he was and see what I can learn. Then we can go, okay?"

Sol said, "I'll meet you near the front door in, say, half an hour. I want to catch part of the Middle Eastern rap session." I nodded and made my way through the stamping, swaying, and chanting mob to the door. Once outside, I was not alone. The clutch of female fans Sol had been ogling hovered nearby, the girls chatting and laughing among themselves. In the glow cast by the parking lot lights, I recognized LaShawn. From where I stood I could see goose bumps on her skinny exposed arms. Wasn't she too young to be out so late? Did she have a ride home?

Before I could move into full Jewish mother mode, I overheard one of the young women call out, "Yo, there's Dream. P-Nutz 'n' them must be comin' right behind her." Her voice was barely audible over the propulsive blasts of sound emanating from inside, where the featured performers had begun exhorting the crowd. If those rappers did succeed in bringing peace to the Middle East, it was not going to be accompanied by quiet. I wasn't sure I had heard correctly, so I followed the girls as they clustered near the door. Standing on the periphery of the group, I felt like the chaperone at a prom. The young woman in the tube dress, whom I'd been observing earlier, emerged and stood there at the top of the three steps surveying the gaggle of stage-door Jennies. Someone, perhaps the same person, called out, "Yo, Dream, where the party be at tonight?"

"Ain't gonna be no party. He mad." From my new and closer vantage point I knew I had heard correctly. The girl on the steps was named Dream. It was her name that P-Nutz had tattooed on his shoulder. They must be an item. Dream hadn't moved from the top step, so when P-Nutz strode through the door he very nearly knocked her over. Sweat still streamed from his face as he stomped down the three steps and pushed his way through the crowd of fans, scattering them. Doug followed, navigating his chair down the ramp and through the crowd. I heard one of the girls say, "Dream right. Ain't gonna be no party tonight. P-Nutz got a beef wid Doug."

The two men came to a halt about ten feet from where I stood, and I watched them. P-Nutz, his teeth literally flashing in the parking lot lights, was flailing his arms and pointing at himself, at Doug, at the club. Then Doug threw his hands in the air, brought them to the wheels of his chair, and propelled himself away, leaving P-Nutz to fume alone. Dream left her post on the steps and walked right past Doug on her way to P-Nutz.

I moved out of the shadows and approached Doug as he neared the ramp. His face brightened when he recognized me. "Hey, Melissa. Glad you made it. Sorry about that little scene over there. Would you believe that wannabe 50 Cent is so jacked up on attitude he expected the TV crew to get here in time to showcase his gig? Like it's my fault they aren't interested in some buster white boy with a blaccent flapping his grilled gums about yet another homey turning up dead in the hood." Doug shrugged. "Hell, I did him a favor letting him open. He just doesn't get it." Doug lowered his head, shook it, took a deep breath, and looked up at the club. We could hear cheers and stomping even over the tympanic tumult of the music.

"Poor P-Nutz. He's lost his old friend and he isn't going to be able to tell about it on TV. Well, at least his girl seems to appreciate him." I was aware even as I spoke that I sounded like a hopeless Pollyanna.

Doug snorted. "Dream? Give me a break. She was 'appreciating' Nas-T until he left." Doug propelled himself up the ramp while I was still muttering my thank-yous and taking in this new information. Had the return of the wounded war hero turned the cozy coupling of P-Nutz and Dream into a tortured triangle? Had P-Nutz killed Naftali in a fit of jealousy?

 **Chapter 21**

To: Bbarrett@circle.com
From: CharB@juno.com
Re: Screened Out
Date: 05/26/04 08:54:09

Believe me, Screened Out, I hear you. My boy Barry has three phone lines, home, office, and cell, and he doesn't pick up or return my calls on any of them. And when I e-mail him, I get a message saying that he's gone for the day. It's easier to connect with a real human being at my health insurer's office than with my Barry. And I really need to reach him. Our new neighbor has a daughter, Florence, and I'm dying to introduce her to Barry. She's maybe twenty-eight, a tenured math teacher at the middle school here, and a very pleasant person, not at all like my friend Hilda's girl, the feral one who growls a lot or my niece's finicky friend, who eats only uncooked food and fasts on the weekends. I know Barry and Florence would hit it off if I could only make contact with him. It's making me crazy.

Charlotte

After reading Charlotte's e-mail, I identified with poor Barry and felt even worse than I had when I logged on, which was pretty bad. I began to wonder what I had done to turn my daughter away from me, especially in her time of need. Had I, perhaps, overdone it when I told Rebecca that watching even a little TV each day was going to make Abbie J illiterate? Or was Rebecca hurt because I had sided with Keith when they argued about invading Iraq? Had my faraway daughter gone far right and chosen to limit her contact with "bleeding heart liberals" like her mother? Or had I simply called her too often? Not often enough? With these doubts plaguing me on the drive to Betty's house, I wasn't very chipper when I arrived.

Betty had suggested that because we now had such different diets, Illuminada and I should each bring our own food. That was why, when we gathered around her table, she set before herself a wedge of triple cream Brie and several generous slices of rare steak. Illuminada had brought a big fruit salad, and I made do with a sliver of cold leftover salmon and some day-old greens that were just a few hours short of compost. The only thing we shared was a bottle of Argentinean Merlot.

After we had raised our glasses to offer what had become our ritual toast to world peace, Illuminada said, "So, *chiquita,* you've infiltrated the hip-hop community. I still can't imagine how you, who know nothing about rap, managed to get anything out of them. It must have been like trying to spy on the Iraquis without speaking Arabic. Tell us."

"I can't," I said. Both Betty and Illuminada widened their eyes in unison. We didn't have a lot of secrets from each other.

"Let me guess," said Illuminada. "As we say in the trade, you're lawyered up now, right? And Dick Halpern has muzzled you."

I nodded. "But the good news is that he's going to try to get access to the Port Authority's surveillance DVD of people who went through the turnstile the night Naftali was killed. He says if I'm not on it, it may help, and, of course, I won't be on it since I was home in bed." Betty, who avoided taking the subway at all costs, looked a little befuddled. "To discourage people from jumping the turnstiles without paying, the Port Authority security uses video cameras for surveillance and as crime deterrents too. We can see how effective that is."

After we all smirked, Betty said, "So what's the bad news?"

"Halpern says I can't talk about my case to the press, to my boss, to my union rep, or even to my friends and family." Betty frowned, obviously distressed at the prospect of not hearing the latest news of my struggle to stay out of jail. Seeing her face, I quickly added, "So this conversation is not happening, right?"

A smile of complicity banished Betty's frown, and she raised her glass again. "Here's to the conversation we're not having." Illuminada and I joined her in another toast.

"So, *chiquita,* don't tell us how you figured out what was going on in hip-hop territory, and for God's sake don't let on what you learned there." Illuminada grinned, and her tone was playful.

For once I didn't mind talking instead of eating because I really wasn't hungry. I didn't even begrudge

Betty her beef and Brie. "Sarah's friend Doug Equivera was a real resource. They worked together on the paper years ago. He used to be a music critic."

Now Betty and Illuminada's eyes rolled in unison beneath their raised brows, a signal that I'd better get to the point. Illuminada, her good humor already exhausted, spelled it out. "Skip the foreplay and cut to the chase, Bel. You have no classes tomorrow, but we both have to go to work."

"Doug is a part owner of the club and runs something called the Rap Room Hip-Hop Academy, where they teach kids how to write and perform rap. It's a kind of after-school program." Despite my listeners' impatience, I continued to provide the background I thought they needed to understand what I had learned. "Derek and Naftali took classes there, and Naftali even taught there. So does a friend of his, P-Nutz, a white rapper who's watched *8 Mile* one time too many. This P-Nutz character looked familiar, so at first I thought he might've been a former student of mine like Naftali, but I changed my mind. This guy's got enough gold on his teeth to save Social Security. I would have remembered him. Now get this," I said, leaning forward and talking faster. "When I met P-Nutz in Doug's office, I noticed that he had the word 'Dream' tattooed on one shoulder. He kept rubbing it whenever I mentioned Naftali. I figured it was a gesture of empathy because after I saw Naftali had lost his arm, I kept doing that too." As if to illustrate, but also because I couldn't help it, I kneaded my own shoulder.

Betty and Illuinada nodded. No doubt they had noticed me doing this before. "So what did he say? It must be hard to lose your best friend when you're that age." Betty had made short work of her steak and was nibbling her Brie. "Did he have any ideas about who might have killed Naftali?"

"Actually, I think P-Nutz might have done it himself." I spoke quietly, as if voicing my speculation softly would somehow give it weight and credibility, but both Betty and Illuminada still registered surprise. Betty's eyebrows threatened to intersect her hairline, and Illuminada put down her fork and took a big swig of her wine.

"So tell us, *chiquita,*" said Illuminada. "Why on earth do you think Naftali's old buddy would have wanted him dead?"

"Well, as I said before, when I first met P-Nutz in Doug's office and noticed the tattoo on his shoulder and the way he was rubbing it, I thought the tattoo referred to a song. Maybe the one by the Everly Brothers, remember?" I began to sing the refrain of the old tune.

"*Díos mío,* Bel, scrap the serenade. So the guy has a tattoo? So what?" I knew Illuminada's patience was really waning then because her words were clipped, and she did not call me *chiquita.*

"It turns out that P-Nutz's girlfriend's name is Dream, so that's why he has that word tattooed on his arm." Having put in place what I thought was a significant piece of the puzzle, I forced myself to take a bite of salmon.

"I don't get it. That's no biggie. He's not the first guy to have his girl's name tattooed on his body," said Betty. "But I have to admit that Dream is an offbeat name. It's pretty, though." Illuminada's cerise nails were tapping rhythmically on the table, so Betty cut short her digression.

"It also turns out that Dream was involved with Naftali before he left for the service." In the speculative silence that followed my delivery of what I thought of as the clincher to my argument, I picked at my dinner. Being charged with murder can suppress the appetite of even the most determined gourmand.

"How did you learn that?" Illuminada's question indicated that she was still curious about how I had penetrated the hip-hop nation.

"Doug told me. I saw him and P-Nutz arguing after P-Nutz's performance, and then I talked to Doug. He was still fuming. I was surprised because he had seemed so tolerant of P-Nutz the other day." I gave Betty and Illuminada a second to take that in and went on. "P-Nutz is pretty volatile and something of a prima donna. He has what I would call entitlement issues." I winced to hear myself using this overworked phrase, which has been applied to everyone from pushy drivers cutting off the less aggressive to Holocaust survivors reclaiming land appropriated by the Nazis.

"Like what entitlement issues?" As was often the case, Illuminada designed her question to force me to be specific and focused.

"Like those of a two-year-old. A fuse blew cutting off power, and Prince P-Nutz had to get Doug to go and flip a switch in the fuse box. He either couldn't or wouldn't do it himself, but he expected this older and disabled man, a kind of daddy figure really, to do it for him." I could hear the disgust in my own voice as I recounted P-Nutz's behavior.

"What kind of disability does this Doug dude have?" asked Betty.

"I didn't mention it before because you were rushing me, but Doug Equivera is in a wheelchair as a result of a car accident. He also has a respiratory disease, probably emphysema." Betty and Illuminada nodded as they absorbed this new information. "P-Nutz barged into Doug's offices without knocking and had no qualms about interrupting our conversation. After his part in the concert, he had a tantrum and ranted at Doug because the TV station didn't cover his gig. He's taken on all the pretensions of a rap star, but he isn't one. He's really infantile," I added in case they weren't already convinced.

"If he has no alibi . . ." I allowed myself a moment to savor the delicious possibility that P-Nutz could not account for his whereabouts on the night of Nafatali's murder. It would be so lovely to have my personal nightmare come to an end and to have a truly toxic killer behind bars. "And you know how I said he kept rubbing his tattooed shoulder? At first I thought it was an empathetic gesture, but what if it's a reflexive guilty reaction, a kind of Lady Macbeth thing? After all, he stole his friend's girl and then killed the friend, who was an injured veteran. He even made up a rap about his victim. How cold is that?" I handed them each a copy of P-Nutz's oeuvre and noted Betty's grimace at the title. Betty was not in favor of rappers or anybody else using the "N"word.

"How do you propose to find out if he has an alibi?" Betty was being pragmatic now, perhaps because she too was beginning to see P-Nutz as a viable suspect.

"He's pretty hot for publicity, and he thinks I'm a reporter. I could just tell him I'm doing a piece on him this time and ask for an interview and then work the question of his alibi into the conversation. It's not very original, but he's so eager to see his name in the paper that it will probably work. What do you think?" I asked the question and waited, hoping to have my strategy validated or, perhaps, improved upon.

"It's a plan," said Betty, chewing on her lower lip. I knew she had more to say, so I waited. "But don't forget about his dream girl." I made a face at her wordplay and wondered what she was getting at. "Dream might have been upset when Naftali left her, and maybe she harbored a grudge. Who knows? She might have been pregnant. Then when Naftali came back, she might have sought to punish him for having left her."

I found Betty's construct of strung together "might haves" unconvincing. But my unspoken resistance to Dream as the killer didn't prevent Illuminada from reinforcing Betty's point of view. "*Chiquita,* Naftali left Dream to enlist, but who knows, maybe he found himself another sweetheart over there and sent Dream a 'Dear Jane' letter. Did she look like the kind of girl who would take that lightly?"

When I shook my head, Betty said, "So talk to her too for your fake article about P-Nutz. It makes sense to interview the celebrity's girl, right?" Betty looked pleased to be directing me once again, and I didn't try to stop her. She and Illuminada were right. It wouldn't hurt to establish an alibi for Dream.

Having agreed to consider Dream a suspect until we could rule her out with certainty, I was taken aback when Illuminada said, "Listen, *chiquita,* you've got to talk to that wacky fortune-teller again, the victim's sister. And isn't there a brother you still haven't met?" I nodded, suddenly too tired to talk. In my eagerness to bring closure to a dreadful experience, I'd tried to take shortcuts, and my friends weren't having it. I was grateful for their vigilance, but that didn't change the fact that a lot of work lay ahead, and I would have to do most of it myself. And I'd have to do it soon because of something that Dick Halpern had told me that I hadn't shared with anyone, even Sol. I'd kept it to myself because to say it aloud would make it seem more real than I could handle. An indictment was imminent.

# *Chapter 22*

Edwina Kittenpenny, Chair
Board Personnel Committee
River Edge Community College
PO Box 4416
Jersey City, NJ 07307

Date 05/27/04

Professor Bel Barrett
205 Park Street
Hoboken NJ 07030

Dear Professor Barrett:

Your presence is required at a special meeting of the
Personnel Committee of the RECC Board of Trustees
on Tuesday, June 8, at 7 P.M. in Room 404 of the
RECC Academic Building.

Yours Truly,

Edwina Kittenpenny

cc: Dr. Ronald Woodman, President
John Stacey, Attorney-at-Law

This missive, delivered via certified mail, arrived when I was in the shower, and Sol signed for it. When I came downstairs, he handed the document to me without a word. There wasn't much to say, given the return address. The Board of Trustees had tired of reading my name in the paper followed by the phrase "awaiting indictment on a homicide charge" or, worse yet, simply "alleged murderer." One particularly rabid reporter referred to me as the "Killer Prof," while another speculated that, maddened by "hormonal fluctuations," I was on a "menopausal murder spree."

Thanks to this relentless barrage of pulp press, I'd begun to get hate calls at home. So, not unlike the kids, I stopped answering the phone. Instead Sol, who was so worried that he too no longer slept or smiled, answered and screened all incoming calls. I dutifully refused to share my side of the story with any of the media vultures swarming around me, including the one from *The Chronicle of Higher Education.*

"How are you supposed to convince the Personnel Committee that you're innocent if you can't talk about your case?" Sol asked, peering over my shoulder at the letter to confirm my interpretation of the cryptic summons. We couldn't believe that my long career as a dedicated and effective educator was about to end in disgrace—and worse.

"Beats me. And whatever happened to 'innocent until proven guilty'? I was pacing back and forth and waving the letter as I spoke. "I've taught at RECC for decades and this coldhearted one-liner is the thanks I get? No one even gives me the benefit of the doubt. They don't care about what really happened to Naftali and they sure don't care about me." I was literally too depressed to cry.

"Your students care. Your colleagues care. Your union cares. You should send a copy of this to your union rep," Sol squawked, his usually deep voice a casualty of anxiety. "Use my printer," he added quickly. He was so eager to do something—anything—to help.

"Here. Give it to me. I'll do it." I scrawled NOW WHAT? on a Post-it note, slapped it on the copy Sol handed me, put it in an envelope, and addressed it to my trusty union rep, Jewel Corona. I would mail it on the way home from synagogue.

I hadn't been attending Sabbath services as often as I had when I was preparing for my adult bat mitzvah, but whenever I did make the effort, I was glad. In Hoboken's lovely old synagogue I reconnected with history, ritual, and community. That Friday evening I felt drawn there, seeking comfort in the familiar songs and ancient prayers that were part of every Sabbath celebration. For once Sol didn't protest when I asked him to join me.

Rabbi Ornstein-Klein's sermons were often so relevant to my life that I felt as if she must have written them especially for me. The talk she gave that evening was no exception. She spoke of our frenetic lives and reminded us of the importance of letting go of at least some of our workaday concerns to allow the spirit of

the Sabbath to bring us respite after the long hard
week. But rather than asking those of us who had resisted the lure of the Sabbath so far to go cold turkey
and forego all labor for twenty-four hours, she advo-
cated a modified and decidedly modern approach. She
suggested instead that we each select just one pressing
concern and agree not to think about it until after sun-
down on Saturday.

I knew I couldn't stop worrying about the murder
charge or curtail my efforts to learn who really did kill
Naftali. And I couldn't control my fretting over Rebecca's silence and her problems either. No way. But I
just might manage to table my anxiety about losing my
job, not because I didn't need and love my work, but
because there was nothing much I could do at the moment. Besides, being fired paled when compared to
going to prison for a murder I didn't commit.

So on the way home when I dropped the envelope
addressed to Jewel Corona into the mailbox, I felt
some relief. Letting go of my anxiety about being ter-
minated gave me a much-needed sense of control over
my life at a time when, in reality, I had none. As I
walked away from the mailbox, I was ready to concentrate once again on finding Naftali's killer.

I made an appointment with Olivia for another palm
reading that Sunday, even though it was in the middle
of Memorial Day Weekend. I had no time for holidays
and apparently Olivia didn't either. Her door was open
when I got there, so I rang the bell and walked in. The
once-orderly living room was crowded with a mattress
and box spring, a bureau, a small table and two chairs,
several suitcases, and stacks of taped cartons. Someone was moving in or out. Had Jude been evicted? Or

had he chosen to leave? Whatever had happened appeared to have affected Olivia. As she pushed her chair away from the kitchen table, I could see that she looked older and thinner than I remembered her. She greeted me with a nod and motioned to me to take a seat.

I hesitated because a pouty-eyed young white woman in denim shorts already occupied the chair across from Olivia's. She wore a shiny neon green blouse with baby-doll sleeves. Spikes of black hair framed her face, making her small features appear even smaller. I felt awkward joining them at the table, but their session must have been finished because Olivia stood. She had no need to shift into her palmist's persona this time. She was already there. Her eyes had that somewhat inscrutable look I remembered, her face was angular, and her expression severe.

She came around the table and took the younger woman's chin in her hand. When she spoke, I recognized the stilted use of the third person that Olivia adopted in her guise as seer. "Ariel, Olivia tells you this is for the best. Your thumbs are so flexible, but my brother, his thumbs don't give. Couples like that . . ." She shrugged, wrinkled her nose with distaste, and made a thumbs-down gesture in case Ariel didn't get her message. "Olivia wishes things were different . . ." She shrugged again. "But I told you that your luck is going to change."

It was all I could do not to give away my excitement at realizing that I had actually come face-to-face with Ariel, the ex-girlfriend of Marcus. It was Ariel, I recalled, who had made the colorful oilcloth coverall Olivia draped over her salon customers, Ariel whom

Betty and Illuminada had insisted I talk with. I was so pleased that I almost missed the shadow that darkened Ariel's eyes at the mention of Marcus. She abruptly lowered her hand from her head, where she had been fingering her hair.

"I sure hope so," she said, not at all intimidated by my presence. "But I better go before he comes back. I don't want him to think I'm, like, you know, following him around." She shoved her chair away from the table abruptly and stood. "Thanks, Olivia. Thanks for everything. And let me know if you hear of any places I should look at. I can't take it at my sister's place much longer." She picked up a wallet and a set of keys from the table, and, with a nod to me, left the kitchen. Olivia had not even had a chance to introduce us.

Before Olivia sat down again, I noticed the marks on her little toes. Even though, I knew that, like Naftali, she probably had her siblings' names writ small there, I resolved to ask her about it if I needed to direct the conversation to Naftali. Soon she took her place across the table from me and said, "Hello, Martha. Olivia welcomes you back. The trace of a smile exaggerated the new lines in her face. "Olivia apologizes for the mess, but her brother Marcus is moving in." When I didn't reply, she continued, "The rent on his place has gone up."

"It takes two salaries to support an apartment nowadays." I was trolling for information. "Doesn't his girl work?"

"His ex-girl, you mean. That was her who just left." Olivia sighed and then frowned. I could tell from the prickly edge to her voice when she spoke next that my question had offended her. "Sure, Ariel works. She works at Good Deal. But remember I told you Marcus broke off with her after . . . after our brother was killed." Olivia lowered her head and massaged her temples as if trying to literally rub this confluence of unwelcome facts into her own head. "Ariel's staying with her sister until she can find a place." Olivia sighed again and shook her head. "If you hear of a place for her, Martha, let Olivia know?" I nodded. Then, squaring her shoulders, she added, "Marcus is coming to stay with Olivia. There's an empty room here now, Naftali's room." I nodded solemnly to show that I remembered. "And Marcus doesn't want Olivia to be living alone." I was right. Jude had left.

"I can understand that," I said. "Naftali's death must be very hard on Marcus too."

"Yes, Marcus is the oldest, and him and Olivia raised Naftali like he was their child. Marcus worked as a roofer during the day and held a security job at night for years to help Olivia buy this house so Naftali would have a comfortable home. Marcus has taken Naftali's death hard. He broke off with Ariel on account of he can't get over it. So now he's all alone too. It's only right that Marcus should come back here to live." Olivia looked directly at me and raised an eyebrow, and I knew that our conversation about her family was over, and she was ready to speculate about mine.

Olivia extended her hands palms up on the table, and I once again extended my own and placed them in hers. I felt as if I had accepted an invitation to dance with a partner who knew all the steps and expected me to follow her lead. "Things have improved for your poor daughter," she said almost at once. I didn't reply.

With a sigh she began to palpate my palms and scrutinize the lines that crossed them in patterns only she could discern, let alone interpret.

Meanwhile, I took a closer look at Olivia. Her own roots were coming in gray and a faint redness and puffiness competed with the black smudges accenting the circles around her eyes. She looked like a woman who was letting herself go, a woman who was crying a lot and not sleeping much. Had Jude's departure been her idea or his? Either way, was that what was causing her to go gray rather than color her hair and to sob herself red-eyed? Or was she unmoved by Jude's absence but mourning still the death of Naftali? Or, most likely, was she reacting to the double whammy of losing a beloved brother and a long cherished partner?

"Martha, Martha, there is hope for your daughter. See the lines crossing her line? They're less pronounced this time." She ran her thumb over the edge of my palm beneath my little finger. I made a pretense of leaning over to see the lines she indicated. Again, even with my reading glasses, the markings were barely visible, tiny tracings, a micronetwork of intricate and natural skin folds.

When Olivia spoke next, her voice was as excited as that of a longtime lottery player realizing that he finally has a winning number. "And look, Martha! You have the Mark of the Teacher!" I squinted at my hand again as she pressed her thumb this time across the fleshy part of my palm just beneath my little finger. "See these two parallel lines?" She didn't wait for me to answer before she gushed on. "Most people have the first one because all of us teach somebody: our kids, our friends, our colleagues. But this second line, right here under your mount of Mercury . . ." She bore down slightly with her thumb. "Right here, see?" I couldn't see, but I could feel the pressure of her thumb on the pad of flesh below my pinky. "This mark means you're one of those people with the gift of empathy, the power to help people define their life choices, to make a difference."

Suddenly Olivia relaxed her grip on my hand. She leaned back and looked at me out of eyes brimming with real tears. When she finally spoke again, her voice was low and tense with sorrow and rage. "Olivia wishes her brother Naftali had had a teacher like you, Martha, instead of that bitch who drove him out of the classroom and into the army and . . ." I stiffened in my chair, leaving my hands outstretched on the table. She reached into her pocket for a Kleenex and blew her nose. "If it weren't for her . . ." Olivia didn't finish the sentence.

Part of me wanted to shout, "I *am* the teacher your brother had! He skipped my class, nearly failed, and blamed me all the way to Iraq." But the other part of me was only too aware of how hard it would be to get M&M's in prison, so I kept quiet. When a moment passed and Olivia still hadn't resumed reading my palm, I spoke. "Your brother's death was tragic. What a loss for you and your surviving brother, for your whole family and for Naftali's girlfriend, for all his friends."

"His 'girlfriend'?" Olivia lowered her chin, raised her eyebrows, and favored me with one of those one-woman-to-another-you-know-what-I-mean looks. "Naftali broke off with that piece of trash before he left. That was the one good thing about his enlisting. He told her it was for her own good, so she wouldn't be tied down while he was over there, but he had, how do you say it?" Olivia paused, frowned, and then, having settled on the phrase she wanted, went on. "Naftali had outgrown her. He had started college. And he wanted to write rap lyrics about war, to change the world through his rhymes. But all Dream could talk about was getting endorsements to sell sneakers."

Olivia brushed back the diagonal stripe of hair that sometimes strayed down her forehead and tried to smile. "Sorry, Martha, but when Olivia saw that you have the Mark of the Teacher, she couldn't help her thoughts. Since Naftali died, Olivia's thoughts are hard to control." She pocketed her Kleenex and took my hand in hers once again. "But your Mark of the Teacher is faint right now, diminished by whatever is affecting your mount of Mercury, your ability to communicate."

Olivia sighed and dropped my hand. "Don't try to have any important conversations today. Soon, though, you will communicate freely again, and your Mark of the Teacher will become more pronounced, you'll see. And then you'll be able to connect with your daughter and with the other person in your family who, I see here, is under a shadow."

I started and blurted out, "What other person in my family? What shadow?" Olivia stared at my palm in silence, shaking her head. Then, looking into my eyes, she spoke slowly in a voice so low that her words sounded like an incantation. "In time, you will be able to lift the shadow. Trust Olivia." It occurred to me then, sitting there with my hand still open on the table, that maybe I should trust Olivia. The instant this heresy entered my mind, I banished it. To credit Olivia with clairvoyance was to open the door to superstition and supernaturalism and God knows what other enemies of reason and science. As a sign that our session was over, Olivia released my hands and stood.

"Thank you, Olivia," I said, getting out my wallet. "I guess I feel a little better. How much do I owe you?"

"Thirty dollars this time," she said. "And it's thirty dollars from now on unless you have a double session. That's fifty dollars. You save ten dollars." I took out a twenty and a ten and handed the bills to her, hoping that my extreme reluctance to part with them was not apparent. She looked drained as she greeted a client who had just entered. Perhaps the effort of fabricating something out of the webbing of lines on my hand had tired Olivia, but I suspect it was really her grief that continued to deplete her. Naftali was gone. Jude was gone. Ariel had just left. Only Marcus remained.

Chapter 23

To: Bbarrett@circle.com
From: RHalpern@msn.com
Re: Indictment
Date: 06/02/04 19:24:04

Copy: IguttierrezPI@juno.com

Bel,

You'll be getting a letter from my office, but I wanted to give you a heads-up myself. I'll be out of town for a few weeks, so I asked Judge Azzarini to agree to postpone your appearance before the grand jury until I get back. My contact at the PA better have those surveillance DVDs by then. He hasn't produced them yet, but I haven't given up. Also the people whose names you submitted to serve as character witnesses are all cooperating, including Ron Woodman. So sit tight and remember, Bel, Nixon was right about one thing. Loose lips do sink ships.

Dick

"Look, Sol," I called when I read Dick Halpern's e-mail message. "My lawyer's going fishing, so I've got a little more time to follow up on the leads I have. What a relief!"

Sol leaned over my shoulder and read the letter I still held. When he straightened up, he frowned and said, "Your high-end lawyer gets to go on a vacation we've funded while we spend the summer eating our hearts out over this whole thing. What's so good about that?"

Ignoring Sol's grousing for the moment, I mused aloud. "I wonder what made Woodman decide to serve as a character witness for me. Maybe Jewel and the union got to him. Or maybe Wendy sicced the Faculty Senate on him." Now that the Sabbath was long over, I had given myself permission to worry about losing my job again. "How can he initiate my termination over this Naftali thing and still serve as a character witness?"

"It's got to be Betty who's behind Woodman's change of heart," said Sol. "He can't afford to lose Betty, and to prevent her from leaving he'll buck the Board."

"You think she really told him she'd quit if he didn't support me in court?" I said. Incredulity charged my voice, so my question came out louder than I'd intended. "Betty didn't say anything to me about that."

"Of course," said Sol with a smile I hadn't seen in weeks. "Woodman can't cross Betty. He can't function there without her. Even Ron's wife acknowledges his dependence on Betty. Alice Woodman told me at the party after our wedding that when Betty's out sick, Ron goes nuts."

"Who would have thought he'd stand behind me

after he as much as told me to resign? I'll have to thank
Betty," I said with a catch in my throat. "I'll call her at
home tonight. Right now I've got to find out if five
people have alibis, and that's going to take some time.
That's why it's good that Dick's vacationing. I've got
to check out Jude Lafayette, P-Nutz, Dream, Ariel, and
Marcus Thompson." I was counting them down on my
fingers as I spoke. "And I don't even have a real name
for P-Nutz or a last name for Ariel."

I reached for the phone, but before I could pick it up,
it rang. "*Chiquita,* I just read Dick's message. Don't
sweat the PA surveillance DVD. I'll get it. I collected
child support for Dorothea Hamilton."

"Who the hell is Dorothea Hamilton?" I asked. I
never ceased to marvel at the vast network of previous
clients who were not only willing but also able to do
favors for Illuminada.

"She's a honcho in Human Resources at the Port
Authority," Illuminada said. "She can make people
there do things. If the DVD exists, Dorothea will get it
for me. I'll ask her to send it right to Dick's office.
He'll have it when he gets back. I just e-mailed him.
Also, before you go too crazy trying to find out if Jude
Lafayette has an alibi, read the police report. I checked
my copy last night, and he does."

"You will go to heaven," I said. "But dammit, I spent
a whole afternoon interviewing him for nothing." Before Illuminada could lecture me on the value of background information, I said, "I know. I know. It wasn't
a total loss. But still, he was a prime suspect. Damn."
Then, having vented my frustration and disappoint-
ment, I moved on. "Okay, so I need another bit of information if you have someone free to work on it." I

was beginning to feel guilty about exploiting Illuminada's resources. "Do you mind?"

"Yes, I'd rather see you spend years in prison than ask one of my staff to spend a few minutes on-line searching for something," snapped Illuminada. "What do you need?"

"Marcus Thompson wears a uniform with 'Kinney' embroidered on it, so I assume he parks cars at one of their garages. I need to know which one," I said.

"Gottcha. I'll put someone on it now and get back to you. Ciao, *chiquita*." Illuminada hung up before I could thank her.

I reached for the police report Illuminada had given me and that I had filed on the shelf over my PC. I made myself a cup of tea and read the report. I learned a few things I hadn't known before. It was good to have Jude's whereabouts on the night of the murder confirmed, especially if I didn't have to expend a lot of time and energy confirming them myself. Jude had an ex-wife and granddaughter living in Paterson. He spent the evening in question at their home, celebrating the little girl's birthday. After the party he'd gone out for a few beers with his son-in-law and two of the younger man's friends. They confirmed that Jude had indeed been with them at the time Naftali was killed.

Naftali's older brother, Marcus, was not questioned since he was not a suspect, but the author of the report mentioned that Marcus had not known of his brother's death until Olivia had called him at home, where he and his girlfriend had been asleep until the phone rang. I wondered if the police, so focused on implicating me, had even bothered to interview Ariel.

I also learned that the night he died Naftali was on

the way home from a meeting with a potential producer named Montgomery Duvalle at a club in
Newark. According to Duvalle, Naftali left the club at
midnight after several drinks. Duvalle had agreed to
listen to a demo CD called tentatively *i-raq traks* as
soon as Naftali finished it. The last thing I learned was
that Detectives Fergeson and Rago had not viewed any
of Naftali's friends as suspects. I wasn't going to make
that mistake. I was convinced that P-Nutz had killed
Naftali.

According to the Hip-Hop Academy schedule Doug
had given me, P-Nutz would be teaching there the following afternoon, and that seemed as safe a place to re-
connect with him as any. So I called the Rap Room and
left P-Nutz a message saying that I wanted to do a feature on him and asking to meet with him after his class
the next day. In the hope of checking out Dream as
well, I added, "Oh, and I'd like to get a quote from
your girlfriend too. If she could be there, that would
save me tracking her down. Please call me if that
doesn't work for you." I left my home and cell numbers and added that I was bringing a photographer. I
figured P-Nutz wouldn't be able to resist having his
picture in the paper. This time Sol agreed to go with
me and pose as the photographer. "I'd rather go with
you than stay home and worry about you meeting
alone with some psycho" was how he put it.

But we had plenty of work to do before meeting
with P-Nutz the next day. We drove to Good Deal,
parked, and headed for the shopping carts. As I
reached for one, I heard a loud, "Yo, Professor B. Long
time no see." Before I could blink, I was enveloped in
a hug by a tall young African-American man in wide-

legged carpenter jeans, a dark green T-shirt reading PHUN HOUSE," and low-top work boots with the laces untied. He wore a Pittsburgh Steelers baseball cap sideways. When he let go of me so I could get a look at him, I thought I recognized him as a former student, and I was beginning to dredge my memory in the desperate hope of bringing up his name. But when he grinned a grin that was as glitzy as P-Nutz's, his face seemed that of a stranger.

"Whassamatter, you don't recognize me? It's Nathan, Nathan Futura, your all-time favorite student." I stared at him blankly. Suddenly he reached up and stuck two fingers into his mouth and wiggled his head. When he pulled his hand away from his face, he said, "Here, now check me out," and grinned again. This time his grin exposed only the welcome white of naked teeth. His bling was bogus, the gold crowns removable, and I knew exactly who he was.

"Of course, Nathan, it *is* you." I was only too happy to return his hug. Nathan really had been one of my favorite students, and he'd been a great help when I was investigating the murder of a young corporate spy several years ago. Maybe that was why Nathan hadn't avoided me in spite of the bad press I'd been getting lately. He knew I hadn't murdered anybody. It felt so good to be warmly greeted by a former student once again that for a moment I stood there just savoring the pleasure of our reunion. Recovering, I introduced Sol.

Laughing, Nathan declined to shake hands. "No offense, man, but I got a golden grip right now." He held out his hand and in his palm nested several gold, tooth-shaped nuggets. In a second, he had replaced them and his smile was, again, aglow. "Now don't you worry,

Professor B. I ain't no thug. But I gotta dress gangsta for work."

"Where are you working now, Nathan?" I asked, reminding myself that it was gratifying that Nathan, whom I had coached for months in Standard English grammar, had graduated and was out in the world, even if he did dress and speak like a refugee from the Rap Room.

"I'm working in marketing at Phun House." When I stared at him blankly, Nathan explained. "You know, the hot hip-hop fashion designer. We sold our line to Good Deal, and we got a big promotional event going down here today." Nathan's chest puffed out just a little as he touted the accomplishments of his firm. "So I gotta wear product. But when I negotiate with the Good Deal honchos, I'm in a suit, talkin' grammar like you taught me, and my bling is home in a box on my bureau." Nathan pointed at his golden incisors and laughed. He looked so pleased with himself that I felt tears well in my own eyes. "I gotta get back to work. You take care now, Professor. And if there's anything I can do . . ." Nathan nodded a goodbye to Sol and hugged me again. His offer of help was the only indication that Nathan was aware of my fall from grace. And unbeknownst to him or me at the time, Nathan had already done quite a bit to help.

Meeting up with Nathan had elevated my mood, so I felt purposeful as Sol and I made our way around the store, picking up a few staples we knew Ma and Sofia could always use. Before checking out, I pushed our cart into the snack area labeled EMPLOYEES ONLY, sat down at a table with Sol, and waited for someone to notice and evict us. Within a few moments, a young man whose nametag read CURTIS approached. In the unctuous voice of an employee who has sat through one too many customer service training sessions, he said, "Sir, Ma'am, this area is reserved for employees. Would you like me to escort you to the customer food service area?"

"Thanks, but we're waiting for Ariel," I said without budging. "She works here and she told us to meet her here during her break." I looked at my watch. "We're right on time."

Curtis took a moment to reflect on his options and then called to a woman sitting at the table he had vacated when he approached me. "Chris, do you know somebody who works here named Ariel?"

Chris, a woman in her thirties whom I recognized from my many sample-tasting forays, smiled at me. She did not have to think for long before she answered. "Yeah. Ariel Quintana. She's off today and in tomorrow. You know her, Curtis. She works the register. She's a chunky girl with jaggedy black hair." Chris raked the sides of her face with her fingers to illustrate, I supposed, how Ariel's hair spiked toward her face.

Curtis had not nodded until Chris described Ariel's distinctive coif. But before he could react, I said, "Oh no! She must've meant tomorrow. We must be a day early. I'm so sorry. We need to start writing things down, dear." I addressed this last remark to Sol. Without waiting for him to respond or for Curtis to offer further assistance, I got up. Sol stood too and propelled our shopping cart out of the forbidden space. Once out of sight of Curtis and Chris, I shot an exultant look at Sol. We now knew Ariel's last name and when and where we would find her at work.

I relished the feeling of accomplishment that followed the morning's fruitful fact-finding foray to Good Deal. Even a little success was encouraging, and I needed encouragement to keep going. Feeling optimistic for the first time since I'd become a murder suspect, I dropped Sol off at home while I delivered the groceries to Ma and Sofia. "Can you stay for lunch?" Sofia asked before I'd even bent over to unbuckle my sandal. I noticed a pair of men's black high-tops next to Ma's Esprit loafers and Sofia's black patent spike-heeled pumps in the vestibule. "Your mother is so worried about you."

"No thanks, Sofia, not today, I'm sorry. I'll take a rain check, though," I said. "I just wanted to leave these." Hoping to avoid having to remove my shoes, I remained in the vestibule and handed Sofia the groceries. "Is Paul here?" I asked, pointing to the sneakers.

"Yes, thank God. He's almost done. He's just finishing my bedroom. Do you want to meet him?" said Ma over her shoulder. She was at the sink.

"I really can't stay, Ma. Next time, though, I promise." I felt guilty, but I was sure Ma understood.

"Sybil, before you run off, tell us, is there anything new?" Ma's slight frame was still hunched over the sink, so I couldn't see her face, but I could tell from her tremulous voice that her eyes were brimming. She hadn't sounded this upset since she called to tell me my father had died. It would kill her if I went to prison. Maybe this was what Olivia had been referring to when she'd warned me that someone in my family beside Rebecca was "under a shadow." In spite of the early summer warmth, I felt a chill. I reminded myself that I didn't set any store by Olivia's fairy-tale fortunes.

"Nothing I can talk about," I said. "But yes, things are looking up. Don't worry. Everything's going to be fine." Empty-handed now, Sofia crossed herself silently.

"From your mouth to God's ears," said Ma, making her own pitch to the deity. I forced a smile, blew them both a kiss, and let myself out, nearly tripping over the high-tops on the floor.

As I walked down the steps, the smile froze on my lips. By the time I got to the car, double-parked in front of the house, I could hear my heart beat. I called Sol. "Meet me in front of the house right away," I barked into the cell phone. In a few minutes when I picked him up, my hands were shaking so hard I couldn't continue to drive.

"What the hell is the matter, love?" Sol asked, getting in on the driver's side as I ran around the car. "Is is it Sadie? Is she okay? Did something happen to Sofia?"

"No, not yet," I said, "But I think I just left those two helpless old ladies alone with a psycho killer. Drive, please."

"What the hell are you talking about?" asked Sol, paling but taking the wheel.

"I'll tell you later." Grabbing my cell phone, I then called the Odd Couple. Ma answered. "Ma, don't ask me any questions, just do what I tell you. Is Paul still upstairs?" When she said he was, I went on. "Good. Go look at his sneakers in the vestibule and see what label they are. And see if you and Sofia can find out what his last name is before he leaves."

"I know his last name. It's Nutz with a 'z.' " I gasped. Then I prayed that P-Nutz had a brother, a twin. "Hold on. I'll go look at the sneakers." I held on. Ma was gone for about a minute. When she came back slightly breathless, she said, "His sneakers are Nike Dunk High Premiums. What difference does it make?" Her curiosity would have to wait. But I recognized the name and the sneakers Mark had worn decades ago. P-Nutz had been wearing them when we met.

"I'll explain later. I'm staying on the phone until you tell me he's gone," I said. Sol had gotten the idea and had already driven to Ma's block and pulled up at the hydrant two doors away from her house. Parking in front of hydrants was, of course, illegal, but it was also commonly done in a city where parking spaces were almost as hard to find as affordable apartments.

"Nice talking to you," said Ma in a louder voice. "I'll call you later." She didn't hang up though, and I knew Paul had come downstairs. I could just barely hear the buzz of the goodbye chit chat that meant Ma and Sofia were paying him and thanking him. We waited. I figured it would take him a few minutes to lace up those high tops, so Sol and I remained in the car, braced to run into the house if Ma hollered. But she didn't. What she finally said was, "He just left." Sure enough Paul walked out, calling something over his shoulder and grinning.

As he strode up the street toward our car, his affable grin disappeared. From behind an old newspaper I'd grabbed from the backseat, I studied his beaklike nose, his disproportionately small chin, and his bespectacled black eyes. I noted his height and build, the way he moved. Then he passed the car, one of his arms only about a foot away from my face. From the sleeve of his T-shirt to the tips of his fingers, the arm was innocent of tattoos. But on the upswing of his arm, the sleeve hiked up a little, revealing a semicircular sliver of blue that could have been the curve of a dragon's belly or the arc of a rose petal. I was willing to bet that on the shoulder beneath that sleeve the tattoo DREAM was etched in purple.

Unless he had a clone, house cleaner Paul Nutz was also hip-hop hero P-Nutz. I almost hadn't recognized him wearing glasses and without his signature gold teeth. But thanks to our run-in with Nathan, I knew that P-Nutz could remove his bicuspid bling at will along with his blue-tinted contact lenses. Olivia was right again. A member of my family was under a shadow. Ma's cleaner was a killer.

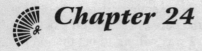

Chapter 24

To: Bbarrett@circle.com
From: hlundergren@hotmail.com
Re: Screened Out
Date: 06/03/04

Hi, Screened Out,

You're lucky your daughter screens her calls. Mine doesn't. Whitney takes calls from me when she's driving the jeep on the LA Freeway with the twins in their car seats in the back. While she's talking to me, Whitney negotiates traffic and changes lanes at high speed, checks her global-positioning map, picks up toys the boys have dropped or thrown, changes the CD, and gets snacks and more toys out of her backpack for them. I bought her a headset so she could have two hands on the wheel occasionally, but she said the twins broke it and she hasn't had time to get a new one. I beg her to call me later, but she says the only chance she has to talk is when she's driving. Whenever we talk now, I'm always listening for the sound of a crash. I'm considering medication. Trust me, it's better to be screened out than freaked out.

Louise

I was freaked out full-time anyway. The discovery that a viable murder suspect was cleaning Ma and Sofia's home on a regular basis was chilling. I wanted to call the cleaning service right away and have Paul (aka P-Nutz) replaced. Sol suggested a different approach. "Confront him with this tomorrow when you interview him. By talking about his alter ego as Mr. Clean, we just might catch him really off guard," said Sol.

"But what about Ma and Sofia?" I asked, unable to exorcise Olivia's prophecy from my head. "We can't let P-Nutz go there again. It's too risky."

"Bel, he's not due at their house again until next week, so let's see what we learn tomorrow," said Sol, his deep voice resonating reason. "He doesn't have a key to their place, right?"

"Right," I said. "But still they could be at risk."

"They're not," Sol insisted. "If he doesn't have a convincing alibi for the night of Naftali's death, then we can make sure that he doesn't clean for your mother and Sofia anymore."

"Okay," I agreed. "We'll try it your way. But now, let's talk strategy. I need to plan the questions I'm going to ask him. And also Dream." I paused. "Sol, will you take P-Nutz out of the room for an outdoor photo shoot, so I can talk with Dream alone for a few minutes?"

"Sure. Rappers like headshots against a gritty urban

background." Sol's face lit up. "I'll pose him against one of those graffitied walls of the club. That would make a great website photo, don't you think?"

"Sol, you're going undercover to trap a murderer, not to start a second career as a hip-hop photographer," I said. But his enthusiasm restored some of my own and distracted me from my fears. That night I actually slept a little, but I dreamed of Olivia reading the palm of Derek Wilson (aka IM Kra-Z). Staring at him across her kitchen table, she took one of his hands in hers, scrutinized it, and then dropped it as if it had seared her flesh. She leapt up from the table and backed away, her eyes wild, her mouth twisted. Just as she was about to speak, I heard Sol's voice saying, "Easy, love. It's okay." I woke up, sweating and scared.

When morning finally came, I was anxious and frustrated that we had to wait until that afternoon to see P-Nutz. Rather than waste the morning, I decided to go back to Good Deal to try to catch up with Ariel and arrange a meeting with her. After reassuring Sol that "I'm just going to talk to her about setting up an appointment," I went to the store alone. "Besides, even if she is some kind of a nut, I'm bigger than she is, and we'll be in a very public place," I told him on the way out the door. As I drove, I distracted myself from my anxiety by figuring out how to get Ariel to agree to meet with me. By the time I arrived, I had a plan.

Once again, I flashed my Good Deal membership card and entered the huge store. It was still early, so only a few shoppers were pushing carts up and down the wide aisles. I spotted Ariel right away, at the second register from the end, but before I approached her I did a little shopping, picking up a pair of sweatpants, a camisole, and several bottles of wine almost randomly. Then I helped myself to enough M&M's to last Wendy and me through retirement. When my cart was plausibly full, I pushed it to Ariel's register. There was no one ahead of me and no one behind me, an extremely rare break at Good Deal, where the lines at the register are legendary.

"Good morning. Did you find everything you were looking for today?" Casting only the most cursory glance at the photo on my ID card, Ariel followed her perky scripted greeting by a grin and personalized it with the jokey question, "Got enough M&M's?" She made a pretense of struggling to lift the hefty bags to pass them over the scanner.

"These should get me through the week," I quipped in response. Then feigning surprise, I exclaimed, "Oh, you're Ariel! How nice to see you." Ariel's eyes narrowed. "Remember me?" Her suspicious squint became an anxious tic. "I met you at Olivia Durango's." At the mention of Olivia's name, Ariel's face relaxed. Her eyes widened out of the squint, and the tic subsided as quickly as it had come. "I came in for my reading right after yours last Sunday. My name's Martha Salem. Remember?" Without giving her a chance to respond or to glance at my ID card, I rushed on. "It's incredible running into you like this. I was about to call Olivia and ask for your number."

Ariel glanced around, perhaps to be sure that no supervisor was observing her chatting away precious minutes with a customer. Again, I barreled on, leaving her no opening. "Olivia mentioned you were looking for a place. I've got a room to rent in my house in Hoboken, and I'm looking for a good solid tenant.

Olivia speaks very highly of you, so I wondered . . ." Seeing her eyes widen even further at the mention of a room to rent in Hoboken, I finally stopped talking and let her speak.

She cast another furtive glance around and began to ring up my purchases while she replied. "Yeah. I'm lookin' for a place. I can't stay on my sister's couch much longer." Ariel lowered her eyes. Clearly she was distressed to find herself among the homeless. When she looked up, the glance she shot me was once again wary. "How much you askin'? When could I see the room?"

Thinking "Come into my parlor," I struggled to conceal the jubilation I felt. Aloud I said, "We can talk rent after you check out the room and the house. How about tonight? Would that work for you? What time do you get through here?"

"Not until nine. Today's my long day," she said. "But I gotta baby-sit my sister's kids tonight." She thought a moment and then said, "I'm off tomorrow, though, so I could come during the day. Anytime, really." Without even looking at the numbers, I ran my debit card through the machine.

Suspecting that Ariel might check me out with Olivia, and remembering that Olivia thought I had a day job, I said, "Well, I have to work tomorrow, so how about you come by some time after five?" When Ariel nodded, I added quickly, "Here." As the customer who had suddenly appeared behind me unloaded the contents of her cart onto the counter, I grabbed the pen that dangled from the chain near the register and scribbled my address and phone number on one of the Post-it notes I always carry. I reclaimed the ID card and receipt she handed me, grateful that Ariel had been too distracted to notice that the name I signed was not that of the fictitious Martha Salem.

"Tomorrow at five-thirty," I repeated. "See you then." Once again I left Good Deal elated—and not by the cartful of M&M's that I had acquired. Although, I had to admit, they did have a certain appeal.

Chapter 25

To: Bbarrett@circle.com
From: Geekmom@comcast.net
Re: Screened out and mad
Date: 05/03/04

Dear Bel,

I know how you feel. All through college my son instant-messaged me all the time. If he needed help with a paper, he'd IM me, and I'd get back to him right away with relevant websites and links. If he had a problem with a roommate or a girl, he'd IM me, and I'd give him instant advice. I telecommute, so I'm on-line a lot and we were in close touch. Now he's moved to New York City, has an apartment in the East Village, a new roommate, a new girl, and a job as assistant stage manager of an off-Broadway production. But he's never home, never on-line, and doesn't answer or return my phone calls or e-mails. I sent him a new cell phone so I could text him and just ask RUOK, but I guess he doesn't check his messages. I was thinking of getting us both *Skype.com* software, so we could actually talk to each other on our PCs for free. It's even better than phoning. But now I'm not so sure. Last week I wrote him a snail mail letter suggesting that I get us some video software so we could see one another when we chat on the phone, but he hasn't answered. I'm ready to call the police. Any advice?

Sheryl

When I checked my e-mail there was still no word from Rebecca, only Sheryl's geeky lament. I wanted to e-mail her to let her son grow up and live his own life, but my reply would have to wait. I had pressing problems of my own. Sol was not altogether thrilled that I had invited Ariel to our home, so I had to reassure him. "Listen, love, it's not as if she's really a suspect. Think of her as an uncrossed 't,' a dotless 'i,' someone I've got to talk to just to make sure I've covered all my bases and left no stone unturned." Not surprisingly Sol didn't respond to this string of clichés, so I tried again. "It'll be fine. She'll come here, and I'll show her Rebecca's old room, and try to get her to talk about Naftali and Marcus and the whole family. And who knows? Maybe Ariel has an idea why Olivia and Jude broke up."

"Who cares why they split up?" Sol asked. "Neither of them is a suspect."

"I know," I said. "But I'm curious. I wouldn't mind knowing why Ariel and Marcus split up either." Sol had never fully understood my inner yenta, so I didn't try to explain why these romances interested me. There wasn't time just then anyway. I pulled the car into the

Rap Room parking lot and slid into a spot near the
door. Once I had removed the key from the ignition, I
patted down my blonde wig and smoothed my color-
splashed tropical-print silk shirt over my cropped
black slacks. "Are you ready?" I asked.

"I've got the camera," Sol said, patting his pocket.
"That's all I need. You have your tape recorder?" I nodded. He smiled and said, "Okay, Sherlock. We're good
to go." We walked up to the door, rang the bell, and
waited.

After what seemed a long time, the door opened and
LaShawn stood there, a smile on her thin lips. "You
come to see P-NutznDream?" The way she spoke their
names as one word made them sound like a candy bar
or a new nut-based drug. I nodded. "You from the
newspaper?" I guess she wanted to be sure. I nodded
again and flashed the press card Sarah had given me
when we interviewed Jude. I had brought it just in
case. I could tell, without looking at him, that Sol was
impressed. LaShawn stared at the card solemnly and
then, satisfied, held open the door.

"I'm Melissa Dworkin and this is Mel Brooks," I
said, pointing to Sol. We hadn't discussed an alias for
Sol, and when I reached into the grab bag that was my
brain to find one, that's the one I latched on to. Again,
I could tell that Sol was impressed, this time by my
quick thinking. He extended his hand to LaShawn as
he passed through the door. After a moment of hesita-
tion, the young woman reached out and took it in hers
very carefully, as if Sol's pudgy paw was a rare and
fragile artifact. I wondered if she had ever shaken
hands with anyone before.

We followed our slender guide along the low-lighted

corridor past the closed door to Doug's office and stopped outside the same classroom I'd been in before. "P-Nutz in dere. He waitin' on you."

After thanking LaShawn for admitting us and shepherding us to our destination, we entered the classroom. P-Nutz had dressed for the occasion. He was in full hip-hop regalia, from his flyaway dreads to his lavender track suit and those now unlaced signature high-tops. I pictured the tips of his gold teeth gleaming behind his unsmiling lips. If he had appeared at Ma and Sofia's door in this getup, they would have thought he was trick-or-treating. He was seated in a chair alongside one of the tables, his legs sprawled straight out in front of him, the backs of his heels on the floor, his toes angled up, his hands in his pockets, and a headset in place. His upper body bobbed back and forth to a beat that only he could hear. When I came in, he looked up, but did not stand. Sol entered right behind me in a crouch, snapping photos of P-Nutz, rapper at rest.

Pulling off his headset and letting it dangle around his neck, P-Nutz acknowledged our presence with a nod. "Dream ain't here yet." P-Nutz had no qualms about stating the obvious. "She comin' from work. You can start wid me." Keeping his elbows at his waist, P-Nutz spread his lower arms and hands in front of himself as if inviting our scrutiny. There was something arrogant about the gesture. Sol, who was practically doing a duck walk to photograph the seated man, caught that pose, and I was glad. It was the essential P-Nutz. "Mel Brooks, P-Nutz. P-Nutz, Mel." The two men nodded at each other.

Having accomplished this minimalist introduction, I sat down across the table from where P-Nutz lolled and took out my tape recorder. Pointing to it, I said, "You don't mind if I tape our conversation, do you?" Not deigning to answer aloud, P-Nutz shook his head. I pushed the machine to the middle of the table and began. "What made you decide to be a rapper?"

"Beat pimpin' and dealin,'" P-Nutz answered, barely concealing his contempt for such a predictable opening question. "I ain't much good at shootin' hoops or boxin'. Them's the other career options in the 'hood." I wondered if, like his friend Naftali, P-Nutz was bidialectical. Ma and Sofia had never mentioned him speaking nonstandard English.

"Who inspired you?" I asked.

"Joe Budden 'n' Eminem," said P-Nutz. In spite of the fact that I nodded in recognition of both names, P-Nutz explained. "Joe a local dude got signed by Def Jam. He come up right here in Jersey City just ahead of me 'n' Nas-T. We opened for him last time he here." As he spoke, I remembered Doug saying that P-Nutz did not make up rap songs spontaneously, and it occurred to me that in spite of his carefully cultivated cool, P-Nutz had anticipated my questions and prepared answers to them. He was following a script.

"Did you attend classes at the Rap Room Hip-Hop Academy with Nas-T?" I asked, figuring I'd give a few more easy questions before I tried to find out if he had an alibi for the night Naftali was murdered or about his day job cleaning houses.

At this P-Nutz snorted. When he spoke, his tone wavered between insolence and incredulity. "No way, man. I hadda work after school. Like Eminem, not like Nas-T. Nas-T had Olivia and Marcus slavin' for him." P-Nutz paused, shaking his head, perhaps at the memory of Naftali's good fortune. "But Eminem, he work in a factory. Me, I got a job cleanin' houses. I worked wid my moms until she die." I was very surprised that P-Nutz had brought up his day job, but not so surprised that I didn't notice the effort he made to maintain his stony, sullen demeanor while talking about the death of his mother. At that moment, "Bad boys don't cry" was written all over his contorted face. "I been doin' it on my own ever since." He regained control of his facial muscles and said, "Last year I sign wid a cleanin' service." P-Nutz's aggrandized image of himself signing with a cleaning service as if it were a record company would have amused me if I weren't so focused on catching and interpreting his every word, facial expression, and gesture. "They insure me and get me gigs. I gotta pay rent and buy bling." He fondled the super-sized gold peanut dangling from his neck and then opened his mouth and flashed his gold teeth in what was intended to be a winning grin. "Bling take real paper."

Undazzled by his dental display, I posed a question I thought might bug him into an unscripted revelation. "I understand that another local rapper, IM Kra-Z, has signed with a producer. Do you have any immediate prospects for attracting a producer?" Sol captured on film P-Nutz's sneer at the mention of IM Kra-Z.

"IM Kra-Z, he a faggot rhymin' 'bout stayin' 'n' school 'n' Jesus 'n' whatnot. Nas-T, he a fool joinin' up ta rhyme 'bout the war in i-rak." P-Nutz shook his head at the folly of his friends and rivals. "Me, I rhyme about the war we got right here in Jersey City. Every day a war in the 'hood. Sure, I got a producer wanna sign me, a dude in Newark, Montgomery Duvalle."

When he said this name, P-Nutz finally straightened in his chair, and again I glimpsed the glitter of gold when his lips parted in a thin smile.

"So you're inheriting Nas-T's producer and his girl-friend," I said. I still hoped to crack his smug and sar-donic façade, to goad him into straying from his lines.

This time it worked. He began rubbing his shoulder, and when he replied, he directed his reply to Sol, even though it was I who had posed the question. I felt as if I were eavesdropping on some sort of primal male bonding ritual. "Man, that wack. Dream mine since backintheday in high school. But then I did some white bitch who been followin' me aroun' 'n' Dream fine out. That white ho she nothin' to me." I saw Sol's jaw tighten here as P-Nutz's voice lowered to a snarl. "But Nas-T, he see what goin' down 'n' he all over Dream. He want her 'cause she mine, tha's all. He jus' playin' wid her. She play him before he jet. Dream 'n' me, we cool now." Sol nodded to indicate his understanding of P-Nutz's man-to-man talk.

Before P-Nutz could return to his script, I said, "Did you go with Nas-T the night he met with Montgomery Duvalle?"

P-Nutz treated me to one of his scowls. "I tol' you, I work for a livin'. I got a regular gig cleanin' offices on Thursday nights. I met wid Duvalle myself jus' dis week. He call after he hear me at the club rappin' 'bout Nas-T."

Relieved that I had finally gotten P-Nutz to state an alibi that I could confirm with the cleaning agency, I was struggling to think of more questions to ask him. Suddenly I saw Sol turn toward the door. Dream had arrived. To my amazement, she looked nothing like the sultry hip-hop queen we had seen at the concert. In fact, her fashion statement was decidedly unhip as well as unhip-hop. She wore loose-fitting white slacks, a prim navy blue tunic, and sturdy sandals. Her long hair was pulled back from her face into a tight chignon atop her head. Even the small golden peanuts dangling from her ears looked more like whimsical charms than blatant bling. Before I could make any introductions, Sol snapped her picture. Dream reflexively put her hand to her head to smooth her hair and smiled belatedly for the camera. I said, "Dream, I'm Melissa Dworkin from the *Jersey City Herald,* and this is our photographer, Mel Brooks. Thank you for agreeing to talk with me about P-Nutz."

"No problem," she said. "Sorry I late, baby. I hadda take the bus from the Heights." I ignored the fact that Dream directed her apology to P-Nutz rather than to Sol and me. She bent down and he nuzzled her neck in response.

"Oh, is that where you work?" I asked, flashing Sol a smile that was meant to signal him to get P-Nutz out of the room.

"I'm a home health aide. I work all over. The patient I got now, he live in the Heights," she said. There was no mistaking the weariness in her voice.

"Hey, man. Whaddya say I take some headshots outside the club with the grafitti in the background?" Sol jerked his head in the direction of the door as he spoke. "I'll take a few extras and send you the prints. Make a great CD cover."

P-Nutz grunted his assent, and the two men left the room. Dream sank into the chair across from mine that P-Nutz had vacated. "Do you mind if I tape your responses?" I asked. When she shook her head, I said, "So tell me, Dream, what's your real name?"

"Tha's easy. I hope alla questions gonna be that easy. Darlene Adams is my gov'ment, but P-Nutz been callin' me Dream since backintheday. He say I his dream girl." She smiled and tilted her head to one side. It was clear that she felt she deserved the compliment implicit in the name P-Nutz had given her and that she far preferred it to her government or given name. I wondered how her folks felt about that. Like P-Nutz, Dream had plenty of what my students called "attitude" and psychologists might call self-esteem.

"I understand. And how long have you known P-Nutz?" The question seemed logical here.

"P-Nutz my first boyfriend. He hung wid my brother, Tal. Tha's how I met him. Tal brought him 'round. When Tal go to jail, P-Nutz look out for me on the street, you know?" Dream looked at me with raised eyebrows to make sure I registered understanding. I nodded. She had spoken of her brother's incarceration so casually that I was shocked until I reminded myself that doing time was practically a male rite of passage in the 'hood.

"And you two have been together ever since?" I asked. She nodded, but then, apparently thinking better of it, she laughed and said, "Well, almos'. P-Nutz friend, Nas-T, the rapper who die?" I nodded yet again to acknowledge that I knew who she was talking about. "Nas-T tell me P-Nutz did a white bitch who been followin' after him like she in heat." She hesitated again and added, "I put that two-timing playa out on his sorry white ass. Nas-T try to get wid me, but he crazy alla time talkin' about goin' to i-rak to rhyme about the war. But I got P-Nutz payin' attention again. An' tha' fool, Nas-T, I dump him and the nex' thing you know, he up 'n' jet." Dream raised her hand in an imitation wave.

"I wonder why Nas-T would rat on P-Nutz," I said. And I really did.

"It ain't right to dis someone dead," said Dream primly. But she barely hesitated before going on. "But Nas-T, he tell P-Nutz he high when he tell me 'bout the bitch, but he lie. He jus' say that so P-Nutz don't whip his ass. P-Nutz believe him, but jus' between you 'n' me, Nas-T was always puttin' moves on me." A slight rise in Dream's chest was the only sign that she considered being desired her due. "Tha' playa used to gettin' whatever he want. And he always want what P-Nutz had. P-Nutz had me." Dream smiled, but when she spoke next, there was no mirth in her voice, only scorn. "Nas-T, he want everythin' P-Nutz got but P-Nutz's damn day job." I heard echoes of Jude's words in Dream's description of the work-phobic Naftali.

"But P-Nutz 'n' me, we come to a understandin'." Dream gave me a knowing, age-old look. It was a timeless look that spoke of standing by your man, of giving him another chance, and of castrating him if he betrayed you again. "He gonna be a bigtime rapper, you see. He tell it like it really is 'roun' here, jus' like Joe Budden."

"Would you like that to be your quote?" I asked. "I'd like to have a quote from you about P-Nutz in the article, and that's a nice one."

"Sure," said Dream, reaching up to fondle one of her golden peanut-shaped earrings. " 'Cause I really believe P-Nutz gonna make it to the Grammys."

Chapter 26

To:Bbarrett@circle.com
From: Jorge@juno.com
Re: Results
Date: 06/04/04 09:18:34

Bel,

When my son, Jorge Jr., went to grad school across the country, he didn't return calls from me and my wife, and my wife went off the deep end. Like you know, she thought the kid was sick or dead, she wanted to call the dean. First I told her to cut the kid a little slack and let him get used to his housemates and his classes. But after a while his mother was starting to get, you know, a little crazy, and I got mad. I left Jorge Jr. a message that if he didn't have time to return our calls or e-mail his *mamacita*, I wasn't going to make time to send in his car payments. Guess what? He called that night.

Jorge Sr.

On the way home from our interview with P-Nutz and Dream, Sol and I stopped at nearby Tania's. We hadn't planned to eat there, but after the metallic chill of the huge and nearly empty Rap Room, the small storefront restaurant seemed like a haven. Tania's was as good a place to process what we'd learned from P-Nutz and Dream as anywhere. It was a little early for the supper crowd, so we had the sunny back garden all to ourselves. We ordered some chilled Ukrainian borscht, cheese pierogies, and iced tea. In pots all around us bright pink impatiens and red geraniums blossomed. Dazzled by Mother Nature's summer bling, I blinked. Like a convalescent, I soaked up the warmth of the sun on my skin.

Up until that moment, misery over my sorry plight had numbed me to the many pleasures of early summer. I had not raked our own small back garden or planted the petunias, pansies, and impatiens that usually splashed it with color. I had yet to visit the Hoboken Farmers Market to garner the last of the rhubarb or sample the early lettuce, radishes, and strawberries. Sol and I hadn't spent a single lazy afternoon lounging on the deck of Betty and Vic's summer place in Ocean Grove. The threat of actually being charged with murder had imprisoned me even before I had been found guilty or sentenced.

"Dammit, Sol," I exclaimed. I felt my eyes tearing up.

The look he shot at me was anxious, concerned. With one hand he smoothed the thinning hair back from his brow. With the other he reached across the table to hand me one of the old-fashioned cloth handkerchiefs he still carried. "What's the matter, love? I thought that whole session with P-Nutz and Dream went well. You were really focused with him, and I bet you got her to spill her guts when I took him outside, right?" I nodded. "So what's wrong?"

"It's stupid, really," I said. "But I just realized that I'm missing summer. Fighting this damn murder charge has got me so busy and so depressed that I haven't had time for anything else." I could hear the whine of self-pity in my voice, but I couldn't seem to repress it. "Besides, what was so great about that interview we just had with those two? P-Nutz has a damn alibi for the night of the murder." I hadn't let on how much I had counted on being able to place P-Nutz on that subway platform on the night Naftali was killed. "And I really don't think Dream killed Naftali. From what she told me, he was interested in her because she was P-Nutz's girl. When she was teaching P-Nutz a lesson, she had a fling with Naftali, but after a sample of whatever he was offering, she dumped him. That was right before he left for the military."

"But isn't that what we wanted to know? Didn't we want to find out if P-Nutz had an alibi?" Surely Sol had grasped the fact that P-Nutz's alibi had to be bad news for me. But even so he wanted to nail it down so we could move on. "Do you want me to confirm it right now? I'll call the cleaning service and see if he showed up and worked that night. I'll check the hours he worked too." Sol had his cell out and was dialing directory assistance. I could tell that he was trying to talk me out of a total meltdown. I did some yoga breathing and tried not to second-guess what he was going to learn.

Our borscht came while Sol was on the phone, and

I tasted mine. It was as delicious as it was colorful, a bowl of sweet and savory soup the color of fuchsias, a brew that had fortified my Eastern European peasant ancestors. I sampled two or three spoonfuls and pushed it away. When all this was over, I would write a blockbuster diet book about how to lose weight while fighting a murder indictment. I had just begun to wonder if Martha Stewart, with whom I had come to identify very strongly, also lost weight during her preincarceration period. I wondered if, like me, she mourned the missed season, the precious months out of a too-short life. I heard Sol's voice. "Earth to Bel. Hello. Anybody home?"

"Yes, love, I'm sorry. What did you learn?" I inhaled peace and exhaled love one more time and looked expectantly across the table at him.

"I just talked to the coordinator of commercial services at Spotless Cleaning. On the night Naftali Thompson was killed, Paul Nutz was cleaning offices with a crew at Johnson Fitch just over there." Sol jerked his head in the direction of the new office towers that lined the Jersey City waterfront. "He was picked up at home at 8:45 P.M. and brought to the offices in the Spotless van. The driver collected the crew at 3 A.M. and took them home." I nodded, remembering when I had gone undercover as an office cleaner to investigate the murder of a dotcom CEO. I knew the grueling nocturnal drill only too well.

"Well, that's just great." My tone had the sarcastic edge of the proverbial nagging fishwife, but I felt like a four-year-old about to erupt in tears of frustration and panic. "I really thought P-Nutz killed Naftali. He even had the time-tested motive of jealousy, your favorite.

But no . . . P-Nutz had cooked his own goose by cheating on Dream. Maybe he was mad at Naftali for telling Dream about his transgression, but it sounds like Naftali talked his way out of that." I shrugged and began shredding my napkin. "But, don't you get it, Sol? None of that matters because P-Nutz has an alter ego and an alibi. He was Paul Nutz on the night of the murder. Even if his friendship with Naftali was fraying, P-Nutz has an alibi. And Jude Lafayette wasn't exactly crazy about Naftali either, but he has an alibi too. And Dream has no motive." I felt tears well. I reached again for Sol's handkerchief. "We're running out of suspects."

"Well, you're going to check out Naftali's brother and his girl tomorrow." Was Sol just trying to cheer me up or did he really think the next day's inquiries might lead to something? I couldn't tell from his voice. "Remember, love, Illuminada's always saying that homicide begins at home. Maybe it's a Cain and Abel thing."

Still on the verge of blubbering, I said, "I don't even know where to find Marcus Thompson."

"Yes, you do. Illuminada faxed over the name of the garage he works in. I took it off the machine before we left the house." Sol pulled a slip of paper out of his shirt pocket and handed it to me. On it there was an address in the Village and the notation 10 A.M.–6 P.M. "At least it's downtown, so we won't have to travel far."

" 'We'?" I said, filing the scrap of paper in my wallet.

"Yes, 'we.' I'm going with you. You can't go by yourself to meet with a murder suspect. And that's nonnegotiable." Sol's face was grave. Beads of sweat covered his upper lip, and his words were clipped, so I didn't bother to argue. Besides, it would be a long, hot day, and I would be glad of his company. "How are you going to approach him?"

"I'm going to drop you off near the garage before Marcus begins work. Then I'll park in the garage and lock my keys in the car. After that I'll meet up with you and we'll have breakfast. When I return by myself to the garage sometime after ten, Marcus will be there." I saw Sol tense, but when he opened his mouth to protest, I reached over and covered his lips with my hand. "Don't worry, love. You'll be right across the street. You'll be able to see if anything goes wrong. But it won't. He'll never know who I really am." Reassured, Sol planted a kiss in my palm. I continued to think out loud. "Okay, so I'll pretend to discover that I've locked the keys in the car. I'll call my husband and ask him to bring his keys. And I'll hang out right there gabbing until you show up in about an hour. I'll chat up Marcus and see if I can get him to talk about Naftali's death, try to find out if he has an alibi or, for that matter, a motive."

Sol signaled the waiter. When he came, Sol pointed at our practically untouched soup and pierogies and said, "We'd like to take this food home, please. It's delicious, but we're not as hungry right now as we thought we were." I felt my spirits lift just a little. It was reassuring to have a plan, to try to help myself rather than to sit passively by weeping and whining about my tragic plight. My strategy was simple and, based on past experience, there was no reason it shouldn't work. I tried not to think about what would happen if my ruse to engage Marcus Thompson in conversation succeeded, but he revealed nothing to link him to his brother's death.

On the way to the car, Sol asked, "But what if Marcus offers to open your car with one of those tools the cops use? He might have one. Or he might even suggest calling a cop to open it." Sol was a good devil's advocate, and I welcomed his questions. He was giving me a chance to prepare for possible snafus.

"I'll tell him my husband doesn't want anyone fiddling with the lock. Another man will certainly buy into that, right?" Sol smiled. "And besides Marcus is probably bored to death sitting there by himself all day. He might just be glad to have someone to talk to."

"You'll have to pay for the time you're waiting for me," said Sol.

"I know, but it'll be a lot cheaper than paying Dick Halpern to defend me if I go to trial." Sol smiled again, partly at my quip and partly because he was relieved that I had made an attempt at humor.

He couldn't resist going for a chuckle of his own. "Meanwhile, look at the bright side."

"What bright side?" I asked as I got into the car.

"Well, because P-Nutz has an alibi, your mom and Sofia still have their precious house cleaner."

Neither of us could sleep very well that night, so it was no hardship to rise early and try to beat the rush-hour traffic into the city. Illuminada had established that Marcus would begin work that day at ten and stay until six. But I was afraid that if I arrived after ten, the garage would be full. So at 8:10 A.M., I dropped Sol off at a diner on Sixth Avenue and West Fourth Street. The garage was a few blocks away and served primarily NYU students, faculty, and visitors. Fortunately for Marcus, this parking garage had not yet become so fully automated that it required no employees. But unfortunately for me, it was a garage in which the attendant presented you with a claim ticket and then parked your car himself somewhere in the multistoried building's mysterious nether regions. This same attendant kept the keys, presumably in the car, so he could move it to make room for other vehicles. My whole scheme was doomed.

I was rattled and annoyed that I hadn't checked out the garage beforehand. I could feel the adrenaline surging through my body, triggering a retro hot flash that left me damp, but alert. I could almost hear the wheels whirring in my brain. By the time I walked the few blocks to the diner, I had revised my original strategy. I hit the booth talking. "Okay, Sol, Plan A isn't going to work." He blinked and furrowed his brow in an unspoken question. "This is a fancy garage. The attendant parked the car and left the keys in it. When I go to pick it up, he'll get it for me. Why didn't I think of that?"

Before Sol could answer, I said, "But it's okay. Here's Plan B. First of all, when I was leaving the garage, I checked out the apartment building across the street. There's a bench just outside its front entrance. You can sit there and make like you're reading the paper and see partway into the garage, okay?" Sol nodded. "And I'm still going to pretend that I'm waiting for someone and he's late. I'll hang out around Marcus's cubicle where he sits and collects the claim tickets and the money when he's not jockeying cars. But this time I'm not going to be waiting for my husband. I'm going to be waiting for my lover." Sol's shrug signaled resignation rather than enthusiasm. "But my lover is standing me up. I may have to have a nervous breakdown right there. I'm going to get that man to talk to me. I have to."

In response to my desperate declaration, Sol nodded, but his hand shook when he lifted his coffee cup. I knew he was concerned about my ability to extract useful information from a total stranger without a more convincing hook. But he needn't have worried. I wasn't finished. "Don't worry. Just listen. I'm going to tell Marcus I recognize him from when I saw him outside his sister's house. Then I can introduce myself. After all, I'm a client of his sister's. He'll have to be civil to me. It's perfect. It's even better than the charade with the keys. I always prefer to use the truth rather than a cover story, if possible." I was so excited that I gulped some tea before I realized how hot it was and scalded my tongue.

Sol cocked his head to one side and gave me a quizzical look. "Bel, you went to that fortune-teller's house undercover. You're not a client of hers. Martha Salem is. And you're not Martha Salem. Your cover story is just that, a cover story. It's not true."

"I know," I said as patiently as I could. Did he think I was losing touch with reality? Was that why he was quibbling and nit picking? I realized that this was not a good time for Sol and me to argue. "Of course, I know I'm not Martha Salem, love, but Marcus doesn't. Dropping Olivia's name worked with Ariel and it will work even better on him. You'll see. There's no reason why Martha Salem shouldn't be parking her car in New York while she goes to a business meeting. And there's no reason why she shouldn't be rendezvousing with a lover later either. I'll have lots to talk about with Marcus. I can express my condolences. I should have thought of this in the first place." Sol concentrated on his English muffin, and I ordered a bagel and cream cheese to go with my tea. When the bagel came, I actually ate half of it. After breakfast, it was too hot to walk around the Village, so Sol bought a paper and we sat on a bench in Washington Square Park. My preoccupation with the conversation ahead made me less than good company. We sipped water, fanned ourselves with the newspaper, and waited in silence.

At 10:15, I parted from Sol back at the diner and walked to the parking garage alone. He planned to follow in a few moments and position himself across the street on the bench outside the high-rise. When I reached the garage, I could see from the pedestrian entrance that the attendant who had parked my car earlier was gone. In his place in the cubicle was Marcus Thompson, the man I'd seen leaving Olivia's.

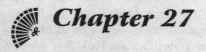 **Chapter 27**

To: Bbarrett@circle.com
From: Sholztman@hotmail.com
Re: 54 Candles
Date: 06/04/04

I hear ya, Bel. When my daughter Tracey blew off Mother's Day this year, I tried not to take it personally. While my friends in the office compared their phone messages, bouquets, and restaurant meals, I told myself that Mother's Day was just a dumb Hallmark holiday anyway. My kid (well, she's twenty-five) had just relocated to Colorado to take a demanding new job, and I knew she had to hit the ground running. When she didn't get back to me by phone or e-mail, I just figured she was busy adjusting to her new life. But that was weeks ago, and last Tuesday was my birthday. I figured for sure she'd at least call to say happy birthday, but she didn't. I got cards and calls from lots of friends and relatives. Even my ex, Tracey's dad, sent a card. But the call from Tracey that would have made my day didn't come.

Sue, who's still waiting

Sue's sad e-mail flashed through my mind as I stood in the pedestrian entrance to the garage. Like her, I'd had a lot of practice waiting, so it wasn't hard to pretend that's what I was doing that morning. I patted my hair, wiped sweat off the back of my neck with a Kleenex, looked at my watch, and glanced up and down the street. I feigned making two cell-phone calls. Then, after about ten interminable minutes and after Marcus had glanced my way a couple of times, I approached him.

I was close enough to read KINNEY embroidered in yellow script on the shirt pocket of the same short-sleeved brown uniform I remembered. But that day his dark hair was drawn back at the nape of his neck into a ponytail, and he wore a navy blue bandana twisted into a sweatband around his wide forehead. The youthful hairdo and headdress were at odds with the crows'-feet and laugh lines that seamed his face. His arms and upper body seemed puffy rather than sturdy, as if the muscles and sinews that had been visible beneath his light brown skin when I'd last seen him had turned to sponge. He could easily pass for forty-five. Like Olivia he looked older than he probably was. "Excuse me, but has a gray-haired white guy about your height been in yet?"

When Marcus looked up, I noted again that his eyes were close-set like Naftali's and the gaze he turned on me was cool and distant. "No, lady, but I only just got here." Most likely, Marcus had been even younger than Olivia when he arrived in this country because his speech had no trace of the island lilt that sometimes transformed hers. Instead his voice had that defensive whine peculiar to New York City cabbies and other service providers who contend with an occasionally obtuse and rude public on a regular basis. "I'm sorry. I should have mentioned that he drives a silver Lexus." He shook his head. Although Marcus certainly hadn't asked, I continued. "He was supposed to be here fifteen minutes ago. Damn." Clearly unmoved by my pouting and uninterested in my plight, Marcus was scanning the headlines in *The Daily News*. He took a swig from a tall thermal cup bearing the ubiquitous Starbucks logo. Then, looking over my shoulder, he shrugged and rolled his eyes. I turned. A bearded red-headed man stood behind me, poised for flight, sweating, his car keys in his outstretched hand. "Oh. I'm sorry. I didn't mean to block your way." I quickly moved aside.

Marcus exited the cubicle. When he came out, a rush of cool air followed him. His office wasn't much bigger than a phone booth, but it was air-conditioned. He closed the door behind him, grabbed the redheaded man's car keys, and handed him a claim ticket before trotting over to the car. "Thanks, Marcus," the man called over his shoulder as he rushed off.

"No problem, Professor," Marcus muttered. In what looked like a single easy motion, he pulled open the car door, slid into the driver's seat, and slipped the key into the ignition. The engine purred and Marcus drove down the ramp and out of sight.

I looked at my watch and leaned against the door at the same time. The door didn't give. I hadn't really expected it to. It had to be locked to safeguard the exorbitant sums of money people paid for the privilege of parking in New York. Just below the opening through which Marcus had spoken to me I saw the drawer where he stored this treasure. That was undoubtedly locked too. Above it, next to Marcus's newspaper, were two small machines, one for translating claim tickets into statements and the other for processing credit cards. On the floor behind the stool provided for Marcus to sit on when he wasn't moving cars, I spotted a worn-looking olive green backpack. Next to it was a black plastic portable radio. I knew it was on because from where I stood, I could faintly hear the throbbing beat of a hip-hop harangue. On the wall above the radio was a calendar. Next to the calendar were four pieces of Scotch tape and the torn corners of what might have been a photo.

When Marcus returned in about five minutes, he swept the pedestrian entry area with his eyes before reentering his cubicle, probably to make sure no one else awaited his services. He showed no reaction when his glance took me in standing near the door to the booth. Once he had reentered his encapsulated workspace, I approached the opening again. "Excuse me, but I think we've met before." Marcus elevated one eyebrow. Like Ariel before him, Marcus did not recognize or remember me. It is often said that women over fifty are invisible, and I was beginning to believe it. My annoyance lent urgency to my voice when I insisted, "Yes, I'm sure we have. It was at your sister's house in Jersey City." Suddenly I had the man's full attention. His lips twitched up at the corners of his mouth just enough to accent his laugh lines. This promise of a smile did not reach his eyes.

"Aren't you Olivia Durango's brother, Marcus?" He nodded but had no chance to speak because I was still talking. "Well, we didn't exactly meet. We passed each other on the steps one day when I was coming and you were just leaving. I'm a client of Olivia's. Your sister saved my life!"

His smile widened very slightly as his eyes brushed over the curls that framed my face. "Yeah, my sister gives a nice haircut."

This limited and almost grudging response was not exactly the outpouring of clues I was looking for, so I smoothed my hair and pushed on. "That's for sure. I get so many compliments on this haircut. But that's not how she saved my life," I added. As soon as I spoke, I realized that Marcus had not asked for the details of Olivia's intervention in my personal affairs, but that didn't stop me from continuing. "She studied my hand and told me something that . . . that really helped me." Trapped in his tiny box of an office, a captive audience to any unwelcome confession I cared to make, Marcus recoiled ever so slightly from the glass between us. I had to back off to relieve the anxiety my soap operatic introduction had obviously triggered in him. I made my next line a generalization. "She really understands people."

Marcus's initial response was a curt nod, but, having been spared an accounting of my intimate problems, he let his body relax forward, closer to the window, and added, "Olivia's okay at reading palms." His tone was agreeable, but a couple of blinks obscured his cool gaze just long enough for me to realize that perhaps Marcus had a less exalted view of his sister's insight into the human heart than I had expressed. Had he always been this laconic, this guarded? Or had grief over the death of his brother and the breakup of his relationship with Ariel shut him down? Or was there something else weighing on him?

I tried a more direct approach to what interested me. "Oh. Marcus, I'm so sorry. I should have offered you my condolences for the loss of your brother right away. Olivia told me how much the boy meant to you, how hard you both worked to give him what he needed."

Marcus blinked rapidly a few times again and took a deep breath. He was fondling the corner of his newspaper absently, as if it were the silken slip of a woman he had hoped to make love to but who was about to leave. It required no special powers to see that Marcus wished I would go away too. "Thank you. Thank you very much." He lowered his head. "We'll be okay."

"You're very brave. Olivia said she hated to be the one to tell you he was dead. She especially hated to tell you on the phone." Olivia hadn't told me this. I had read it in the police report, but Marcus wouldn't know that.

"Thank you." Marcus lowered his head once more.

I was disheartened by his uncommunicativeness, his impenetrability. I couldn't afford to even consider the possibility that Marcus had nothing to hide. So I decided that cracking him was going to be much harder than I had thought. And it was going to require a more invasive strategy. Damn, I'd probably have to find a way to search his room at Olivia's. But until I could figure out how to do that, I wanted to see what was in his backpack on the off chance that it contained something—anything—that would connect him to Naftali's death. It was a long shot, but I was desperate. So when Marcus looked up, he saw me staring at my watch again and scowling, perpetuating the pretense that I was waiting for somebody. I extracted a Kleenex from my purse and began to wipe my face and neck. "God, it's hot," I exclaimed.

Then, turning to Marcus, I said, "Your brother suffered so much from his war injury, and then just when he was getting his life back together, to die like that . . ." I paused. "It's so, so unfair." At the word "unfair," Marcus flinched. Clearly I'd finally struck a nerve, albeit a perfectly understandable nerve. "Olivia told me how you soundproofed and rewired his room to surprise him when he came home from the army hospital." Marcus's mouth twitched. Was he trying not to cry?

"You are so lucky to have that AC," I said, changing the subject, but keeping my eye on the prize. "It's so hot. Lately I just can't take this heat." I leaned heavily against the cubicle and took short loud breaths.

"You all right, miss?" Marcus's use of the formal "miss" reinforced my impression that I had not made much progress with my "I'm a friend of the family, tell me everything" campaign. But the quickening in his voice told me that, for whatever reason, he really didn't want me to collapse from heat prostration on his watch. Just as I was trying to figure out how to capitalize on his unexpected solicitude, an ebony-skinned woman of fifty or so came into the garage, talking on her cell phone, and holding out her claim ticket in her free hand. In her purple- and blue-striped turban and matching caftan, she was an exotic and regal figure.

Marcus appeared genuinely torn between getting her car immediately, as she clearly expected him to, and doing whatever he had to do to keep me from passing out. "You all right, miss?" he repeated, already out of the cubicle and reaching for the woman's ticket. "I'm on it, Dean Stiles," he said, not moving. "I'm just worried about this lady here." He spoke as if I were deaf. "She's waitin' for somebody, and she don't look so good. Turns out she's a friend of my sister's," he added, as if he had to justify his concern.

"I'll be all right," I whispered, my voice barely audible, my hand pressed against my chest. "I just need to catch my breath." I tried to will the blood out of my cheeks so they would appear dangerously white.

I was about to beg Marcus to grant me access to his lifesaving air-conditioning, when Dean Stiles spoke. Her diction was brusque, her tone authoritative. "Marcus, let her sit in there where it's cool with her head between her knees until you get back." She pointed at the cubicle. My new best friend, Dean Stiles, was clearly a problem solver. Marcus's cool eyes actually brightened at the brilliance of this suggestion and then narrowed when he realized the security implications of allowing me access to the treasure hoard he guarded. Reading his expression, she said, "Oh, don't worry. I'll be right here. I'll keep an eye on your ill-gotten gains, Marcus. Just get my damn car, please. I have to be at Columbia for a meeting in twenty minutes, and the traffic on Sixth Avenue at this hour will be impossible. I'll have to take the West Side Highway." Waving me into the cubicle with the imperiousness of a longtime administrator, Dean Stiles returned to her phone conversation. Dutifully, Marcus turned and headed toward the stairwell. It occurred to me that Dean Stiles hadn't paid him yet, so perhaps she was a monthly customer, and she and Marcus had a relationship of long-standing.

Feeling like a cross between the consumptive Camille and an ark raider, I staggered into Marcus's Plexiglas cage, leaving the door ajar. The slightly acrid smell left by Marcus's sweat evaporating in the stale chilled air threatened to lend some credence to my pretense of faintness. Again Dean Stiles's voice rang out. "Close that door to keep the cool air in. And put your head between your knees." As I obediently lowered my head, I saw her face out of the corner of my eye. She was leaning over and peering in to make sure I was complying with her command. As soon as her turbaned head disappeared, I turned off the radio. Then I could hear that Dean Stiles had resumed her phone conversation. She was far enough away from the cubicle so that I couldn't make out her words.

Staring at the grime-streaked floor just inches from my nose I cringed, and, for a few seconds, gave in to despair. How had I literally sunk so low? And for what? Only desperation would lead me to imagine that Marcus had killed his beloved brother and was still carrying around evidence linking him to the crime. But I was desperate. And desperate times call for desperate measures.

I raised my head slightly to brush away a welling tear and found myself eyeball to buckle with Marcus's backpack. Searching it was a risky move, but one I had to make. Furious with myself for having squandered even a few of the precious seconds I had before Marcus returned or Dean Stiles checked on my health, I worked the strap free and opened the flap. My fingers brushed across what proved to be a hairbrush, an old

Daily News, and a pair of chinos. More interesting was a photo of Marcus, Olivia, and a teenaged Naftali in a cap and gown. The corners were missing, as if the picture had been ripped from the wall. Perhaps it had once been taped to the wall just above me.

Quickly I rifled through the pockets of the chinos. Years of going through the kids' pockets before tossing their clothes in the washer had made me proficient at this. One pocket contained change and a set of keys, probably Marcus's house keys. Reluctantly I left them there. The other pocket held a package of gummy bears. The rear pockets were empty. His wallet was undoubtedly in his uniform. Feeling around in the bottom of the bag, I came upon a few wads of balled-up paper, probably gummy bear wrappers and other trash. When I carefully and quickly pried one of these open, it turned out to be a flowery Valentine's Day card signed: WITH ALL MY LOVE FOREVER, ARIEL in neon pink. Another wad of paper proved to be a multipaged apartment lease that had been crushed until it was the size of a golf ball. And the last, compacted into a really small black and white wad, was a photo. I gently teased it open, glanced at it, and gasped. My desperate long shot had paid off big time. In seconds I had balled the photo up again and jammed it back into the recesses of the backpack. In less time than I would have thought possible, I buckled the straps and made sure that the backpack was positioned on the floor exactly as it had been before. I switched on the radio.

Then I sat up and glanced around. Even though my world had literally been turned upside down, everything looked just as it had a couple of minutes ago. Marcus had not yet returned. Dean Stiles was still yakking on her cell. I caught her eye and smiled at her to indicate that I was feeling better. Without interrupting her phone call, she nodded and smiled back. I exited the cubicle, taking care to close the door behind me. It was time to call Sol. Just as I reached for my cell, I saw him striding across the street, his phone to his ear, and mine buzzed. It was good to hear his voice. "Oh! There you are, love! You disappeared into that booth, and when you didn't come out right away, I got worried. Is the heat getting to you? Are you all right?"

"I've never been better," I said. Pocketing his phone, Sol entered the garage and I walked into his arms for a very long and decidedly extramarital kiss. We disentangled when Marcus drove up in a lime green updated VW Beetle. He turned it over to Dean Stiles, who swooped into the tiny car in a swirl of purple silk, waved goodbye, and drove away without missing a word of her phone conversation. "Marcus, thanks so much for letting me cool off in your office. I'm feeling a lot better, and my friend is finally here. Mel Brooks, Marcus Thompson." I rushed through the perfunctory introduction, and the two men nodded at each other. "So I'll get out of your hair now. Would you please bring my car? It's a blue Toyota RAV 4." I had the claim ticket ready.

Sol and I stood there in silence until Marcus returned with the car. I didn't even flinch when he produced a statement indicating that I owed the parking garage almost fifty dollars for less than three hours. Not wanting to give away my identity by using a credit card, I handed him cash. As I turned to leave, I said, "Thanks, again, Marcus, and please give my best to Olivia." He opened the drawer where he stashed cash and was about to hand me my change when I said, "No, please keep it. And thanks again." When I piloted the car out of the garage, I was grinning for the first time in weeks. It felt so good to be back in the driver's seat.

 **Chapter 28**

To: Bbarrett@circle.com
From Mbarrett@hotmail.com
Re: Missing Link
Date: 06/04/04 12:34:46

Yo, Ma Bel,

No, I haven't heard from Rebecca lately either. Last time I talked to her, she was totally stressed out what with Abbie J out of school for the summer and trying to land a real job. I remember what that was like. But not to worry. My big sister may be a wayward wench and a drama queen, but she'll talk someone into hiring her. Dad called last night when we were out and left one of his tirades masquerading as a message. He's wired about Rebecca too, but I'll get back to him before he loses it totally and his pressure goes up. Remember, Ma Bel, inhale peace, exhale love,

Mark

I didn't know that Lenny had blood pressure problems, but it didn't surprise me because he had always
been excitable. It didn't surprise me either that Mark,
the peacekeeper in our family, would try to soothe his
dad so as to prevent an attack. And it certainly didn't
surprise me that Mark was downplaying Rebecca's
disappearance from the familial radar. I recalled the
time Rebecca had been back from her freshman year at
college just long enough to announce that a summer at
home was "like a death sentence." When she missed
her curfew that night, it was her kid brother who made
excuses for her. But there was no time to muse on my
ex's aging circulatory system or my second born's long
experience covering for his AWOL sister. Seeing the
photo of Ariel and Naftali had changed everything.

I wanted to talk with Illuminada and Betty before my
meeting with Ariel that evening. I was now convinced
that Marcus was the one responsible for Naftali's death.
In light of my discovery, Ariel had gone from being a
bit player in the Durangos' family drama to a leading
role. "I've drawn the Get Out of Jail Free card, and I'd
really like to meet with you before my appointment
tonight" was the message I'd left for both Betty and Illuminada. President Woodman was on vacation, so
Betty had no problem leaving the office for lunch immediately. Illuminada wedged us into her schedule between a session with a new client and a late lunch with
her accountant, who happens to be her husband, Raoul.
To accommodate her, we met in a conference room in
her busy Jersey City office. "No thanks, Mike," I said to
her secretary's offer of iced tea or coffee.

"I'd love some iced tea, Mike," said Betty. "And
please bring Bel some too. She needs a little caffeine."

I was so elated by my discovery that I didn't even argue when Betty overrode my refusal. Mike's eyes widened in confusion for a moment, and he turned to Illuminada for help in dealing with the mixed messages Betty and I were sending.

"Just bring in three iced teas, please, Mike," Illuminada said, rolling her eyes. He left and she turned to me. "If you don't want it, *chiquita,* don't drink it." Her arch delivery of the old mommy-line made both Betty and me smile. Still looking at me, Illuminada asked, "So what did you get from Marcus? Something good, it sounds like."

"Yeah, girlfriend, out with it," Betty echoed.

For once I went straight to the point. There would be plenty of time later to regale them with the details of my sleuthing. "I got into Marcus's backpack and found there, among other things, a picture of Ariel and Naftali, both naked and in a very compromising position." Illuminada greeted this announcement with her I-told-you-so nod, but Betty's mouth dropped open, and she made a show of closing it with the back of her hand.

"So Naftali and his older brother's girl were getting it on?" Betty needed confirmation of what she clearly found hard to believe. "This is the brother who worked so hard to support Naftali, right?"

"That's what the photo says," I replied. "Go figure. I was literally flabbergasted myself."

Illuminada was beaming. "*Chiquita,* this just might keep you out of jail, but before I get too excited and relieved, I have to ask why Marcus would hold on to something so incriminating. It's the only evidence we've seen of a motive. Why didn't he just set a match to the dirty picture?"

Illuminada's question was one that had bothered Sol and me, so I had already considered it. "It's as if he couldn't stand to look at it, so he crushed it, but he couldn't bring himself to throw it away either." Illuminada made a cranking motion with one hand, indicating that she wanted me to say more. "That photo is his motive, but it's also his justification." Both Illuminada and Betty leaned forward and knitted their brows, so I continued. "Someday Marcus may want to explain himself to Olivia, but without proof she would never believe Naftali betrayed him, or Ariel either, for that matter. She thinks Naftali walked on water, and she really likes Ariel. But you know the old saying, 'A picture is worth a thousand words.'" Betty and Illuminada nodded. "Marcus might figure that if he is ever actually accused, he could make Olivia understand and, possibly, forgive him by showing her that photo. And maybe looking at it helps him to forgive himself as well," I added. "After all, Marcus loved Naftali too."

I had barely finished my sentence before Betty fired questions at me. "How did he get ahold of that photo? Who took it? Is it recent?" She had crossed her arms in front of her and was waiting for me to respond when Mike came in carrying a tray with a pitcher of iced tea and three tall glasses. I didn't answer until he had filled the glasses, placed one in front of each of us, and left the room.

"Sol wondered about that too. I figure there are several ways that photo might have gotten into Marcus's hands. According to Olivia, while Naftali was in the hospital getting rehab, Marcus and Jude rewired and soundproofed Naftali's room to surprise him when he came home. To do that, they had to take out all his stuff. Maybe when they were packing it all up, Jude came across the photo and sent it to Marcus. Or, maybe Marcus himself found it in Naftali's things. I lean toward that explanation."

While I was ticking off these possibilities, a new and even grimmer one occurred to me. "It's even possible that Naftali himself showed the photo to his brother." My friends' eyebrows jumped in unison, so I rushed on to explain. "We know Naftali was a real piece of work. When his old buddy P-Nutz cheated on his girl, it was Naftali who told her about it. And then while Dream was angry with P-Nutz, Naftali hit on her." I paused, letting this sink in, before I took it one step further. "And if Naftali was the one who showed that photo to his brother, and Ariel found out, then it's possible that Ariel got so furious at Naftali for ratting on her that she killed him herself." Betty and Illuminada were nodding again now. "But one way or the other, that photo explains why Marcus broke up with Ariel." The iced tea looked pretty good after all the talking I was doing, so I helped myself to a long swig.

When Betty and Illuminada didn't refute my explanation, I continued, addressing another question of Betty's. "The photo was taken before Naftali lost his arm, so it dates from before he went to Iraq, probably not too long before he left because his hair is long, just like it was when he was in my class." I sighed, wishing I could turn back the clock and undo all that had happened since then. To answer Betty's final question, I said, "I don't know who took the picture, but Sol speculated that it was either Naftali or Ariel. You know how you set the camera to flash and then you quickly run around and pose in front of it?" Illuminada and Betty nodded and sipped their iced tea.

I interpreted their silence as an invitation to bounce ideas off them, so I began thinking out loud. "Okay, so Ariel, who may or may not be a murderer, is coming over tonight to see about renting a room from me and Sol. She's in a funny position. If the police question Marcus, he needs an alibi. If he wasn't at work, he needs to have Ariel say he was with her. But what if he wasn't? If he doesn't have another alibi . . ."

Illuminada broke into my chain of speculations. "First of all, *chiquita,* would you like me to have someone find out right now if Marcus was at work? That's easy enough to do. Then you'll know before you talk to Ariel tonight." It was my turn to nod. As I did, I savored the possibility that Marcus might have no alibi, and I might actually be off the hook. Illuminada pushed a button on her desk, and in a moment Mike appeared at the door. She jotted something on a pad he carried, and he read it and left.

"Wait a minute." There was a new urgency in Betty's voice. "If Marcus Thompson believes Ariel cheated on him with his brother, isn't she at risk? I mean, he just might turn around and do her in too."

"It could happen." Dizzied by the array of grisly possibilities that photo had opened our eyes to, I spoke slowly. "He's still got a Valentine's card from her and a lease, probably from their apartment. And both of those are crumpled up like the photo. Her betrayal hit him pretty hard." I shivered slightly, recalling how distant and detached Marcus's eyes had been whenever I saw him. "His eyes are always somewhere else."

"She must be a pretty nasty number to cheat on a guy with his own brother," said Illuminada.

"Could be. Maybe she and Marcus had a fight, and she showed him the photo to hurt him or make him jealous." I mentioned this only because I remembered Dream's effort to get back at P-Nutz by hooking up, however briefly, with Naftali. Although Illuminada's scenario was not out of the question, it was hard for me to imagine the perky and playful young woman I'd bantered with at Good Deal as a vengeful virago.

"She's a lot younger than Marcus," I said, shaking my head. "But who knows? That's why I want to talk to her. I just wish there were some way I could definitely place Marcus on that subway platform on the night of the murder before I meet with Ariel. That would exonerate her in my mind and it would also give me more credibility with her."

"Placing him on that platform would also give you more credibility with a grand jury," said Betty, practically purring with satisfaction. Suddenly her eyes widened and she plunked her glass down on the table. When she spoke next, anxiety had turned her purr into a squeal. "Oh my God, Bel, what if Marcus comes to his senses and destroys that photo before he's arrested?"

"Not to worry. He has no reason to suspect anyone is on to him and, as I said before, that photo is the only hope he has of ever making Olivia understand why he did what he did." In response, Betty held up crossed fingers, her way of saying that she hoped I was right but wasn't at all sure.

Just then Mike returned. He and Illuminada conferred at the door for a moment. "Two pieces of excellent news," Illuminada proclaimed with a grin when she retook her seat at the end of the conference table. "Marcus Thompson left his shift at the parking garage at 11 P.M. on the night of Naftali's murder. That would have given him plenty of time to get to the subway, conk his brother over the head, and toss him onto the platform." She and Betty exchanged a somber high-five. "And we're really on a roll because Dorothea Hamilton called. She's arranged for Bel and me to see the subway surveillance DVDs as soon as we can get to the Port Authority Terminal in New York. I just have to bail on my accountant for lunch and I'm ready. Maybe you'll get your wish, *chiquita*."

By the time Betty had bought herself a sandwich and returned to her office to eat a solitary late lunch, Illuminada and I were driving through the Holland Tunnel in Illuminada's car. I had resigned myself to forking over yet another chunk of change to park in Manhattan, so Illuminada pulled into a garage on Fortieth Street. From there we practically sprinted the block to the terminal.

Dorothea had agreed to meet us at the top of the escalators in front of the large glassed-in surveillance center. A tall and large-boned brunette, Dorothea had a broad, unsmiling face. She wore khaki pants with a crisp white blouse, an outfit that screamed, "I am not a sex object." Her knuckles on the hand clutching her brown leather briefcase were white, leading me to believe that the briefcase held either the Hope diamond or the archived surveillance DVD. After a hasty greeting, she led us through the terminal into a small windowless office where she had arranged for our screening.

Closing the door, she opened her briefcase and extracted a DVD. Before she popped it into the computer, she motioned us to sit down and said, "I practically had to guarantee a promotion to Tiffany Karpertian, our archivist, to get my hands on these." Illuminada was about to respond when Dorothea continued, "Not to worry, Illuminada. Tiffany's due to make a vertical move anyway, so I didn't really compromise myself."

Having reassured Illuminada that her own integrity was still intact, Dorothea hesitated a moment and went on, still speaking mostly to Illuminada. "You probably know that a couple of detectives from Hudson County Homicide already screened these, and they didn't find what they were looking for. Tiffany says they acted like it was her fault." Illuminada nodded at Dorothea to show she sympathized with Tiffany and gave me a thumbs-up. We both knew that the detectives of whom Dorothea spoke were Fergeson and Rago and that they had been hoping to find my image on the screen. "And now she says some lawyer wants the DVDs. They're a really hot item."

"We appreciate your showing them to us," I said. Dorothea wasn't exactly personality plus, but she was doing me a big favor, and I was grateful. "How many are there?" I asked. I had been surprised by her use of the plural.

"Two. Illuminada asked for the one showing turnstile traffic, which is, of course, on the upper level of the station and the one that shows activity on the platform below." Dorothea directed her response to me. I squeezed Illuminada's arm in appreciation of her thoroughness. "Tiffany suggested we watch them in the dark." Dorothea switched off the light as she spoke. The three of us sat there in the blackness while on the

monitor the date and the hour flashed: 04/30/04 12:56
A.M. I knew perfectly well there was no way my image
was going to grace the screen, but my stomach
churned, and the hairs on my arms began to prickle
anyway. These DVDs might very well be all that stood
between me and jail. I felt my body warming. When
the empty turnstiles appeared, we stared at them for
what seemed like a long time.

"Not much passenger traffic at that hour on a week-
night," said Dorothea, almost apologetically, as if she
were a hostess at a poorly attended party. A couple
more year-long moments passed. Perhaps discomfited
by our silence, Dorothea announced the obvious.
"Look, there's somebody coming." It was Naftali. His
one-armed body was unmistakable, even though his facial features were slightly blurred. But his grin, though
fuzzy, was discernible. It was the beatific grin of a
young man whose dreams are finally coming true. Naftali had just met with the producer who had agreed to
hear his demo, *i-raq traks*.

Naftali fumbled for a few seconds, trying to get the
PATH fare card into the slot with his remaining hand,
his left. Was this so hard because he had been drink-
ing? Or smoking? Or had Naftali been right-handed?
As I watched the young man struggle, I found myself
once again massaging my own shoulder. When Naftali
finally succeeded in making the turnstile admit him
and return his card, I felt like cheering but instead
found myself choking on a sob. The image on the
screen seemed suddenly a figure in a ghoulish computer game. The smiling young vet could not have
known that his triumph at the turnstile was to be his
last.

We stared for a while longer and another man, older, dark-skinned, bespectacled, and wearing a light-colored business suit, passed through the turnstile. For the next few minutes, no one else entered and then the screen went blank. "Closing time," said Dorothea, once more sounding apologetic. She switched on the light. "I hope that was helpful."

"Oh yes," I said, brushing my hand across my eyes. I didn't want Dorothea to see how upset I'd been at the sight of Naftali. He had not been the nicest person, but he had not deserved to be maimed and then murdered either. Had he lived to grow older, he might have matured into a kinder, gentler man. "It really was." Illuminada nodded in agreement.

"So are you ready for the next one, the one showing the platform?" Dorothea had removed the DVD we had just seen and was inserting the other.

Illuminada and I signaled agreement by rearranging ourselves in our chairs. Once again Dorothea turned off the light. Again we saw the date and the time. Then the late-night subway platform filled the screen. There were three people visible. One appeared to be a homeless man stretched out on a wooden bench, his face covered with a newspaper. Another was the dark-skinned fellow in the light suit whom we had seen go through the turnstile. The third was, of course, Naftali. The newspaper covering the face and chest of the man on the bench rose and fell with his breath. The suited dark-skinned man paced back and forth near the platform's edge. Naftali leaned against a pillar, his head bobbing up and down, perhaps rhyming to beats sounding in his brain. So far there was no sign of Marcus.

A subway headed for New York pulled in and

stopped. The camera must have been on the other side of the tracks because for the few minutes the train was in the station, the monitor showed only the outside of one car. Once the train left, it was clear that no one had disembarked and no one else had arrived via the turnstile above. The suited man had boarded. It had not been the train Naftali was waiting for because after it rushed out of the station, he remained on the platform. He was alone, except for the homeless man still asleep on the bench. Just then the predictable rush of air blowing in from the tunnel in the wake of the departing train disturbed the newspaper covering the face of the sleeping man. It slid toward the floor. His hands moved swiftly to reposition it as the screen went blank. I blinked, not trusting what I had glimpsed. It was too good to be true. But I wasn't going to say anything until I was sure.

"Now in an ideal world, somebody from PA security saw that vagrant asleep there and rousted him out." Oblivious to my excitement, Dorothea spoke as she flipped the light switch. She still sounded like a hostess, this time apologizing for the appearance of a roach in the *vichyssoise*. "We can't have them staying there all night, especially not after 9/11. He could be a terrorist."

"I suppose," said Illuminada with a sigh. "But he looked like a homegrown homeless man to me. I'm starting to see a fair number of homeless folks on the streets again. With the job market so tight and rents so high, it's no wonder." Dorothea pursed her lips, but she didn't argue. Illuminada stood.

I remained seated, but reached out and put my hand on my friend's arm. Illuminada's face registered surprise, and then she smiled. She looked at her watch, but she didn't protest as she sat down again. "Dorothea, would you let us see those images of the platform one more time, please?" I tried to keep the elation I felt out of my voice.

"Yes, of course," Dorothea said. She flipped the light switch, and once again we stared at the figure stretched out on the bench, the dark-skinned man pacing, and Naftali leaning against the pillar rapping to himself. Again we saw the train pull in and then leave, its roar inaudible except in our imaginations. And once more we saw the newspaper slide down, revealing for a few seconds the wide-eyed and tight-lipped face beneath it. This time I was sure. The man on the bench was Marcus Thompson.

"You've been so helpful already, Dorothea, that I hate to ask for anything else, but . . ." I paused. "Could you find out if your security people did actually go down there and make that man leave? And did they identify him? Or take him to a shelter?" Illuminada was quiet, suspecting my agenda.

"Sure," said Dorothea. "I'd like to know myself. Give me a minute." She picked up the phone on the desk opposite the DVD player and pushed a few buttons. Illuminada and I waited in silence while Dorothea posed several questions. When she put the phone down, she was smiling.

"Well, according to the log for that night, a security officer went down to the platform and found that the bum had left." Dorothea sounded relieved that her agency had done what she considered the right thing. "He probably got on the last train, the one your victim was waiting for. They can be pretty canny, you know.

Or he could have just walked upstairs after the camera went off for the night but before the guard went down to check." In spite of her help, Dorothea was beginning to bug me. I didn't like the way she designated the man she thought to be homeless as a bum or her use of the third person plural pronoun "them" to refer to the homeless. And under the circumstances, the phrase "your victim" didn't sit well with me either, even though I understood that she had not meant it literally. We thanked her profusely and left.

As soon as we were outside, Illuminada said, "So, *chiquita,* was that sleeping beauty masquerading as a down-and-outer our man? I know you recognized him when the newspaper blew away from his face."

"You got it," I said, sniffling and struggling to quell my tears of relief. "The man on the bench was Marcus Thompson, Naftali's older brother. He's the one who knocked out Naftali and dumped him onto the tracks."

Illuminada handed me a Kleenex saying, "Here, *chiquita,* stop sniveling. I hate to say it, but I'm not surprised. I never write off relatives. You know that." And I did. Illuminada really believed that in human relationships, anything was possible and that kinship was no guarantee against murder. "And speaking of family, call Sol and your mother. They both deserve to know that things are finally looking up. Then we can talk about how to handle Ariel when she shows up at your place tonight."

Chapter 29

Producer Shares Rhyme of Slain Vet

Late Rapper's Farewell Lines Live On

i-rak traks numba 1

college drop out wid no job n no plan
got rhymes for sale but no contrak in hand
musta fucked up, made a big erra
cause tomorrow I gon off ta fight terra
no girl back home gonna write me no letta
say how she miss me, knit me no sweata
but uncle sam he say he want me
need me ta fight for god n my country
that recruter dude, he think Nas-T way cool
say the army gonna be better n school
say they gonna train me n give me a skill
give me a gun n teach me ta kill
but I got my reasons for gon ta war
gonna do rhymes like neva before

gonna spit bout how it feel by the tigris riva
when it come time to stand n deliva
gonna rap bout bombs n missles n rockets
gonna make rhymes n put green in my pockets

"When Nas-T showed me these lines and said he
had lots more that he wrote while he was stationed
in Iraq and later after he was wounded, I was blown
away. I knew I would sign him," said producer Montgomery Duvalle. Duvalle had agreed to hear the latest demo tape of the late rapper, otherwise known as
Naftali Durango. Durango was knocked out and
pushed onto the subway tracks, where he was run
over by an oncoming train. Hudson County Homicide
detectives claim an indictment is pending. "Even
without the beats, I could tell that Nas-T speaks for
lots of recruits in his generation. Before his death,
Nas-T was working on . . ."

While Sol and I waited for Ariel, I automatically
glanced at the *Jersey City Herald* to check on the
seemingly endless coverage of Naftali's murder. I
didn't know then that Duvalle had not been the only
audience for this rhyme in which poor Naftali had said
goodbye to civilian life and anticipated his military career. When I put aside the paper, I said, "Soon I'll be
out from under this murder rap and I can just mourn
that poor kid." But when five thirty came and went that
evening with no sign of Ariel, I began to fret. "Where
the hell is she?"

Sol's explanation was not reassuring. "Maybe she
figured out that you were a phony and decided not to
come."

"More likely she's just running late," I countered, hoping I was right.

I couldn't tell if Sol was relieved or not by Ariel's failure to show. Now that I'd told him about the incriminating photo of Ariel and Naftali and the surveillance DVD placing Marcus Thompson on the subway platform on the night of Naftali's death, Sol's relief made him less than practical. "Let's just phone Dick Halpern, tell him about this evidence, and leave the matter in his experienced and capable hands," my husband had urged. "Surely that snapshot and the surveillance DVD will put the kibosh on your indictment and refocus the whole investigation. Then this nightmare will be over. We can reclaim our lives."

"No way," I'd snapped. "I charge a lot less than Dick Halpern does. Besides, we did all the leg work. I'm not going to let him come back from his vacation just in time to play hero." I didn't add that I wasn't about to forgo the pleasure of following up on the loose ends of this investigation, so I could personally wrap them around the necks of Detectives Rago and Fergeson. But if Ariel didn't keep her appointment, this might not be so easy to do.

When our doorbell rang at a little after 5:45, I was relieved. Ariel stood there on our stoop. She was out of breath and her words rushed out in spurts. "Sorry I'm late. I got on the wrong PATH train and ended up on Christopher Street in New York. I shoulda called," she added apologetically. "But my cell don't work in the train, and then I figured I'd make better time if I just ran. I'm sorry." The excuses and apologies rolled off her tongue almost glibly, as if she had been apologizing all her life. Sweat had plastered spikes of her hair to her flushed cheeks, where they lay like black arrows pointing to her nose. She wore the same neon green cropped blouse with the baby-doll sleeves she'd had on when I'd seen her at Olivia's, only now the armpits and back were sweat-stained. Ariel had traded her denim shorts for a denim miniskirt that bared almost as much of her solid thighs as the shorts had.

"Not a problem," I assured her. "I just got home a few minutes ago myself. Come in, Ariel. This is my husband, Mel Brooks." We'd agreed that Sol would play hard-nosed landlord to my softhearted landlady and that together we would try to break her down, get her to talk about her and Naftali. Sol glanced at his watch, scowled, nodded perfunctorily at Ariel, and grunted a monosyllabic greeting. Then he looked her up and down in silence, taking in her blotched blouse, her disheveled hair, and her shortness of breath. Under his critical eyes, her greeting was reduced to a tentative nod of her head. "Why don't I show Ariel the room?" I said, directing this question to Sol. "And then we can all talk." I turned to the young woman, who had begun running her fingers through her hair in an effort to smooth it. "Come on, Ariel, follow me. The room's in the rear of the house. It has a view of the garden."

When we reached Rebecca's old room, I threw open the door. Rebecca's tattered Don Johnson poster was still on one wall and a yellowing *Playbill* from *Chorus Line* remained wedged behind the mirror. "This was our daughter's room, but she's moved out. The mattress is fairly new, and there's a big closet. See?" When I pulled open the door, a pair of roller blades and a headless Barbie doll on the top shelf threatened to precipitate an avalanche. Getting Rebecca to claim and cart away the contents of that closet had been on my to-do list for years. Ariel had just stepped forward to peer inside when I slammed the door, saying, "Oops! I'll pack up my daughter's stuff before you move in. But you saw how roomy that closet is. And look! There's a view of our garden." I'd forgotten that there was no garden that year. I had been too busy trying to stay out of jail to plant even a single annual, so the bedroom window looked out on a patch of brown earth, barren except for a few weeds that had sprouted around the trash cans. Ariel moved toward the window and stared wordlessly out.

Completely into landlady mode, I said, "I'll empty the bureau drawers too." Her eyes swept the chest of drawers I pointed to and focused on the small black and white TV on top of it. "The TV comes with the room," I added. "It's the only one in the house." A slight hunch of her shoulders was the only apparent reaction to this news that Ariel allowed to show. Sol had certainly cowed her into silence. "Do you want to see the bathroom? It's right down this hall." She nodded and followed me out of the room.

After she had checked out the bathroom, I led the way back to the kitchen. "Would you like a cold drink? Of course, you'd have access to the kitchen." I added this as an afterthought when I realized that, as a roomer, Ariel would have to eat.

"No. But thanks. The room is real nice. This is a beautiful house." Ariel sounded wistful as her eyes moved over the cherry cabinets and her fingers traced a pattern on the sleek granite surface of the countertop. "It's like in one of them magazines."

Sol had been sitting on a stool at the sink island

reading the paper when we joined him. "Yes, it is," he said, all traces of his usual endearing modesty gone. "We like our home too. That's why we have to be very particular about who we have living here. They'll be sharing our home."

"It's probably too expensive for me, anyway," she said, examining her chipped green nails. Sol stared at her nails, making no effort to hide a slight shudder. "I don't bring in a lot of money." Ariel's voice was soft now. She raised her head to look at me as if expecting me to bear witness. "You saw, I'm a cashier at Good Deal."

"We should get five hundred dollars a month for the room, but we'd settle for four hundred dollars in exchange for some help with the house work," Sol said evenly. A room in yuppified Hoboken at that price was a rare find. Ariel's eyes brightened until Sol added, "That is, assuming your references check out. We'd need to talk to your previous landlord. Where are you living now? And why are you relocating?"

"I'm at my sister's place. She's letting me stay as long as I help out with her kids. I'd rather do housework than take care of them three brats, believe me." Now it was Ariel who shuddered.

"I can't ask your sister for a reference." Sol made his deep voice stern. "Where did you live before that?"

"In Jersey City on Grand Avenue. My fiancé and me, we rented a place in a three-family house. The landlady's name was Garofolo, Caridad Garofolo."

Sol made a pretense of jotting down the name. "And why did you leave there?" He was relentless.

I made my voice tremulous, as if I were fearful of speaking out. "I told you, dear, Olivia said her boyfriend . . ."

"I don't care what you told me," Sol barked. "And I sure as hell don't care what some flaky fortune-teller told you." He glared at me and spoke his next words deliberately in a tone heavy with menace. "Martha, I told you. I'll handle this."

After Sol's deep growl, Ariel's response sounded faint and weak, but I had to hand it to her. She stood her ground. "But it's true. Olivia is my fiancé's sister. When we broke up, he moved in with her." Ariel lifted her chin a little, as if she thought her reference to Olivia would make the palmist credible to Sol. He just raised his bushy eyebrows and remained silent, waiting for her to go on. Looking down again, Ariel continued. "Anyway, without my fiancé, I couldn't make the rent." Having actually uttered the words that signal disaster to every landlord, Ariel brushed away a tear and then another. "That's why I went to my sister's."

"Just suppose we do a credit check on her and her credit rating is actually decent and the Garofolo woman says she was no trouble . . ." But Sol was shaking his head, even as he posited this rosy scenario. "And that's unlikely, since it sounds as if the two of them bailed on their lease. How do we know that when Romeo has a change of heart and takes her back, Juliet won't bail on our lease too?" Sol spoke as if Ariel were not sitting right there between us at the table, as if she could not hear the contempt in his voice. But she was and she did. Two tears that she had brushed away earlier proved to be the prelude to a torrent. Sol grunted in disgust, stood, and left the room. As if he had not already broken her spirit, on his way out, he called over his shoulder, "You sure know how to pick 'em, Martha."

I handed Ariel a Kleenex. "Aren't men something?"

I said, feigning embarrassment. "But he's wrong about this, isn't he? Your fiancé really is gone for good, right?" Ariel, still suffering after Sol's demeaning diatribe, cried harder. I handed her another Kleenex. Before she pulled herself together and took off, I needed to say something to keep her there and keep her talking. "Did your fiancé find another woman?"

Ariel blew her nose and, red-eyed, looked up at me. "No. I don't know. Olivia says there's nobody else, but even Olivia doesn't have a clue why he left me. One day we was planning to marry, to have a family. And the next day Marcus, that's his name, Marcus never wants to see me again. He packs up his stuff and leaves." She shrugged, as if to say, "Go figure."

Hoping to catch Ariel way off guard, I played my ace. "Do you think he came across a photo of you and his brother Naftali having sex?" I spoke softly, but even so, the dead man's name and the crass question sounded loud and harsh in the quiet room. Ariel's eyes closed and her nostrils began to quiver. Her face paled, and for a moment I feared she might faint. Then she opened her eyes and glared at me. "Who the hell are you? How do you know about them pictures of me and Naftali?" Her voice was a harsh rasp.

"I'm one of the people trying to find out who killed Naftali," I answered. There was no point in telling her more. "And I learned that Marcus carries around an incriminating photo of you and Naftali in his backpack. It's all crumpled up, but I saw it." Ariel put both hands on the counter, as if to steady herself. I filled a glass with cold water and brought it to her. The hand she took it with shook, but she lifted the glass to her mouth and drank.

When she put the nearly empty glass down, she said, "Damn that Naftali. He swore to me on his mother's grave he'd get rid of those photos." But even as she spoke, she was confronting the fact that the dead man had not kept his word. Her shoulders slumped, and she inhaled deeply, taking in the truth as she took in more air. Finally, with her lips pressed tightly together, she squeezed out a question, avoiding my eyes as she spoke. "Does Olivia know? About the picture?"

"Not yet, but she will have to know before long. It will have to come out in court." Again I had delivered a big message in a small voice.

The eyes Ariel raised to meet mine were suddenly those of a bewildered child facing a punishment she does not feel she deserves. " 'Court'?" I could see her trying to figure out what court had to do with her indiscretion with Naftali, with her and Marcus, with Olivia. She repeated the word a few more times, shaking her head. But she must have finally understood because when she looked up next, her eyes were round and with her right hand she crossed herself. "No! No!" She repeated the word over and over, even after she had lowered her head onto her arms. Hunched over the counter, the young woman was a picture of abject grief, even though she was silent. She appeared too defeated even to weep.

I patted her shoulder awkwardly and placed the Kleenex box within easy reach, just in case. I refilled the water glass. After a few moments, Ariel winced and covered her mouth with her hand, even though it was me she wanted to stop talking. "Marcus probably found it in Naftali's room when he soundproofed it," I said. Ariel gasped and crossed herself again.

"Anyway, on the night Naftali was murdered, Marcus left work at eleven. That left him plenty of time to make it to the subway platform and wait for his brother. He appears there on a PA surveillance tape." Ariel was shaking her head again, preferring the comfort of disbelief to the pain of facing up to her role in the events that led her former fiancé to commit fratricide. "Ariel, what time did Marcus come home that night?" I asked. "Do you remember?"

Ariel kept shaking her head while she spoke. "I was in bed," she said. "But it was late. I remember because Marcus had said, 'Don't wait up for me.' But I did. I always did." She blushed. Apparently sex with Marcus had been worth staying awake for—and merited a blush. Ariel had not blushed at the memory of sex with Naftali. I filed this away to think about later. "But that night Marcus said he didn't feel good." Again Ariel's cheeks flushed red as she relived this rejection. "I didn't think nothin' about it at the time. He slept in the next day 'cause he didn't have to be at work until ten.

"So when Olivia called about, you know, about Naftali, Marcus was still in bed. He sounded surprised when he heard her crying and when she told him what happened. Marcus acted like he was upset, sad. And he stayed like that for weeks. He'd just come home, have a few beers, and go to bed. He didn't want nothin' from me, no conversation, no sex, no meals even. Olivia said he was depressed like her, and we figured he would get over it. But he didn't."

At this point in her story, Ariel's speech became singsong, as if she'd repeated this part of it often. "And then one day I came home from work, and he was packing up his things. I said, 'Marcus, baby, what're you doin'?' And you know what he said?" I shook my head. "He said, 'I'm outta here, bitch. Me and you, we was a mistake.' And he took off." Ariel snapped her fingers. "He came back one day when I was at work and took the furniture."

"Were you in love with Naftali?" The answer to this question probably didn't matter to the investigation, but I was curious about what had moved Ariel to have sex with her fiancé's brother.

"No way," she said dismissively, as if my question was preposterous. Her voice took on a dreamy quality when she continued. "I love Marcus. I loved him from the first day I saw him in the line at the unemployment office. We was both between jobs. He needed a pen, so I lent him mine." Ariel's voice softened further at the memory of this landmark moment. "He treated me so good, and he's not afraid to work either. Marcus and me was gonna get married, have kids. But now he'll go to jail and it's my fault." Ariel's voice was so low that I barely picked up her last few words.

"Why did you have sex with Naftali?" I asked. I was touched by her avowal of love for Marcus and more curious than ever about why she would jeopardize that relationship for a roll in the hay with Naftali.

Ariel shrugged. When she spoke, her voice was brittle and her words clipped. She might have been describing the activities of two strangers: characters in a movie or a book. "The night before he left for basic trainin', Naftali came by the apartment to say goodbye to me and to pick up this new Polaroid Marcus and me were givin' him to take with him. I got it at the store with my employee discount." At the thought of the terrible price both Naftali and Marcus would eventually

pay for this gift, Ariel covered her eyes with one hand
and took a deep breath.

Then she continued. "Marcus was workin' that
night. Him and Naftali had already said their goodbyes
anyway at a party Olivia had, but the party was on a
Sunday, and I couldn't get off work to go. Anyway,
that night Naftali brought over some weed. Naftali and
me, we was friends mostly on accounta every now and
then we'd smoke a couple of tokes together. Marcus
don't like to smoke, but I like a little weed now and
then, you know, to relax." I nodded, beginning to see
where this familiar story would end.

"So we had a few drinks and shared a coupl'a joints.
Naftali was rappin' about how Dream had broke off
with him, how he done bad in school, and how he
couldn't get a producer to sign him. But I was feeling
pretty good from the hooch and the weed. Naftali always had pretty kind bud." Ariel grimaced at what was
now a painful memory. "From the way he was rhymin,'
I figured he was gettin' pretty blazed too, but then he
stopped spittin' and started going on about how scared
he was. He was sure there would be a war with Iraq
soon, and he wanted to go, but he was scared. I felt real
sorry for him.

"He asked for a goodbye kiss, and next thing I know
we got no clothes on and he's takin' pictures of us. One
minute we was cryin,' and the next minute we was
laughin' like crazy at those damn pictures. I made him
swear on his mother's grave he would burn them before he got home. We got dressed, and I made him
some coffee, and he left. No way him and me had sex.
We was just playin' each other." The photo had shown
two entwined naked bodies, but Ariel, like Bill Clin-

ton, could parse the sex act into so many disparate pieces that maybe she herself no longer recognized it. Or maybe she was telling her version of the truth.

Realizing the absurdity of her denial, Ariel said, "But if Marcus saw those photos, he wouldn't believe we was just playin'. He wouldn't believe it at all." The young woman's shoulders slumped at the thought of how the photos would have damned both her and Naftali in Marcus's eyes. "Nobody will believe me. And now Naftali's dead and Marcus will go to jail." Her own eyes filled, and she lifted both hands to cover them. The enormity of what had happened was overwhelming.

"Ariel, I know you feel responsible for Marcus's predicament, but you're not, not entirely. What you and Naftali did was stupid and thoughtless, but your only actual crime was smoking marijuana. And Naftali should have kept his promise and destroyed all of the photos. But what the two of you did, however dumb and disloyal, does not justify murder." I could tell that my words were not registering with her, so I gripped her by the shoulders and forced her to look at me before I went on. "Ariel, right now the thing is that once Marcus realizes that he's a suspect in the murder of his brother, he's also going to realize that he needs an alibi. He doesn't know we have a video placing him at the scene of the crime at the time of the murder. He'll want you to lie and say he was home at the time Naftali was killed. If he suspects you won't do that, he may decide to go after you. In fact, he may be so unhinged by your betrayal of him that he goes after you, even if you do provide an alibi."

Ariel looked at me as if I had just suggested something far outside the realm of possibility. "Marcus would never . . ." she began.

"You would never have expected Marcus to kill his own beloved younger brother, would you?" I asked.

Ariel shook her head. "No, he spent his life tryin' to make Naftali happy. Marcus loved Naftali." Then, her eyes wild, she looked around and said, "Oh my God, do you think Marcus is going to kill me too?"

"We're not going to take any chances," I said. "We're going to have him arrested on the basis of your testimony and that photograph and the surveillance DVD before he can do you or, for that matter, himself any harm."

Chapter 30

**RECC Prof Cleared in Slaying of Vet
Rapper's Brother in Custody**

Suicide Watch in Effect at County Jail

Hudson County Homicide Detectives Oliver Fergeson and Jack Rago, following leads phoned in by an informant, arrested Marcus Thompson for the murder last month of his younger brother, Iraq War vet and local rapper Naftali Thompson. The victim had been knocked unconscious and pushed off the platform at the Grove Street PATH Station in Jersey City. He was run over by an oncoming train a few hours later. According to Detective Fergeson, "We got enough evidence to put Marcus Thompson away for a long time."

In response to queries about how they had suddenly shifted the focus of their investigation away from chief suspect, RECC Professor Bel Barrett, Detective Rago said, "We let on to the press how we suspected Professor Barrett to give Durango a false sense of security. But we had our eye on him from the start. That's all I can tell you now." Neither Detective Fergeson nor Detective Rago would reveal the identity of their informant, but it is rumored that PI Illuminada Guttierez served as consultant to the officers. When questioned about her agency's role in the investigation, Guttierez said only, "I'm not at liberty to discuss my clients."

Marcus Thompson's attorney, ace criminal lawyer Richard Halpern, has asked Judge Zankar Tripatti to put a gag order on those involved in the case, in order to ensure the defendant a fair trial. "To describe the evidence in the press before my client is even indicted or tried would make it impossible for him to get an impartial hearing." Police Chief Carl Logan confirmed reports that Marcus Thompson is under a suicide watch while he is in custody. Olivia Durango, sister of both the dead rapper and his alleged killer, was unavailable for comment.

At least three copies of the newspaper carrying this article were strewn around the deck of Betty and Vic's summer place in Ocean Grove. In the same edition of the paper, but buried on an inside page, was an article explaining that Sarita Singh had agreed to allow RECC student government reps to monitor *www.pickur-profs.com* for politically incorrect or pedagogically irrelevant content. Sol and I had read both articles and then gone for a long restorative walk on the beach.

After strolling a few miles in compatible silence, we headed back to the house and took refuge from the sun under the umbrella that shielded the cushioned teak

chairs surrounding a matching teak table. Betty poured
me a tall glass of iced tea. Raoul handed Sol a beer
from the nearby cooler. Vic nudged a tray of fruit and
cheese in our direction. I took off my wide-brimmed
straw hat and shook out my hair before sipping the
cold tea. I leaned back and closed my eyes. This was
about as close to heaven as one could get and still be
in New Jersey.

"Before you drift off, Bel, tell us what really happened." Vic tossed aside the newspaper at his elbow.
"All Betty said was that it's true your pending indictment is no longer pending. She figured you'd want to
recap how you persuaded those goons to lay off you
and go after Durango." Vic's request was reasonable,
but I was so tired.

"Yeah, Bel, I want to hear too. Mina just said something about how you turned the tables on those two
morons. But she wouldn't tell me the details. Said it
was your story. C'm on, Bel. You know you want to."
Near the end of this speech, Raoul exaggerated his
Spanish accent and made his voice soft and cajoling in
a perfect imitation of a teenaged Latin lothario trying
to seduce his girl in the backseat of a car.

"It was really simple, almost an anticlimax," I said,
raising the back of my chair so I could literally rise to
the bait as my friends had known I would. When had I
ever refused an opportunity to tell a story? "You know
that once I saw the incriminating picture of Naftali and
Marcus's girl, Ariel, and the surveillance DVD placing
Marcus at the crime scene, we were really ready to go,
right?" The two men nodded.

Sol beamed. His theory that sexual jealousy was behind most homicides had been proved valid in this

case. He chimed in, "But my beauty here wanted the icing on the cake, so with a little help from yours truly, she got Ariel to admit to having participated in a pot-fueled porno photo shoot with Naftali." He stopped talking for a moment and turned the baseball cap he wore around and then back so the visor once again protected his face. "I still have trouble believing Ariel fell for that old 'I'm shipping out tomorrow, so gimme some tonight' routine." I could tell from the faraway look in his eyes that Sol was reliving a memorable send-off from his own long-ago days as a soldier. "Anyway, as Ariel told it, Naftali said he was scared and wanted a goodbye smooch and next thing you know they're naked. And get this. Ariel implied that she never really had sex with that man." We all grinned as Sol pointed his index finger at us in the familiar gesture of Bill Clinton's that had come to be synonymous with lying about sex.

"Part of me really wants to believe her," I said. "I hate the idea that Marcus was two-timed by both his brother and his girl. Marcus worked so hard to make sure that Naftali was well taken care of. He was like a father to that kid. I suspect that Naftali's betrayal was the one that hurt Marcus the most." I paused. "You know, it is possible that Ariel and Naftali were just so stoned that they didn't realize what they were doing. Maybe they didn't really . . ."

"Sure, and if you believe they didn't actually have sex, I have a bridge I want you to look at." Illuminada spoke from the chaise lounge where she had stretched out. Her iced tea was on the floor beside her. "*Díos mío, chiquita,* I hope this whole thing hasn't made you go soft in the head."

"It just doesn't matter if they did or they didn't," said Betty with a sigh. "When Marcus saw that photo of the two of them naked and smiling and all tangled up, the poor dude lost it." We greeted her pragmatic pronouncement in silence, each of us pondering for a moment the tragedy that had resulted from Marcus's fatal confrontation with that Polaroid picture.

"Come on, Bel. Tell them how you put it to our friends from homicide. Once you and Sol had gotten Ariel to open up about the photos, what did you do?" It was Illuminada again, prompting me. The mystery she had been reading lay open across her chest.

"Remember when Illuminada had said my office phone was probably wired?" Everybody nodded. "Well, Wendy thought it was too, so we pretty much stopped using it. We haven't been in the office much this summer anyway," I added. "But when I was trying to figure out how to get backup for us when we went after Marcus or, better yet, how to get Fergeson and Rago to go after him like they were supposed to, it occurred to me to use that phone." I was grinning again, this time at the memory of the satisfying "Aha" moment I'd had when I'd thought of this ploy.

"All it took was one call," I boasted. I didn't mind gloating over outsmarting the two men who'd nearly put me behind bars. "I made sure I spoke slowly and clearly, like this." I slowed down my delivery to show what I meant, as well as to drag out the exquisite pleasure I was taking in reliving my triumph. "I phoned Sarah Woolf at the *Jersey City Herald* and told her that Illuminada, Betty, and I had the goods on Naftali Durango's real killer. I told her about the photo and where it was. I told her about the surveillance tape and who to contact at the PA to get it. I told her about Ariel's admission and gave her Ariel's sister's address and told them where Ariel works." I ticked each revelation off on my fingers and paused to enjoy the way Vic and Raoul were smiling.

"Then I told Sarah that I was going to make a citizens' arrest of Marcus Thompson for the murder of his brother. I mentioned that I was going to apprehend Marcus at his place of work in two days, and I gave the address of the garage. I also mentioned, almost as an afterthought, that I was notifying the NYPD because the arrest would be made in Manhattan, and I expected backup at the site. I said I planned to ask NYPD to take Marcus into custody until the New Jersey authorities could pick him up. Last but certainly not least, I invited Sarah to send a reporter and a photographer, and I mentioned that I was also notifying the local cable station." I stopped for breath and took a long swig of iced tea before I continued.

"In a matter of hours, Fergy called me at home to say that he and his buddy had picked up the DVD, interviewed Ariel, gotten a warrant, searched Marcus's backpack, found the photo, and arrested him. They searched his room and found the hammer he used to knock Naftali out. It was back in Marcus's toolbox with all the other tools he and Jude had used to renovate Naftali's room. Marcus had wiped off the metal hammerhead, but forensics found traces of Naftali's blood on the wooden handle. Marcus broke down and confessed. Even if bail is set low, which it won't be, there's no way Olivia can come up with it." Then, almost as an afterthought, I added, "I also persuaded Dick Halpern to defend Marcus."

Raoul and Vic both raised their eyebrows. "How did you get that notoriously pricey legal eagle to work for nothing?" Vic asked.

"Bel told Halpern that if he didn't defend Marcus pro bono, she would tell the press that Halpern had shortchanged her on her defense because she had to do all the investigative legwork herself while he went fishing!" Illuminada was chuckling as she answered for me. "I have to hand it to you, Bel. That dude was really unhappy at the thought of the public bad-mouthing he was going to get."

"But didn't Sarah want to print the real story? After all, she didn't get to be managing editor by squelching stories." Again Vic's question was logical.

"No, Sarah Woolf got to be managing editor because Bel gave her first dibs on the story of who really killed Altagracia Garcia," snapped Betty. The long-ago murder of her friend and boss still had the power to disturb her. "Right, girlfriend? Sarah owes you for that promotion."

I nodded. "She does, but she's also a good friend and a solid citizen. You know, she and Doug Equivera reconnected and are working together to produce a five-state hip-hop tour promoting peace." No one looked surprised. "Anyway, Sarah gets it. She understands that Fergeson and Rago were trying to avenge the way I set up their former chief detective, Nick Falco. And she also knows that they weren't gifted or diligent crime fighters. Sarah thinks that even if Curly and Moe hadn't been trying to frame me, those two buffoons might not have had the brains or the patience to figure out who really killed Naftali." I shook my head at the memory of the detectives' obtuse blustering.

"When they came to see me to tell me that they had Marcus in custody, they begged me to ask Sarah to run that version of the story." I pointed at the newspaper on the table. "I'd already arranged with her to run it their way if they took in Marcus. She was pretty happy that the real killer was going to be taken off the streets." Sarah had literally whooped with relief when I'd told her that I was off the hook for Naftali's murder.

"It's sad about the fortune-teller, the sister," said Raoul. "She's lost her whole family."

Now that I was no longer in danger, Sol too could spare some compassion for Olivia Durango. "Bel stopped by to see how she was," he said.

Betty and Illuminada exchanged glances. I knew that they thought I was too softhearted sometimes, but I didn't care. "Olivia's in pretty bad shape. She's actually considering moving back to Trinidad," I said. "But I think she'll change her mind. Just as I was getting ready to leave, Jude Lafayette showed up to pay his respects. Now that her brothers are out of the picture, maybe she and Jude can get back together."

"And live happily ever after? Is that what you think?" Illuminada's tone was mocking.

"Well, yes. I do. She told me she missed him. She said Jude left after they had argued about Naftali. Jude had said he still thought she and Marcus had spoiled the kid, and Olivia accused him of having been jealous of Naftali. Jude blew up and moved out. Maybe now that Olivia's heard about that photo, she's caught on to the fact that Naftali had a dark side, and so did Marcus. I'm no fortune-teller, but I bet now she can see Jude's point of view a little more clearly." I shrugged. I still thought it was sadly ironic that while Olivia was busy predicting doom and gloom for my relatives, she failed utterly to notice that her own were in trouble. "But maybe not. Time will tell. At any rate, I feel bad for her. She's agreed to have some grief counseling. I hope that will help."

"I hope so too. She's had so many losses. Her whole world's turned upside down." As an undertaker, Vic had more than a little experience with people mourning the deaths of loved ones, but it hadn't dulled his ability to empathize. I reached over and gave him a peck on the cheek. Just then my cell phone buzzed, signaling that someone from the real world threatened to intrude on our lazy seaside idyll.

"Let it ring," said Sol. "It's probably just another reporter."

"Or maybe it's Edwina Kittenpenny calling to kiss my feet and beg for forgiveness on behalf of the Board of Trustees," I speculated. President Woodman had already phoned, sent flowers, and written me a letter apologizing for even suggesting that I resign. "I wouldn't mind hearing Ms. Kittenpenny munch on a slice of humble pie." I reached into the pocket of my shorts for my cell.

I saw Sol's shoulders tense when he heard me say, "Ma? Are you okay? What's wrong?" My grip on the phone tightened. Ma had wept with relief when I told her that I was no longer being indicted for murder. But maybe my reprieve came too late and the strain she'd been living under had already undermined her fragile health. I pictured my mother, pale and frightened, as she struggled to give my cell phone number to an emergency room nurse. In my mind's eye, Sol and I were already in the car speeding back to Hoboken to be at her side.

"I'm fine, Sibyl." My grip on the phone relaxed. "Paul drove Sadie and me to your house to check on Virginia Woolf. Your message light was on, so I listened to your messages." The fact that I'd not asked Ma to perform this service, along with cat-sitting, did not seem to have deterred her. I'd inherited my yenta-who-has-to-know-everything gene from her. "There are quite a few calls from Rebecca. You better check your messages. She sounds like it's pretty urgent."

Once again my hand on the phone had closed into a claw. The other shoe had finally dropped. Rebecca was in trouble. Or maybe Abbie J was sick or hurt. "Okay, Ma. Thanks, I'll check."

I pushed the button programmed to connect with our message machine and listened.

Mom, Keith, Abbi J, and I just got back from our camping trip. It was way cool. But what's with all these crazed messages from you and Dad? Remember I told you that as soon as I got a good local job offer we were going camping? All those practice interviews I did worked and Virginia Mason came through with an offer. That same day we were outta here. Give me a call when you get home.

Mom, I just checked my e-mail. What's with all the messages? I'm pretty sure I told you we were going camping, didn't I? It was totally awesome to be off the radar in the woods for a few weeks. Keith had no tenants on his case, and I had my first real vacation from the restaurant and school in years. Abbi J loved toasting marshmallows and making s'mores. So call me, and I'll tell you all about it.

Mom, where are you? This is like the third time I've called. I have your cell number on my cell in the car, but Keith's taken the car to pick up some groceries. Where are you? Have you been playing detective again? Are you okay?

Yo, Ma Bel, give Rebecca a call when you get home. She's surfaced, and she's bugging me about where you are.

Sibyl, this is your mother. I just listened to my messages. I've got one from Rebecca too. She's really worried about you, so give her a call.

Just as I was about to call Rebecca, Randy Ramsey and Lourdes Guttierez, their office attire rumpled from the car ride, appeared on the deck hand-in-hand, both looking sheepish. A slight jig in Betty's shoulders was the only indication that she was surprised to see the two kids. Illuminada blinked when she saw them, but she smiled a greeting, as if she had expected them all along. Neither Raoul nor Vic bothered to pretend the arrival of the two kids was anything but a jolt. "Look what the tide washed up," Vic said. He took the edge off his less than enthusiastic welcome by giving Randy a mock salute and winking at Lourdes.

Raoul said, "Lourdes, we thought you were going out of town this weekend."

Lourdes bent down and kissed her dad on his cheek, saying sweetly, "This *is* out of town, *papi*." Then she leaned over and gave her mother a smooch on the forehead.

Perhaps fearing he had been less than cordial, Raoul pointed to the cooler, saying, "Randy, help yourself to a cool one."

"Thanks, man." Randy took out two Coronas, twisted the tops off both, and handed one to Lourdes. Then, turning to Vic and Betty, he said, "Looks like we're crashing a party. I'm sorry. Obviously we didn't know you folks were going to be using the house this weekend." Looking directly at Betty, he said, "I thought you said you were staying in Jersey City, Mom."

"I called to tell you that we had a sudden change of plans, but you didn't get back to me," cooed Betty. "But it doesn't matter. It's great to have you both with us. There's plenty of room. When you bring in your stuff, put it in the living room. You two can crash there or in the sun room or both." Betty's voice held no trace of smugness and her smile of welcome was as warm as the seaside sun. Only the twinkle in her eye betrayed the fact that she was relishing the joys of payback. If Randy had returned her call, he would have planned his romantic beach getaway weekend with Lourdes somewhere else—anywhere else. But he hadn't called back, so now he and Lourdes would have to put up with us all or try to find an affordable B&B on the Jersey shore with a last-minute vacancy, an impossible task.

I was pleased at the prospect of spending the weekend with the two young people. Neither of them had

heard my story yet, so perhaps I'd get to tell it again—
and from the beginning. But first, I had to call Rebecca
back before she started imagining that I was in some
kind of trouble, which, for the first time in ages, I
really wasn't.

The World of Bel Barrett

The "M" Word

The very first Bel Barrett Mystery, The "M" Word, *introduces us to the smart and sassy midlife professor and part-time sleuth. With a sensibility shaped in the sixties and kids born in the seventies, Bel hit the big five-O in the nineties. In Bel's first case, it's hot flashes and a fancy fundraiser that really turn the heat on when Bel's boss, college president Dr. Altagracia Garcia, is poisoned. When the police suspect one of Bel's students of murder, she sets out in search of the real killer, before she becomes his next victim . . .*

We entered and seated ourselves in a corner booth. I ordered a cup of hot water into which I dropped an herbal tea bag from a stash in my purse, and Illuminada ordered black coffee. I looked straight at her across the table and made my move. In the special voice that I use to cajole potential drop-outs to stay in school, speech-phobic students to address the class, and blocked writers to compose research papers, I said, "Illuminada, I just know Oscar Beckman didn't kill Dr. G. And the more I think about her being murdered, the more I want to figure out who really did do it and why. And now here you are, a bone fide private eye sitting right across the table from me. I just have to ask. Will you help me?"

"You mean pro bono?" Illuminada screwed her delicate features into a grimace. "I do this sort of thing for a living. But . . ." she grinned as I whipped out my fan and began to circulate the air around my face, "for the mother of all mentors. To vindicate our shared heritage, mine and Dr. G's," she added hastily as it was my turn to look quizzical, "and finally, because if we do unravel this, it'll be good for business. I'll make a deal. If you let me observe a few of your classes, I'll do a little poking around." Laughing, Illuminada raised her coffee cup in a toast and then we awkwardly clinked cups, sealing our compact.

Still fanning, I said, "I'm going to find out everything I can on my own. Then we'll know where to look further."

"You better be careful, Professor. Like it or not, somebody did poison Dr. Garcia and that somebody is not going to appreciate your curiosity. This is not exactly library research." When had this role reversal happened? Now who was mentoring whom?

I responded to her warning with more confidence than I felt. "Oh, I'm just going to chat up people the way I always do. One of the advantages of being the faculty yenta-in-residence is that people are used to me having my nose in everybody's business. No one takes me very seriously. I'll start with Betty Ramsey. She was very close to Dr. Garcia. She'll help us. Don't worry about me."

Death in a Hot Flash

In Death in a Hot Flash, *Professor Bel Barrett's colleague, popular local undertaker Vinny Valone, shows up dead. Many suspect suicide, but when the police accuse one of Bel's students of the crime, Bel knows that she's the only one who can clear his name. With loads of leads and phony clues that challenge her midlife memory, Bel must face her toughest case yet.*

Just then Gilberto Hernandez arrived, nodding politely at me as if to apologize for his tardiness, but not actually saying anything. Gilberto had been doing an externship at Vallone and Sons, so I assumed that he had known Vinny better than the others. Because he wasn't usually late, I decided not to make an issue of it. There were clearly extenuating circumstances that day.

Gilbert had flashing dark eyes and an easy grin and was handsome in a male-model sort of way. But as he took his seat that day, his eyes were still and his lips were a straight slash across his face.

I resolved to do more listening than speaking, since

I had no insight to offer and since the students clearly wanted to talk. "Please take one of these and pass the rest," I said, handing Alan a sheaf of announcements about Vinny's wake and funeral. The familiar classroom routine of passing around printed material occupied us for a moment or two.

Then, while she was stuffing the handout into her book bag, Joevelyn blurted out, "You know, maybe he got bad news or somethin', like, you know, his health . . ." Her words hung suspended in the room, catching all of us off guard. Of course, she could be right. How much did any of us know about Vinny, really? Vinny had never mentioned a word to me about being sick, but would he have? For all his chattiness, Vinny had always kept his private life private. It was awful to think of him hiding a serious health problem behind a facade of bad puns. Poor soul. Joevelyn must have been thinking the same thing, because her eyes were tearing up again.

"Maybe he was worried about somethin', like, you know, maybe somebody had somethin' on him." It was Henry Granger, speculating so matter-of-factly in his deep voice that Joevelyn stopped blowing her nose and, along with the rest of us, turned toward Henry, a dark face in our circle.

As usual, Alan required more information. "You mean you think somebody might have been threatening to blackmail Professor Vallone?" Alan's voice approached a squeak when he got to Vinny's name. "So instead of calling the cops or paying the blackmailer, he jumped in the river? Is that what you *really* think?" Alan looked incredulous. In his own carefully ordered version of the universe, such a series of events was out of the question.

Mood Swings to Murder

Bel Barrett is once again on the case in Mood Swings to Murder, *when local Frank Sinatra impersonator, Louie Palumbo, turns up dead. When the bogus Blue Eyes' fiancée Toni pleads for help in solving the crime, how can Bel say no? In her own unique style, Bel plunges estrogen-patch-first into the strange world of obsessive Sinatra worship—a move that could prove to be something stupid . . . maybe even fatal!*

"You met while you were doing your research, right? In the Sinatra archives?" I knew she was going to want to tell her tale from the beginning, so I tried to cue her.

"Yes. It was in the archives. Louie knew everything about the Sinatras. It was awesome how much he knew. And he was so helpful." A new teardrop was forming in the corner of her reddened eye.

At the sight of this harbinger of yet another paroxysm of sobs, I quickly interjected a question, "I guess it was love at first sight, wasn't it?"

Big mistake. I could read Sol's critique of my ill-

chosen line of inquiry when I saw him shaking his head.
We waited for Toni to regain control of herself. "No, actually, I was engaged to someone else when I met Louie.
A really awesome guy I've known for years, the boy
next door actually." Toni smiled at the absurdity of this
cliché, and a wayward teardrop slipped from her lash
and splattered on the counter. After swiping at the tiny
puddle with a Kleenex, she took a sip of her lemonade
and continued. "Well, anyway, my former fiancé—John
is his name—is a law student. One night last December,
he was studying for finals, so he couldn't go to a concert
at city hall in Hoboken that this other Frank Sinatra impersonator, somebody new in town, was giving. It was
to celebrate Frank's eighty-second birthday. Louie
wanted to go to check out the competition, you know?
He was a little surprised not to be asked to do that gig
himself, or at least to share it." Toni shook her head, recalling the logic of the dead man, and forged ahead with
her story. "So I invited him to use John's ticket, and we
went together. It was there, that night, listening to Luke
Jonas singing 'All the Way,' that Louie and I fell in
love." For a second my eyes glazed over, and once again
I was in the backseat of Teddy Lichenstein's father's
new T-bird with Frank crooning over the radio about
how glad he was to be near me.

Neither Toni nor Sol had noticed my moment of private tribute to The Voice. When I tuned them in again,
Toni was saying, "So right after that I, you know, I
broke off my engagement to John. It was only right."
For a moment I felt a pang of empathy with the Demaios,
who had probably had some difficulty understanding
why their bright and lovely twenty-two-year-old
daughter would prefer a thirty-something tone-deaf

Frank Sinatra wanna-be to a future lawyer. But had the future lawyer been so unhinged by the loss of his la-dylove that he had stabbed his rival in the back several times and then pushed him over the palisade? Appar-ently Toni didn't think so.

Midlife Can Be Murder

Professor Bel Barett is in hot water again in Midlife Can Be Murder, *when she agrees to help one of her former students prove that a friend's freakish rock-climbing death was no accident. But the only way to find some answers is to go undercover as a housekeeper at a suspect's office and look for clues. Too tired to moonlight, and too feisty to give up without a fight, Bel won't stop until she finds the killer.*

"Hey! How'd you get in here?" It was Greg himself who had glided silently into the doorway on his Rollerblades. Holding onto a doorjamb with each hand for balance and leaning into the room, he filled the doorway, making escape impossible. "What're you doing here, huh? Calling your relatives all over the Caribbean like the last one? You people never learn, do you?"

I realized that he thought I'd been using the phone to place long-distance calls. This was a fairly common practice among homesick evening maintenance workers and even security personnel in Jersey City, who couldn't resist making "free" calls to relatives, friends, and lovers they had left behind in places like Miami, Dominica, Haiti, and Ecuador. At RECC this unauthorized activity had resulted in some pretty high phone bills, so the administration had blocked long-distance access on most of the college's phones. "What's your name? Answer me?"

I smiled idiotically. I did not have to mimic fear. I was terrified. What I had to mimic was Spanish, so I kept muttering, *"No comprende"* and then, in a desperate imitation of Illuminada's accent, I whispered, *"Dios mío,"* lowered my head as if awaiting the guillotine, and crossed myself. Gliding over to the other side of the desk, he picked up the phone and punched a number. "Jack, send someone from security up here to escort one of Delores's girls downstairs. She can wait for Delores outside. I don't want her in the building. I'll call Delores myself and tell her I caught her girl using the phone in my office." I struggled not to let my face show that I understood what he was saying as I moved tentatively from behind the desk in the direction of the doorway.

It took a few minutes for the security guard to get upstairs, so I was able to hear Greg bark into Delores's message machine. "Delores, Greg, CEO at e-media.com here. I just caught one of your girls using the phone in my office tonight. Those offices are off limits. I don't want to see her here again." I was livid. This underaged and underbred techno tycoon had pushed most of my buttons. He'd called me a girl. My blond wig and uniform did not mask the obvious fact that I was, literally, old enough to be his mother. He'd referred to non-native speakers as "you people," lumping all immigrants together as, at the very least, petty criminals. And finally, he'd lied about me using the phone, and his lie would have gotten me fired if I'd been a real employee of Delores Does Dusting.

By the time the security guard arrived, Betty and Illuminada had finished the basketball area without me and were putting away their equipment. I pantomimed to my keeper that I too wanted to stash my maid props, and I did. As I walked out, my escort and I went downstairs in the same elevator as Betty and Illuminada. But there was no question about it. For me it was a one-way ride. From now on Delores would be dusting without me. I had been canned.

Out of Hormone's Way

Bel Barrett already has enough to worry about with her busy teaching schedule, not to mention dealing with the annoying challenges of midlife and menopause. So when she agrees to head up the Urban Kayaking Club, it's just one more thing to add to her already full plate. And when a sweet, shy fellow kayaker is found floating in the water, Bel once again puts her sleuthing skills to the test to find the killer, before she gets sunk as well.

Politicians weren't the only headliners though. There was an equally predictable population of psychopaths who routinely and fatally shot, strangled, stabbed, poisoned, and suffocated their hapless victims. That's why I hadn't really been surprised earlier by Gina's account of a murder at the Outlets. Nor was I surprised now to see that it had made the front page. The victim, a young Colombian-American woman, Maria Mejia, had been found stabbed to death in the parking lot of her place of employment, His 'n' Hers Shoes, presum-

ably on the way to her car after work. Because her
purse was missing, the local police officer summoned
to the scene assumed that she had died resisting a thief.
There were no suspects or witnesses yet. I wouldn't
have paid too much attention to poor Maria Mejia's un-
timely demise had it not been for Gina's heads-up. But
now, reading about it in the paper, I felt a chill.

I poked Sol, who was holding the *Times* with one
hand and his head with the other, distressed by events
in Washington, the Middle East, Africa, and Asia. "Sol,
look, some poor young woman was just murdered at
His 'n' Hers Shoes. That's the outlet where I bought
the black flats I wore to Rebecca's wedding," I added,
hoping that if I put this killing in a personal context, he
would pay attention. "Right in the parking lot. In Secaucus. At the Outlets. Betty said Gina was there when
it happened," I added, trying harder to interest him in
this odd confluence of conversation, shopping, and
death. "Look," I insisted, finally placing my copy of
the *Jersey City Herald* over his *New York Times* so he
couldn't help but eyeball a headshot of the late Ms.
Mejia.

"What the hell did she do? Shop till she dropped?" I
winced as the familiar bad joke rang out for the second
time that day. "Jesus, Bel, she's not the first and she
won't be the last. The Meadowlands has been a body
drop since forever. Before Jimmy Hoffa." Even as he
spoke, Sol gently but firmly pushed my paper out of
his way and immersed himself once again in The Big
Picture.

I didn't bother explaining that Maria had not been a
shopper but an employee. Nor did I say how discomfit-
ing it was to read about this murder on the same day

I'd been reminiscing about shopping at His 'n' Hers Shoes in Secaucus. Sure, it was just a coincidence, but an eerie one. I was chilled by the killing itself and by the fact that the killer was still out there somewhere. *Not at Laurel Hill Park, I hope*, I muttered to myself as I moved closer to Sol.

Hot and Bothered

*The work of a full-time professor and part-time
sleuth is never done. As Bel Barrett tries to cope
with the effect that September 11 had on her
hometown of Hoboken, New Jersey, one of her colleagues turns up dead. But things aren't always
as they appear. The victim led a double life—academic by day, stripper by night—and Bel must
discover which of those lives attracted the murderer. Education and titillation could prove a
most volatile mix, and a murderer may be closer
than she thinks . . .*

The block party fell on one of those perfect Indian
summer days that we had been perversely gifted with
during that cataclysmic fall. The bright sunshine and
unseasonable warmth brought out the neighborhood
neatniks all ready to sweep early in the morning. I was
not among them. Since the terrorist attack on the
World Trade Center, I'd resumed attending synagogue
on Sabbath mornings. Sabbath worship, a habit I'd
only begun cultivating when preparing for my adult bat

mitzvah, had been a casualty of the Saturday mornings I'd spent as faculty advisor to the RECC Urban Kayaking Club the previous spring. I shuddered, recalling the grisly murders that had become indistinguishable from that experience and blighted it in my memory.

The sight of Sol brandishing a broom delivered me back to the present. Unfortunately, since September 11 the present had been blighted as well, and Sol was living testimony to that fact. His stocky frame appeared less substantial and his eyes, normally mischievous, were now more often wary. I was worried about him. Like Betty's son, Sol had been enroute to the WTC on the morning of September 11 and had witnessed the buildings' destruction. But whereas Betty's son had been on the subway, Sol had been aboard the ferry. Badly shaken by what he had seen, he feared more terrorist attacks.

But that morning he had joined our neighbors to prepare for the block party. He was sweeping fallen leaves and scraps of litter from our gate, the vernacular term for the concrete area in front of a row house. As soon as the street was completely cleared of cars, Sol and the other gate sweepers would turn their attention to what was to be our communal patio for the next fifteen hours.

Sol and I were sharing a good-morning hug when Joey P came rushing over to us looking flustered. His simple words would have sounded ordinary a year earlier. That year they had the ominous ring of prophecy. "Jeez. I was tryin' ta move my car but they got cops all over the Avenue." For reasons lost in local lore, Hoboken's main drag, Washington Street, is always referred to as "the Avenue." "Traffic's backed up for blocks."

Delphine, Felice, and Tony, all engaged in sweeping their gates, put down their brooms and gathered around the tall gray-haired man. Sol, his brow suddenly rutted with worry lines, asked, "What's going on?" I resolved to try not to focus on Sol's anxiety. I wanted to believe that, given time, this retired economics prof would recover the self-possession and wry sense of humor that had attracted me to him when we first met. That had been years before, when we were both active in the Citizens Committee to Preserve the Waterfront, a group determined to stave off those developers hoping to play high-stakes Monopoly along Hoboken's strip of riverbank.

"A cop told me," Joey P wheezed, "that there was an unmarked package delivered to Swift Savings this morning. They don't know what's in it. The cops are waiting for the bomb dogs and then if it's not a bomb, they'll take it to examine for traces of . . ."

"Anthrax . . ." everybody intoned in unison, a Greek chorus articulating one of our newest and worst fears.

A hefty woman with tufts of red-orange hair and the social style of an antebellum plantation overseer showed up just then. It was Ilona Illysario, and she spoke with her usual authority, an authority derived largely from being married to the PANA president and mother of last year's PANA scholarship winner. "It's not a bomb and they've already taken it away for testing. So let's get this place cleaned up. Remember, the kids gotta make chalk drawings on that concrete. Move it guys!" She grabbed her broom and headed for the street to begin sweeping the gutters where earlier the cars had obscured the week's accumulation of litter and leaves. Sol looked only slightly relieved, but by the time I left, he had finished sweeping our gate, bagged the debris, and joined several others in the now nearly carless street.

Hot on the Trail

Busy planning her upcoming wedding to her sweetie Sol, the last thing overbooked community college professor Bel Barrett needs is another distraction. But when an older student from her senior citizen writing seminar fails to show up after a death in the family—his own—Bel can't control her urge to investigate. Now she's knee-deep in pigeon poop, investigating the world of pigeon racing, her deceased student's favorite hobby, and with one more false move, Bel won't have to worry anymore about wedding plans—someone will be planning her funeral!

"Poor Flora. She has stress related asthma, but she hyperventilates even when things are going well. This might push her over the edge. Where could that sweet old man have gone?" I muttered. I had addressed this query to myself, but, seated at her desk not two feet away from mine, my officemate Wendy could not help overhearing.

"What sweet old man? Listen Bel, now that you've

finally weaned yourself off estrogen, if you're going to start babbling to your computer, we're going to have to rethink this cozy arrangement." She looked up from the business section of the *New York Times* and gestured around her at the claustrophobic cubicle that she and I had shared since the seventies when we'd both joined the English Department at River Edge Community College in Jersey City, New Jersey. We also shared this "closet" with Thelma and Louise, two feisty philodendrons that thrived on our windowsill despite decades of sporadic watering and long outgrown pots. Their vines meandered over Wendy's cluttered desktop and would have encroached on the pristine surface of mine except that they knew better.

Ignoring her dig, I passed Wendy the jar of M&M's I kept on my side of the divide, and she helped herself to a handful. "Better than estrogen, right?" she quipped. "Maybe if I eat enough chocolate the fact that my IRA has been shrinking like cotton undies in the dryer won't seem so important," she said. The curve of her grin softened her drawn features. "Jeez, Bel, you've completely interrupted my efforts to calculate how old I'll have to be before I can retire on what's left of my portfolio." She pushed the newspaper away as she spoke. "So, what sweet little old man were you just ranting about?" Without waiting for me to answer, Wendy continued. "I hope nothing bad has happened to that old charmer in your memoir class, the one who was bragging about having been an extra in *On the Waterfront*." I'd invited Wendy to a session of "Tell It Like It Was," my memoir-writing course for senior citizens, because she was considering teaching it in the fall.

Hot Flashes and Cold Killers—
The Bel Barrett Mysteries by

JANE ISENBERG

HOT WIRED
0-06-057753-3/$6.99 US/$9.99 Can

When an angry ex-student turns up dead, college professor
Bel Barrett is suddenly the cops' chief murder suspect.

HOT ON THE TRAIL
0-06-057751-7/$6.99 US/$9.99 Can

When one of her senior citizen students dies, Bel can't resist
the urge to investigate . . . especially when his distressed
daughter insists the old man's demise wasn't accidental.

HOT AND BOTHERED
0-380-81888-4/$6.99 US/$9.99 Can

When one of her fellow judges in a scholarship contest is
found dead—a woman who lived a strange double life as an
academic by day and stripper by night—Bel decides to
investigate both worlds.

MOOD SWINGS TO MURDER
0-380-80282-1/$6.50 US/$8.99 Can

One of Bel's favorite students is the prime suspect in the
murder of Louie Palumbo, a sorry imitator of the late local icon
Frank Sinatra.

DEATH IN A HOT FLASH
0-380-80281-3/$5.99 US/$7.99 Can

Before Bel can help Vinny Vallone teach a class, the part-time
Funeral Services Education instructor turns up deceased himself.

PERENNIAL DARK ALLEY

Like a Charm: Karin Slaughter gathers some of the hottest crime fiction writers around in this suspense-filled novel in voices.
0-06-058331-2

Men from Boys: A short story collection featuring some of the true masters of crime fiction, including Dennis Lehane, Lawrence Block, and Michael Connelly.
0-06-076285-3

Fender Benders: From **Bill Fitzhugh** comes the story of three people planning on making a "killing" on Nashville's music row.
0-06-081523-X

Cross Dressing: It'll take nothing short of a miracle to get Dan Steele, counterfeit cleric, out of a sinfully funny jam in this wickedly good tale from **Bill Fitzhugh.**
0-06-081524-8

The Fix: Debut crime novelist **Anthony Lee** tells the story of a young gangster who finds himself caught between honor and necessity.
0-06-059534-5

The Pearl Diver: From **Sujata Massey**, antiques dealer and sometime sleuth Rei Shimura travels to Washington D.C. in search of her missing cousin.
0-06-059790-9

The Blood Price: In this novel by **Jonathan Evans**, international trekker Paul Wood must navigate through the world of international people smugglers.
0-06-078236-6

An Imprint of HarperCollins*Publishers*
www.harpercollins.com

DKA 0905

Visit www.AuthorTracker.com for exclusive information on you favorite HarperCollins authors.